Hippocrates
Wept

Hippocrates
Wept

WILLIAM F. QUIGLEY, M.D.

To order additional copies of this book, contact:
Xlibris Corporation
1-888-795-4274
www.Xlibris.com
Orders@Xlibris.com
18005

Contents

PREFACE

Ecclesiastics: Chapter 10, verses 19-20.

> *"More weighty than wisdom or wealth is a little folly.*
> *The wise man's understanding turns him to his right;*
> *the fool's understanding turns him to his left.*
>
> *When the fool walks through the street, in his lack of*
> *understanding, he calls everything foolish.*
>
> *Should the anger of the ruler burst upon you forsake*
> *not your place for mildness abates great offenses.*
>
> *I have seen under the sun another evil, like a mistake*
> *that proceeds from the ruler: a fool put in lofty position*
> *while the rich sit in lowly places. I have seen slaves on*
> *horseback while princes walked on the ground like slaves.*
>
> *If the iron becomes dull, though at first he made easy*
> *progress, he must increase his efforts; but the craftsman has*
> *the advantage of his skill.*
>
> *Words from the wise man's mouth win favor, but the*
> *fool's lies consume him. The beginning of his word is folly,*
> *and the end of his talk is utter madness; yet the fool*
> *multiplies words."*

～

And now the gospel according to the Department of Health, Education, and Welfare: Chapter – irrelevant, verses – ad nauseam.

"The Northwest Connecticut Health Systems Agency (NWC/HSA) will be addressing the issue of health status indicators in document #2 of its Health Systems Plan, annual implementation plan (HSP/AIP). Toward this end function one, objective two of the NWC/HSA Work Program requires the determination of a list of health status indicators to be kept as a long range data base for the region. The task is a complex one. At the present time no official guidelines exist from HEW as to which health status indicators should be collected by HSA-V, although section 1501 of PL, 93-641 calls for them to eventually be provided. The Rand Corporation of Santa Monica, California, is under contract to study the matter, but preliminary results are not expected until late 1977, too late for use by the NWC/HSA in it's first HSP/AIP.

In the interim the NWC/HSA may refer to a document entitled, "Recommended Data Sets for Effective Health Planning and Resources Development," printed by the Bureau of Health Planning and Resource Development," (BHPRD) in October of 1975. However, the document is reported to be undergoing major revision at this time. The Boston University Center for Health Planning has provided training and technical assistance in the matter, but at one session the Director of BHPRD's Division of Planning Methods and Technology, in effect, told the HSAs to, "do their own thing," with HEW's blessing. Since the indicators chosen will represent a long term commitment to the manner in which the NWC/HSA will be monitoring the health status of the population in it's region, careful consideration should be given to this process".

∽

"The beginning of his words is folly, and the end of his talk
is utter madness; yet the fool multiplies words."

In that tranquil and nostalgic era of the Nineteen Fifties, Hollywood produced a hackneyed but charming tale of a troubled Ireland, *The Quiet Man*. It starred none other than John Wayne, supported by Maureen O'Hara and Barry Fitzgerald. What brings the film to mind is the invitation a wizened and elfish Barry Fitzgerald extended to John Wayne "to come to the pub and talk a little treason."

"Ladies and Gentlemen, members of the Waterbury Medical Association come to your meeting and talk a little treason."

∽

The foregone is the text of my presidential address to the Waterbury Medical Society upon the completion of my tenure in that office in the summer of 1977. In its own way, it defined the opposing sides in a struggle for the soul of the medical profession, a struggle of mammoth proportions over the last quarter of the twentieth century. Though there have been many skirmishes and battles in those twenty odd years with a few wins and many losses, the campaign has inexorably been downward in favor of increasing regulation and control by corporate and governmental entities. By this year, 2002, corporate America has an iron grip on the economics of medicine, and government agencies have embarred its soul within a prison of self-fulfilling bureaucratic regulations and red tape.

The purpose of this narrative is to offer a prediction of what might transpire in the upcoming five years, with its effect on both providers and beneficiaries of medical care in these United States. It is, of course, purely conjecture; but I would suggest, quite reasonable in light of what has transpired in the preceding decades.

If there were an underlying theme, I would say it is hyperbole, but exaggeration only to prove a point; with an analogy to an instance of hyperbole, which indeed was fact along a road our country traveled more than a century ago.

In this endeavor, I will be forever grateful for the patience of my wife, Maggie; the encouragement of my sons and daughters; and for the diligence and ability of the staff of the medical library at St. Mary's Hospital for researching an appropriate trial and verdict which took place in the Commonwealth of Pennsylvania one hundred and sixty years ago. A special, unique gratitude must go to Leigh Aronin, secretary in the Division of Surgery at St. Mary's Hospital, for her patience and understanding in typing the hen scratches of my written pages.

As for myself, I am and have been a general surgeon who has labored in the vineyard for many years and is now in the twilight of his career. Without vainglory, I can say that I served my profession well, but not well enough.

INTRODUCTION

FALL OF 2012

The cotton candy fog played hide-go-seek with a solitary seal playing the buffoon on the ghostly shore to the port side of their Boston Whaler. The laughter of his pod playmates could be heard to starboard, beyond a rocky point hidden in the same iridescence, as a kaleidoscope of changing rainbow hues testified to its losing battle with a resurgent sun. In the short time left before the clarity of a delightful October morning the distant dirge of a ship-board klocsin defined the deeper waters of Nantucket Sound to the West. An answering avian chorus from the minty mist surrounding them was accented by the mournful cry of a humpback whale basking in the already sunlit ocean to the East of Monomoy Island.

"I betcha that's the Nantucket ferry. Right, Grandpa?"

"Can't fool you. Can we, son? Hey! What've you got on your line? That's quite a tug!" Ricky's pole had suddenly arched downward, almost touching the calm surface of their secret cove. "Acts like a striper, and a keeper too!"

"Dad, what should I do? It's gonna pull me off the boat!"

Dan had been baiting his own line but immediately came to his son's aid. "Give him plenty of slack. That's it. When he calms down, reel him in just a little at a time, okay? Pretty soon he'll get tired and you can get him close to the boat."

Suddenly the fish broke the surface as he flipped over to dive deeper. "Wow!" He's over forty inches. We'll have a feast tonight! Grandma's an expert at cooking striper."

It had been well before 6 A.M. when Ted, his son-in-law Dan, and grandson Ricky, had weighed anchor from the dock at the foot of a small peninsula crowned by the O'Hara's vacation home. At that wee hour a seasonal cocoon of the Cape's familiar gray-white aerosol obliterated visibility throughout Stage Harbor. Penetrating the impenetrable, thanks to marine knowledge gained over the many years Ted had navigated these waters, they had safely passed the lighthouse guarding the entrance to the harbor, and, by further hugging the shoreline of Monomoy Island, had settled into the safety of their favorite fishing cove.

"My hat's off to you, Ricky. You've already got him in the palm of your hand."

"You're right, Gramps. He's not fighting near as hard."

"Okay, son. Keep reeling him in and bring him alongside. Easy does it now. I've got the net ready." When Ricky had the striper within ten feet he brought him to the surface. His father let out a low whistle. "Whew! I haven't seen one like that in years. He's at least forty-five inches."

They were all smiles as Ricky brought his prize alongside. Its scales now glittered in the sunlight which had finally conquered the October mist. His father expertly trapped the fish in the net and, with more than a little expenditure of muscular energy, brought their evening entrée on board. Several quick snapshots from Ted's digital camera confirmed Ricky's feat for posterity, as he proudly held his catch at shoulder height near the stern.

"You do realize you can take home only one of these a day? We also have a few cod so let's heave anchor and deliver your trophy to nana and your mother. Besides, I'm hungry and could use some breakfast."

"Right, Dan. It's a beautiful morning, and now it'll be a cake-walk getting back to the harbor. Here, Ricky. Take the helm. You've earned it."

Dan hoisted the anchor aboard as Ricky angled the outboard into the water, started the engine, and shifted into forward gear. Gently advancing the throttle and turning the wheel to starboard, he maneuvered the boat from the cove and headed North toward Stage Harbor. Ted relaxed into a cushioned seat to enjoy the warmth of the now unhindered sun.

"So, Ricky, you're pretty well into the new school year. How is it being a junior? Beginning to think about what to study in college? You'll be pretty busy looking them over and picking one out come next spring and summer!"

"Go ahead, son. Your grandfather will be pleased to hear what you've been telling your mother and me. Don't you have some questions you think only he can answer?"

"Aha! What's it to be? Professional golfer or world-class fisherman?"

"Aw, Gramps, I can enjoy those things any time, but I'm pretty sure I want to be what you and Mom are, a physician."

"I'd be extremely proud to see that, Rick, but do you really know what you'll be getting into? I'm sure your mother has told you how tough it is to get there."

"I know it's a big commitment, lots of work in medical school and residency, sleepless nights and all that. When I see you and Mom with the confidence both of you have in dealing with people, and the honor and respect you are held in by others, you know, like friends and patients. Well, that's what I want and at this point I'll do anything to get there."

"All the right reasons for a good start. How long have you been thinking about this?"

"About a year, but over the past summer I read a lot and became serious about it."

"You say you read a lot. What did you read?"

"I went to the public library and borrowed the usual books describing what's necessary to become a doctor and what to expect. Then I raided your bookshelves and found an old copy of *Gray's*

Anatomy and a dream of a book called, *The Century of the Surgeon*. Man, I read and reread every page. Those guys and their discoveries really came to life. What a book!"

"I'm happy for you, Rick. You remind me of myself too many years ago."

"Thanks, but what I wanted to ask you was about something my science teacher brought up last week in class."

"What's that?"

"Well, he told us about an ancient Greek physician named Hippocrates and referred to him as the 'Father of Medicine', you know, something about an oath which doctors still take even today. It seems to me that with all the progress medicine has made, particularly now, how can anything someone said over two thousand years ago have significance today?"

"Why not?"

"Come on, Grandpa. Give me a break!"

"Is that all he said about Hippocrates?"

"Well, he didn't go into any great detail, if that's what you mean."

"Let me do that for you. Okay?"

"Sure, that's why I asked."

The boat had passed the lighthouse and they were halfway across the harbor from where they could see the dock at the foot of the O'Hara peninsula. "How to put it? H'mm! Okay, let's start by accepting the fact that medicine is a profession. Can you tell me what that means?"

"Sure, it's sort of a group of people with a common purpose. Like a fraternity. You know!"

"I admit that would fit most dictionary definitions. However, you asked me why Hippocrates is called 'The Father of Medicine'. Quite simply he was the one who defined medicine as a profession for all time. In ancient Greece, on the Isle of Cos, over three hundred years before the birth of Christ, he permanently separated medicine from the superstition and philosophic mumbo-jumbo which held sway until that time. Actually he promulgated two concepts which changed our profession forever, namely the scientific basis upon which our clinical ministrations are based and more importantly the ethics, without which medical science could readily be transformed into medical anarchy.

"Now what do I mean by 'the scientific basis of medicine?' He was the first to observe and categorize, in an objective fashion, the symptoms and natural course of various diseases and by deductive reasoning assign causation and treatment according to whatever science was available at that time. This concept formed the basis of the quantum leaps we have been witness to ever since, particularly the advance of medical science over the past two centuries. Just to name a few: the discovery of bacteria, viruses, anesthetics, antibiotics, blood transfusions, chemotherapy, genetics, cellular biology, you name it, they all owe their acceptance to the hypothesis he taught in that distant past.

"Even more amazing are the tenets of his oath, as to the manner in which physicians are to conduct themselves in their ministry. They make our profession unique and have been sworn to by all those who practice the art of medicine throughout the subsequent history of Western civilization even by those graduating from medical school today. Individually and as a group, we swear to honor and respect those who have taught us; to respect our patients and always render them treatment that will do no harm; to keep confidential whatever our patients reveal to us and whatever we discover about them; and to lead honorable and upstanding lives, not only in relation to our patients, but with all who come into contact with us. As opposed to the scientific aspect of his teaching, these principles were not meant as a mere beginning for future generations to expand and build upon. Rather they have been a beacon light which has passed through the centuries, undisturbed to the present day, incapable of improvement. Indeed, he admonished that each of us is individually responsible for molding ourselves to these ideals or woe betide those who don't."

"Are you telling me that, even with the advent of Christianity and all the other major religions we have in the world today, these principles have never changed? After all Hippocrates lived in a pagan era in a pagan land."

"Also right, son, but I'm sure you're aware from your history classes that democratic notions also had their origin in ancient Greece. Hippocratic thought centered about the value of the individual and the innate respect due each person. In this sense, I would say he actually pre-empted Christianity.

"There is one thing I think he missed the boat on, but I wouldn't hold it against him, given the dangers involved at that time. Part of his oath forbade a physician to perform surgery of any kind. Indeed this prohibition lasted until the middle of the nineteenth century when the advent of sterile technique and adequate anesthesia made a place for surgeons as physicians. At last, my branch of the profession finally found its niche along with some respect. You should be aware that, in England, surgeons are still referred to as 'Mister,' not 'Doctor.' Oh well, nobody's perfect."

"Gee, I never knew that. I always thought surgery was at the top of medicine."

"And deservedly so! But it took a lot to get there. Barbers did our work until that epiphany well over a century ago. Seriously, the ideals I've been referring to are near perfect. No one can or should change them but many have violated them to the detriment of themselves and our profession. History is replete with examples. I'll just mention a few of the more recent ones.

"During the Second World War a few German physicians, under the Nazi regime, participated in experimentation on prisoners leading to their deaths or permanent disability. More recently in our own country agencies outside the profession have restricted access to beneficial treatments purely because of their cost and have been insisting upon breaches of patient confidentiality in order to carry out the business concerns of their involvement with our profession."

"I would certainly condemn a doctor for doing what you described in Nazi Germany, but when it comes to the cost of medical care isn't some compromise necessary?"

Intent on their discussion, they scarcely noticed that Dan had taken over the helm and singlehandedly docked the Boston Whaler. "Come on, you two. I can smell the coffee from here. Breakfast is at the top of the stairs."

"Okay! Rick, if and when you become a doctor, when you take the oath we have been talking about, you will obligate yourself as your patient's primary guardian and advocate. It will be your personal responsibility to respect his confidentiality and to constantly resist any detrimental treatment, either of commission or omission, no matter who orders or suggests it."

"I can see that could be tough, Grandpa. Seems to me I remember a few years ago, you were involved with a fight against the government when it was doing what you just mentioned. Weren't you and Uncle Joe together on that one? What was going on?"

"You're right. It was a bad time in our history and for my profession. I'll be happy to tell you all about it after breakfast. For now let's just say it was a time when Hippocrates wept."

THE OATH OF HIPPOCRATES

*Y*ou *do solemnly swear, each
by whatever he or she holds*
most sacred:

*That you will be loyal to the Profession of Medicine and
just and generous to its members; That you will lead your
lives and practice your art in uprightness and honor; that
into whatsoever house you shall enter it shall be for the
good of the sick to the utmost of your power, your holding
yourselves far aloof from wrong, from corruption, from the
tempting of others to vice; That you exercise your art solely
for the cure of your patients, and will give no drug, perform
no operation, for a criminal purpose, even if solicited, far
less suggest it; That whatsoever you shall see or hear of the
lives of men or women which is not fitting to be spoken,
you will keep inviolably secret;*

These things do you swear, Let each bow the head in sign of acquiescence, And now, if you will be true to this, your oath, may prosperity and good repute be ever yours; the opposite; if you shall prove yourself forsworn.

"Hippocratic Oath" Microsoft ® Encarta ® Online Encyclopedia 2000 http: //encarta.man.com ® 1997-2000 Microsoft Corporation. All rights reserved.

PROLOGUE

"Methinks Don Miguel is brother to Don Quixote."
"God help us. We are all brothers to Don Quixote."
Act III. "Man of La Mancha"

CHAPTER I

"THE WISE MAN'S UNDERSTANDING TURNS HIM TO HIS RIGHT; THE FOOL'S UNDERSTANDING TURNS HIM TO HIS LEFT."

I t was one of the ten worst days of the year. The temperature hovered in the upper nineties, successfully matching the humidity. Fortunately, there was the promise of a thunderstorm later that evening, the hoped-for relief from a Bermuda high which had long since worn out its welcome. All of which made Dr. O'Hara thankful for the air-conditioned comfort of his office, having finished with his last patient on a busy afternoon late in August. Although Connecticut's "ten best" seemingly exceeded the "ten worst", one's misery index is recorded in steamy hours compared to comfort's fleeting seconds.

His almost tactile awareness of the sauna awaiting him in the parking lot did not deter Dr. O'Hara from recording the defecatory habits of Mrs. Vincent, an otherwise charming woman whom he had just examined. She was forty, a mother of three, who during pregnancy four years previously suffered from hemorrhoids, the symptoms of which had not only persisted but also worsened in spite of conservative therapy, initially by her primary physician and for the past four months by her surgeon, Dr. O'Hara.

The nuances manifested by these varicose veins of the anal canal and lower rectum can run the gamut from mere irritation, to bleeding, severe pain when thrombosed (clotted), or gangrene (tissue death). Further complications of local or generalized sepsis (infection) could ensue. It would be difficult to dispute the necessity for operative removal of hemorrhoids involved to the maximum degree just described. However, short of that situation, a surgeon in the year 2005 had to carefully record the key words needed to justify surgical intervention (thus the parenthetical definitions recorded above). After all, a clerk in the regional office of the National Health Administration, at the opposite end of a telephone line, required words that she (or he) could easily fathom and match with a list of criteria elicited from an appropriate manual. In just such a manner would permission be granted or withheld. God forbid that such a decision be made by a surgeon with over thirty years' experience.

Be that as it may, when he finished dictating the burdensomely detailed note (which when typed would fill the better part of three pages) he reflected for a moment how the same facts would have been recorded years ago when he had first entered private practice in Westbury.

"Forty y.o. (year old), Gravida III Para III (three pregnancies, three live births) *c* (with) 4 yr. history of prolapsing bleeding hemorrhoids. Failed conservative Rx (treatment). Scheduled for hemorrhoidectomy (removal of hemorrhoids). No other medical problems. Explained procedure to patient including possible complications. She has accepted it."

A slight smile crossed his face as he concluded. "After all, didn't that say the same thing?" It seemed a great paradox that as medicine progressed (no, that's not the correct word) as medicine had changed, there had been a distinct metamorphosis in the approach of a physician to his patient.

History taking had lapsed into the gerbil activity of a lengthy check-off list errantly filled out by the patient while waiting to be seen.

Physical examination was now abbreviated and perfunctory for several reasons. With the ever-increasing availability of a technically sophisticated diagnostic armamentarium, reliance on the physician's senses had ebbed and became a subject placed on the back burner in medical school. Indeed, the stethoscope, reflex hammer and related instruments were rapidly gaining antique value, particularly as it concerned the younger Hippocratic generations. In addition, time constraints dictated by a high-volume practice with emphasis on cost-containment and symptom-oriented investigation were locking the museum door behind the antiques being deposited there.

The added time necessary to expand upon these activities and develop mutual trust and confidence had been almost completely curtailed by the regulatory requirements of documentation and approval for diagnostic tests and/or treatment programs. Ted would be among the last to deny the critical importance of an accurate and pertinent record. But when such detail was motivated not by patient benefit but by bureaucratic requirement and inefficiency, they could not be justified at the expense of precious moments spent in establishing the pillars of what in the past had been referred to as "a good doctor-patient relationship".

Turning to the phone on his desk, he pressed the intercom button.

"Sally, is that a wrap for the day?"

"Yes, doctor. Remember you're operating at 9 A.M. tomorrow."

"I know. Mr. Jones' gall bladder and then the breast biopsy on Ms. Vega. Did you forward the 3D mammogram to X-ray so beforehand they can localize the shadow with the laser-staining technique?"

"Three days ago, Doctor, they confirmed it by email."

"Fine. After you log today's notes into the computer, book Mrs. Vincent for outpatient surgery at St. Lucy's next Thursday. She has internal and external hemorrhoids, and I'll be doing a hemorrhoidectomy; epidural anesthesia. Get approval and an admission number from the National Health Administration; and contact Dr. Green or Dr. Morgan for the mandatory second opinion. Any hassle, call me. I guess that's it."

"Not quite, doctor. Remember, office hours start at 1:30 tomorrow."

"Sally, how did I know you wouldn't let me forget? Oh! There is one more thing. Roll the phone over to the service. I'm on call tonight. See ya."

⌒

He was ill prepared for the blast of the Bessemer belching outside the entrance as he quickly exited to his car hazily floating on a lava lake a short distance away. Fortunately he was carrying rather than wearing his jacket, and as he gained access to his Oldsmobile microwave he dropped it on the seat beside him, hit the ignition, and turned the airconditioner to maximum. The car knew the path into the increasing traffic on Main Street by rote. The light at the first corner was accommodating and he was rapidly abreast of Westbury's green. As always, he was struck by the subtle majesty of the surrounding architectural landmarks. They had developed personalities of their own, the quaintness and uniqueness of which had helped attract him to this old New England mill town lo those many years ago.

The Elton Hotel wore its Victorian facade with elegant grace. When it was new, he could readily imagine a wasp-waisted, flamboyant, but chastely attired young woman alighting from a Hanson carriage beneath a stylish, broad-brimmed hat held in place by a diaphanous kerchief. Her parasol would have been a-twirl, more coquettish than practical in protecting her fair skin from the blistering sun. He pictured her mincing steps floating her through the entrance beneath a gingerbread marquee, the top of which served as a balcony accessed from the ballroom behind it on the second floor. It was from this very balcony that John F. Kennedy addressed a jubilant throng of more than fifty thousand people at 3 A.M. on a Sunday morning, the weekend prior to his election to the presidency of the United States.

Alongside, in Mediterranean grandeur, rose the Church of the Immaculate Conception. It was of cathedral dimensions, at least in proportion if not in reality, gleaming in a Romanesque style to rival that of St. Peter's in the Vatican. His eyes were drawn to the words chiseled in granite above the enormous bronze doors at the entrance.

"Domus Dei et Porta Coeli."
"The home of God and the Gate of Heaven".

Words mostly forgotten by the present successors to the city which had produced these very doors in distantly famous brass mills, now lying fallow along the banks of the Naugatuck and Mad Rivers, or converted into quaint malls rife with aphoristic "Olde Shoppes" plying the pitifully few wares not found in the discount goliaths sited on concrete fields at the edge of town.

At the other end of the green, the sun behazed the lofty, slim spire arising from a Gothic nave – St. John's Episcopal Church. Its granite, New England starkness was a perfect complement to the Renaissance excess of the Immaculate. As they gazed upon one another across the tree-lined walks of the intervening green, one recognized the simple ecumenism shared by two saintly matriarchs of advanced years, close enough to eternity to mutually agree that both did indeed worship the same Deity.

Also obvious were the ornate, geometric shapes adorned with weathered green statuary and scrolls, similarly found on all greens throughout New England. They provided memory of those who gave their lives in service of their country; in the case of Westbury a roster passing through time as far back as our own Revolution. In attendance were the usual addicts, alcoholics, and homeless who seemed more interested in whatever slight respite from the heat might be gained from a whimsical breeze or passing cloud.

A final glimpse brought another smile to his face as a certain image of Mrs. Vincent leapt back into his mind, brought there by the monstrous visage implanted around the green. His eyes beheld a four-square block, second-story walkway spanning streets and desecrating the masonry of the landmarks already mentioned, as well all other structures unfortunate enough to front the green. It assaulted one's senses like pornographic graffiti in an urban slum. Through the beneficence of a Federal grant, the current mayor had touted this effrontery as the only solution to traffic congestion and pedestrian safety in the downtown area. A comparison echoed in his mind; this obvious sacrifice of harmony and beauty for perceived efficiency on the one hand, versus the abandonment of an important human relationship for false economy on the other. His smile ended in laughter when the image turned to that of a necklace of Mrs. Vincent's hemorrhoids draped over the building and trees of his beloved green.

"Woah, Ted. This is getting to you. How much longer can you keep up the charade? Surgery and the challenges that go with it remain fulfilling, but the rest of the bullshit is too much!" No longer willing to explore that alley and where it might lead, he slid a CD into the stereo as his car entered the ramp onto I-84 East leading to Longview and a quiet evening with Laura.

⤶

For a surgeon, time existed only to be jealously rationed. For Ted, time spent driving had for many years been transformed by listening to the music of Broadway; not only listening, but singing. He had committed many of the lyrics to memory and it was quite relaxing to boom them out within the confines of this metallic acoustic cage. The activity immensely pleased him in spite of Laura's feigned embarrassment on their many trips to Cape Cod.

The unique tenor voice of Michael Crawford reverberated within the car accompanied by Ted's baritone. The Phantom's invitation to "*listen to the music of the night*", was succeeding when Ted, hypnotized by the moment, *"purged all thoughts of the life he knew before."* A truck driver, alongside, started in alarm seeing Ted's face, his free hand, and overall body-English reacting to the emotion of the lyrics. Ted smiled in return and gave him a thumbs-up sign.

"Turn your face away from the garish light of day. Turn your thoughts away from cold, unfeeling light." His beeper went off, that damnable clarion he had long ago made a Faustian bargain with. The magic of the moment gone only to be enjoyed another time, he turned the volume down and pressed a button on the right side of the steering column. After several rings, a voice filled the silence.

"Dr. O'Hara's service. May I help you?"

"This is Dr. O'Hara. You beeped me?"

"Hi, Doctor, yes I did. Let's see . . . hummm? . . . yes, here it is. The emergency room at St. Lucy's is looking for you."

"Thanks. I know the number." He then pressed a pre-programmed button labeled ER.

"St. Lucy's emergency room. May I help you?"

"This is Dr. O'Hara. You were looking for me?"

"Yes, doctor. Would you hold a moment for Dr. Curtin?"

The atonal notes of an indefinable melody filled his head, continuing for several minutes. He had just been deprived of the enjoyment of real music and he resented this intrusive substitution. Why did anyone feel that such inane noise could be pleasing to the ear? He preferred silence, or a buzz, or even the delicious eavesdropping afforded by an open line, the disjointed sounds and bits of conversation which imagination could transform into a rainbow of comedy, drama, or both.

"Hello, Ted, Brian here."

"Hi, Brian, what can I do for you."

"I have a patient here by the name of Hanway. Says he knows you personally; was even your patient years ago."

"Right. His first name is Joe. Don't believe his golf handicap and whatever else never play gin with him. What happened? Did he fall off a golf cart on the way to the nineteenth hole?"

"I'm afraid not. He came in an hour ago complaining of pain in his back. It came on fairly suddenly about twelve hours ago and has remained constant since."

"Did he strain himself? Any question of an injury?"

"No. The pain awakened him early this morning. Says he felt fine when he went to bed last night. No GI or GU symptoms and his vital signs are normal, no change in blood pressure or pulse, no fever."

What's your best bet, Brian?"

"He's somewhat obese but I can almost convince myself I feel a mass in the upper abdomen which could be pulsatile".

"Did you get any X-rays?"

"Yes, but they're all negative, chest, abdomen, spine. Blood works normal too; Even the EKG doesn't help, I'm ready to get an ultrasound or a CT scan, but he insisted I call you."

"Well, he owes me thirty bucks from a Nassau yesterday, so I'd better protect my investment. Give the surgical resident a call and tell him to meet me there in ten minutes."

"Roger"

"Thanks, Brian."

He pulled off at the next exit, passed left over the highway and turned onto the ramp leading to the westbound lane, back to the city and St. Lucy's ER. As he checked the rearview mirror, he punched the button for his home number.

Laura's voice came on after two rings.

"Hello, O'Hara residence. Laura speaking."

"Hi, hon, it's your ever loving Ted. How's the world's most beautiful and sexy CEO?"

"Why, I do declare. It's that Yankee carpetbagger, Rhett, trying to turn my head again."

"I'd love to do more than turn your head, but there's a slight hitch, darling. Got a call from the ER. It seems Joe's there with a sore back and insists on my seeing him. It doesn't sound too serious."

"Now, darling, you tell that black lothario he's too old to pretend to be 'Don Juan' incarnate. Tell him to give it a rest and give Vicky a rest. Remember the back is the second thing to go. Is Vicky there with him?"

"Okay, okay, I'll tell him, but if Vicky is there, she's likely to sue me for malpractice. Seriously dear, I'll call as soon as I know something. In the meantime, keep my dinner warm and remember: My back is in great shape. Love you."

"Love you back, I'll be waiting for your call."

CHAPTER II

"But the craftsman has the advantage of his skill."

Dark clouds gathering in the West slowly dimmed the incandescent August sun, as an unseen hand slowly turned a celestial rheostat to the "off" position. Ted exited his car as furtive eddies of fitful winds rustled the surrounding trees, lifting the skirts of their verdant leaves and exposing the lighter green of intimate undersides to an atmosphere now alive with the dank odor and sudden coolness of the approaching storm. Stan Brown, the security guard, opened the door for him as Ted entered the ER.

"Hi, Doc, what brings you out at this hour?"

"Duty, my son, duty."

"Well, Doc, you'll find plenty of flesh to work on in there."

It's a living, pal, it's a living."

He waved a quick hello to the triage nurse who returned it with a smile as, looking up from her desk, she pointed in the direction of room 10. The chart outside the room confirmed most of what Dr. Curtin had told him. He was about to enter the room when Dr. O'Leary, the fifth-year surgical resident, arrived slightly out of breath.

"Dr. O'Hara. I didn't think you would get here so soon."

"Well, Jack, let's just say that modern transportation is truly miraculous." With that they both entered the stark, uncluttered confines of the ER cubicle where the abundant frame of Joe Hanway lay overlapping the sides and ends of a gurney.

Joe was black with graying, closely cropped, curly hair framing an intelligent, self-confident face, which obviously wore a pained expression. His bulk, though familiar to his good friend, confirmed the difficulties of examination alluded to by Dr. Curtin. Joe had spent his entire life in Westbury having been born in St. Lucy's Hospital sixty-five years previously. He was descendant from a slave brought to Maryland from Africa in the early part of the nineteenth century. A self-made man, he had taken a high school diploma, a relentless desire to succeed, and an apprenticeship as a toolmaker in the old Century Brass Company, and parlayed them into the ownership of his own successful tool and die company.

He married Vicky, a nurse trained at St. Lucy's, when they were both twenty-three and during their rise in fortune had parented a son and daughter both of whom had long since graduated with honors from college. They had gone on to become successful in the professions of medicine and law. Ted has been proud to recommend their son, Jeffrey, to a premiere residency program in his own field of general surgery. Their daughter, Trina, was now a junior partner practicing corporate law in a prestigious Boston firm.

A slight turn of his head revealed that Vicky indeed was there. She, as always, was a remarkably striking woman with a carriage and demeanor which belied her years. A sensitive face with full features, surmounted by an elegantly styled coif of ebony hair tinged with gray, was marred by the slightest indication of concern and worry, evidenced by the foreign furrows seen in her forehead and the hint of wrinkling at the corners of her eyes.

Joe fortunately had good health throughout his life. There was the emergency surgery to remove an infected gall bladder twenty years ago. Indeed, thanks to Vicky's background and constant insistence, he had dutifully subjected himself to the periodic poking and prodding of Dr. Buonocore, his internist, all such visits being loudly protested to his feigned tormentor and companion in love.

"Well Joe, Dr. Curtin filled me in on the details of your problem. How bad is the pain?"

"Ted, it's like a toothache that just won't go away."

"Exactly where is it?"

"Right in the middle of my back. I can't get comfortable in any position although three Advil took the edge off it, but not by very much."

"Does it go down either leg or into the groin or scrotum?"

"Nope."

"How about deep breathing or coughing? Does that make it worse? Or have you had fever or chills?"

"No and no."

"Dr. Curtin reported no nausea or vomiting; but have you had constipation or diarrhea? Any difficulty voiding or burning when you pass your urine?"

"Not at all. Ted, I've had my share of aches and pains but this one is different. What's going on?"

"That's what we're here to find out, and it better be worthwhile to keep me from dinner and an evening with Laura. First, I'd like you to meet Dr. O'Leary, one of our chief residents in surgery. Dr. O'Leary shakes hands with Joe Hanway and be sure to count your fingers afterwards."

Ted lowered the sheet and lifted the skirt of Joe's hospital gown to expose his ample belly. It did not appear distended and moved normally with each respiration. He took the stethoscope offered by Jack O'Leary and began listening to Joe's abdomen, moving the wider, flat side of the instrument from one quadrant to another including both groins. Seemingly satisfied, he then indicated that Dr. O'Leary should repeat the same maneuvers. Ted then began probing the entire surface of the abdomen with gentle but inquisitive hands, eliciting any tenderness, the size of the spleen, presence or absence of a hernia in the groin, the configuration of the spermatic cords and testicles. Having finished, he again requested that Jack performed a similar examination.

"Okay, Joe. You can turn up on your side so we can get a look at your back!"

"Sure, but I'll have to do it slowly. Left side up okay?"

"Either way, now easy does it. Fine. Right there."

Ted proceeded to thump the back of Joe's chest by placing his left hand on the skin and sharply striking the back of its middle finger with the tip of the middle finger of his right hand. A hollow thud resonated into the room with each blow. This was followed by a thorough examination with the stethoscope over the same region as Joe breathed deeply through his mouth. The same middle finger was used to percuss the entire spine from the nape of the neck to the sacrum.

"Any pain when I do that, Joe?"

"Not really. It's just downright uncomfortable deep down in the middle of my back whether you're hitting me or not."

"Okay, Joe. How about here?"

Ted gently struck both sides of the back at the lower margins of the rib cage with a closed fist.

"Nope"

"Well, Dr. O'Leary, I don't see or feel any deformity of the spine. The lungs are clear as a bell and there's no kidney tenderness, no tenderness over the spine either." As Ted donned a latex glove on his right hand he again addressed Joe.

"This will be a little uncomfortable but I have to examine your rectum with my finger." He applied KY jelly to the tip of his index finger and carefully inserted it through the anus into the rectum.

"Jack. I won't ask you to repeat this exam, but take my word for it. There are no masses, no tenderness; the prostate is normal and the rectum is filled with soft, well-formed stool. As he removed his finger there was a small amount of brown stool at the tip which he rubbed into an absorbent paper surface in the center of a card which Dr. O'Leary offered to him. Jack then placed several drops of a clear liquid from a nearby vial onto the fecal stained paper. No change in color was seen.

"Dr. O'Hara. The stool is guiac negative (no blood in the stool)."

"Joe, you can turn on your back again. I'll get Vicky back in here. Dr. O'Leary and I will return in a moment to talk things over and tell you where we go from here." Outside the room Ted walked over to where Vicky was waiting.

"Hi, angel. Why don't you get back in there and keep Joe company while we get a look at the X-rays which have already been done. We'll be back in a few minutes and then we can talk. Okay?"

"Sure, Ted. But don't be long." She couldn't hide the trace of fear in her voice.

Ted gathered her into his arms and spoke gently to her. "Joe didn't get where he is by giving in to adversity. He's a scrapper and so are you. Now get in there and work your magic on him. I'll see both of you in a few moments."

⌒

Dr. O'Leary was removing the X-rays from the view box when Ted began to speak. "So much for the films of the chest, spine, and the belly. What did you find with your examination?"

"Not much. Everything was quite normal except for some mild tenderness in the upper midline of the abdomen. There was no definite mass, but I thought I could feel fullness in the same area and some pulsation."

"I agree, Jack. Joe's abdomen is rather large and, to say the least, rather difficult to examine. I felt those pulsations also. The question is: Does he have an aneurysm of the abdominal aorta, or are they transmitted pulsations through an overlying inflammatory process or tumor? How would you differentiate the two?"

"An ultrasound might be helpful but my money would be on a CT scan."

"Right. Order it now with IV contrast. If it's an aneurysm, he could have an early leak and if we have to perform surgery tonight, I want an empty stomach, so hold on the oral contrast. Oh, and Jack, would you go with him to radiology and make sure his vital signs remain stable."

"Right. Do you want a central line?"

"Hold on that until we see the results of the CT. Let's go talk with the Hanways.

As he reentered the ER cubicle, Ted could see that Joe's predicament had not worsened. But just as obvious was the continued expression of pain on his face. Vicky's concern was apparent in her questioning eyes as they met his.

"The plain X-rays are all normal and don't help in establishing a diagnosis. However, when I examined Joe, I could feel pulsation in the upper mid-abdomen. Nothing else seemed out of the ordinary other than a sense of fullness in the same area."

"What do you mean fullness with pulsation? What could cause that and the back pain?"

"Well, you're pretty thick from front to back, Joe, and that makes things more difficult to sort out; but there are several possibilities. First, it could be an aneurysm of the abdominal aorta."

"An aneurysm?" Vicky's voice was tight and shrill as she blurted the question out.

"Right now, it's just a possibility. An aneurysm is a swelling of the aorta, the main artery running down behind the abdomen in front of the spinal column. It's caused by a loss of elasticity in the wall leading to weakness, and, eventual dilatation. The primary danger is rupture with bleeding."

"You mean I'm bleeding now?"

"No, Joe. Your abdomen is not distended or significantly tender; your blood pressure and pulse are okay; and the blood count is normal. However, if it is an aneurysm, it can cause back pain under two circumstances. There could be an early sentinel leak of blood in the tissues surrounding the aneurysm or there could be a small ulceration on the back wall with irritation of the anterior spinous ligament lying in front of the spinal column. In either case back pain could result."

"The second possibility is a tumor or inflammatory mass in the pancreas, duodenum, or stomach overlying the aorta through which pulsations could be transmitted to the abdominal wall in front. Dr. O'Leary and I agree the one test which should clarify the diagnosis is a CT examination of the abdomen which we have already ordered. You'll get some dye through that IV in your arm which, when the X-rays are taken, will light up the aorta, kidneys, and ureters. For your part, all you have to do is lie face up on a movable stretcher which will gradually pass through an opening in the CT apparatus. Multiple X-rays will be taken at various levels between your diaphragm and pelvis and a computer will reconstruct images of all your intro-abdominal organs. When we look at the images of the aorta, pancreas and stomach we should have our answer. All of this will be quite painless and the only thing which might bother you is the limited confines of passing through the small opening in the CT scanner."

"I just want to find out what's causing this pain."

"Here's the X-ray tech now. Vicky, you can go with Joe and wait for him outside the CT suite. By the way, you don't have any allergies, do you, Joe?"

"No, just some mild hay fever in the fall."

"Didn't I order a test before I removed your gall bladder years ago, part of which was injecting a dye into your vein?"

"Right, Ted. You did and I don't recall any bad reactions."

"Good. I'll see you when the CT is done and we'll talk more then."

The large bulk of the liver could be seen in the upper right quadrant of the abdomen, hugging the contour of the diaphragm. The shadow was a homogenous gray flecked by an occasional streak or dot of lucency indicative of the vessels and bile ducts lying with its substance. None of them were abnormally placed or enlarged; indeed the main bile duct leading from the liver to the small intestine was also normal.

The stomach was empty and lacked any thickening of its wall, which might indicate a tumor. There were no fluid collections or indistinct areas of muddied fat in front of or behind the stomach to signify an ulcer, which might have perforated and formed an abscess. The head of the pancreas was of normal size and shape lying in the arms of the duodenum (The first part of the small intestine just beyond the stomach). The balance of the pancreas narrowed as it crossed from right to left in front of the vena cava and aorta to tail off and end in the hilum of the spleen. All of the organs mentioned were quite normal.

As Ted's eyes scanned the aorta from top to bottom, he could see that at a point 2 cm. below where the artery to the left kidney branched off, the diameter of the aorta itself suddenly increased from a normal 2.2 cm. to as much as 7 cm. at its widest point. The entire vessel was a brilliant white having been highlighted by the dye injected though the IV in Joe's arm. As his eyes pursued the irregularity downward into the pelvis the diameter just as rapidly returned to normal 2 cm. above the bifurcation of the aorta into its terminal branches – the right and left common iliac arteries. He also quickly noted that both kidneys functioned well.

"Well Jack, there it is – a seven-centimeter aneurysm of the abdominal aorta. Fortunately it starts below the renals (arteries to the kidneys) and ends above the aortic bifurcation."

"No doubt, Dr. O'Hara, but why does he have sudden back pain? I don't see dye leaking into the tissues surrounding the aorta. There's no evidence of a leak much less a complete rupture."

"Flick the switch on the computer to digital subtraction and 3-D, Jack."

Suddenly the structures surrounding the dye-enhanced aorta became muted as one could appreciate the aneurysm gaining depth, making it appear as a large white football on the screen. Maneuvering what appeared to be a small joystick, Ted turned the image in all directions so that the contour of each of its surfaces could be observed minutely.

"Look Jack, right here, on the back wall, just in front of the spine. Do you see this small niche of dye jutting out like a nipple from an otherwise smooth wall of the aneurysm?"

"Now that you mention it, I do. What are you getting at?"

"The back wall of the aorta has ulcerated and the blood flow is in contact with the anterior spinal ligament causing the back pain. It's a good thing for Joe that the ulcer formed before the aneurysm ruptured. The only thing preventing a massive hemorrhage is a few fibroblasts in the flimsy reaction around the side of that ulcer. What would you recommend now, Jack?"

"Well, he needs to have the aneurysm resected and replaced with a graft. He's stable so we could get him ready for tomorrow or the next day."

"You're right on the first count, but I'm not willing to delay surgery. He could blow at any time. Joe hasn't eaten in twenty-four hours and I already called his internist while he was in CT. Dr. Buonocore cleared him."

"Do you want me to book the OR now?"

"Roger, Jack, and after I talk to the Hanways, I want you to place a Swan-Ganz catheter, a nasogastric tube, and a Foley catheter. Also type and cross-match him for four units of packed red cells and have the OR get the cell saver ready."

"Okay, Dr. O'Hara, I'll call now."

"Once the Swan is in place, run a computerized profile and let me know when it's done. We'll both go over it."

"Sure thing."

CHAPTER III

"WORDS FROM THE WISE MAN'S MOUTH WIN FAVOR."

As Ted finished explaining the CT findings, Vicky was on the edge of her seat, the questions fairly tumbling one after another from her dry lips; not knowing if any answers could assuage the underlying volcano in her brain.

"What can be done? Will he be all right? Could we have done something sooner? Did I miss something?"

"Vicky, believe me, I understand your concern, but no one could have appreciated the problem sooner unless you had married a skinny fellow whose abdomen would be a might easier to examine, but you're stuck with Joe here. So let's all be thankful he gave us a little warning. Dr. Buonocore has given his approval for surgery. Joe hasn't eaten in twenty-four hours and I don't want to risk rupture in the next day or so. As far as I am concerned, we're ready to go. I've booked the OR for tonight.

"Joe, before you go to the OR, we're going to place a tube through your nose into the stomach to assure that it's empty. We will also place a catheter into your bladder so we can measure the urine output during and after surgery. Dr. O'Leary will place another catheter beneath your collarbone into a major vein, leading to the right side of your heart and the artery going to your lungs. The catheter will continuously give us information as to how efficiently your heart is working and how much IV fluid you need at any given time. We will keep it in place during surgery and for a few days afterwards. Placing the catheter is an invasive procedure and complications, though rare, can occur. The procedure will be done under local anesthesia and, since we enter a major vein, bleeding can occur. The catheter, when it passes through the right heart, can irritate its lining, causing an abnormal rhythm to the heartbeat. Repositioning will usually solve that problem. When the initial needle is placed beneath the collarbone, the top of the lung, where it rises into the lower neck, could inadvertently be punctured and air can escape between the lung and the chest wall, collapsing the lung. The condition is known as a pneumothorax and should it occur, we would have to place a small tube between two ribs to remove that air and re-expand the lung. The tube would be in place for several days and is easily removed when it's time to do so. In any event the information gained from the catheter is indispensable during surgery and far outweighs the possibility of complication.

"The operation is a big one but at this point there really is no choice. The aneurysm could rupture at any time. Right now, the surgery will essentially be the same as doing it electively when the mortality rate is one percent and complications are much less frequent. I am going to replace part of the aorta with an artificial graft. You'll be asleep the entire time but I want you to know that complications can happen. As with any major operation, infection can occur, either in the graft, abdomen, or incision. Infection can also follow in the lungs or urinary tract. To avoid these problems you will be on antibiotics during surgery and for a few days post-operatively. Of course, there's the problem of bleeding, but we use fine sutures very close together where the graft is sewn to the aorta. A problem peculiar to this surgery is the strain put upon your heart when I clamp the aorta above the uppermost part of the aneurysm. This clamp is necessary so that I can sew the graft in place. It should be removed within twenty minutes or so, and most patients tolerate it without a problem. But we are always concerned about any drop in blood pressure, which could lead to a heart attack or kidney failure. That's the main reason for having that catheter in the pulmonary artery. Again, everything will be done to make this procedure as safe as possible. Should anything untoward happen I assure you we will be on top of it and treat it appropriately. Do you or Vicky have any further questions?"

"Ted, neither one of us would have anyone but you do this. Go ahead before you really scare the bejesus out of me with your depressing recitation of woe."

It was Vicky's turn in a voice now calmer and less strident. "Thanks, Ted, we know we have the best, but you'd better get this lug back to me in good shape. Assuming everything goes smoothly, how long will recovery take?"

"In better shape, Vicky. He should be in the hospital for five or six days following surgery. When he goes home, he'll be up and around, eating fairly well but still taking something for pain. He'll be better than new in five or six weeks, but I can't guarantee any improvement in his bedroom performance or golf handicap."

"Some things can't be improved upon. Just get him back to me."

"Roger, Vicky. I'm going to call Laura and have her come down to hold your hand, okay?"

"Oh, Ted, that's too much to ask of her at this hour."

"Once I tell her what's going on, I won't be able to keep her away. See you upstairs Joe, and Vicky. I'll talk to you as soon as we're done."

～

"Laura, honey, sorry I took so long to get back to you. Stow dinner for tonight. Joe has an abdominal aortic aneurysm causing his back pain. I plan to operate in a few minutes. I'll be busy for about three hours."

"Oh! When I didn't hear from you, I figured something was going on. Give Joe my best and how's Vicky?"

"Vicky is anxious, of course, but holding up fine. Joe's quite stable. He hasn't hemorrhaged from it, but I've got to take advantage of the golden hour he's given me. Could you come down and keep her company during the procedure? She could use all the support she can get."

"Try and keep me away. Tell her I'll be right there and give Joe my love."

"Thanks, darling. I'll see both of you as soon as we're finished. Wish me luck. Love you."

～

Dr. O'Leary slipped the eighteen-gauge needle through the skin just below the junction of the middle and lateral third of the collarbone, aiming the tip in a plane toward the opposite shoulder. Joe didn't feel a thing since the area had already been numbed with a local anesthetic. Jack felt the needle impinge on bone and walked the tip off the lower edge of the collar bone. Then, applying suction by pulling back on the barrel of the syringe, he advanced the needle just over the first rib. A gush of dark, venous blood filled the syringe as the tip entered the subclavian vein. Holding the needle in place, he removed the syringe and covered the open hub with his gloved thumb.

A nurse handed him a flexible wire coiled in its container. Jack slipped the tip into the open end of the needle and meeting no resistance, fed the wire out of its plastic housing into the vein leading to the right side of Joe's heart. Jack then removed the needle over the wire and, using a scalpel, slightly enlarged the skin opening where the wire protruded. A plastic sheath about eighteen inches long was threaded over the guide wire. Actually this was a sheath within a sheath, the inner one having a tapered end extending a half-inch beyond the end of the outer one. As he pushed both sheaths together, the tapered end of the inner one dilated the soft tissues and the puncture site into the vein so as to accommodate the thinner outer sheath. Again, meeting no resistance, Jack passed it over the wire until the hub was at skin level. The wire was then removed along with the inner sheath. The outer introducer sheath was left in place.

The Swan-Ganz catheter is actually three catheters in one. One channel measures pressure at its tip; a second is available for injecting fluid or medications, and taking samples of blood; and a third leads to a small balloon surrounding the tip of all three. Jack attached a syringe to the hub of this channel and injected a small amount of air inflating the balloon to check its integrity. Satisfied, he emptied the air and passed the catheter into the sheath until the end with the deflated balloon protruded beyond the sheath in the superior vena cava above its entrance into the right side of the heart. He glanced at the waveforms on the monitor measuring the pressure at the catheter's tip. The pressure suddenly rose to 12 millimeters of mercury, fluctuating slightly with Joe's respirations. This told him the tip was measuring central venous pressure in the superior vena cava. Jack then inflated the balloon and gently coaxed the catheter further into the sheath. This allowed the flow of blood to float the balloon tip through the right atrium and tricuspid valve into the right ventricle. The wave forms suddenly shifted to a sharp peak of 30 millimeters of mercury as the heart contracted and suddenly dropping to the zero line when the heart relaxed. As he offered further slack to the catheter the right ventricle pushed the balloon through the pulmonary valve and beyond into the pulmonary artery. The wave form on the monitor again changed. The peak wave stayed at 30 millimeters of mercury but when the heart relaxed the pressure dropped only to 15 millimeters of mercury. Seeing the confirmation that the catheter was properly placed, Jack rapidly deflated the balloon and at the same time asked the X-ray technician who was standing by to take a film of the chest.

Five minutes later, Jack and Ted, upon viewing the X-ray, could see the tip properly placed in the branch of the pulmonary artery leading to the right lung. Jack re-inflated the balloon and the tip floated into the opening of a smaller branch, thus isolating the pressure sensing tip from the pulmonary circulation behind the balloon. The monitor immediately recorded a straight line at thirteen millimeters of mercury. This was the wedge pressure which reflected the filling pressure into the left side of the heart.

The balloon was deflated once more and the catheter anchored in place. He then performed a computer profile which printed a number of important measurements helpful in evaluating the heart's efficiency and the status of the fluid volume of the circulating blood. During Joe's operation, the anesthesiologist could follow these parameters on a continuous basis and make adjustments in blood and fluid replacement; use drugs to increase the cardiac output or expand or contract the size of the vascular bed in which the blood flows. He would also monitor urinary output throughout the procedure.

Three other monitoring devices were now being arranged by the anesthesiologist. A clip was applied over Joe's earlobe which would continuously measure the oxygen saturation of the hemoglobin in his red blood cells, a direct reflection of the efficiency of extracting oxygen from the air delivered to his lungs. Secondly, electronic leads were also being strategically placed on his skin so that a continuous electrocardiogram could instantly pick up any abnormal rhythm or changes indicating lack of oxygen to the heart. Lastly a small catheter was being inserted into the radial artery at Joe's wrist enabling the recording of the peripheral blood pressure at a glance.

"Joe, all systems are go. You'll be wheeled into the OR now. Meet your anesthesiologist, Dr. Arthur. He'll have you fast asleep before you know it. I'll talk to you when you wake up in the recovery room. Good luck, pal."

"Do your best, Ted – and Dr. Arthur, doesn't your daughter work for me?"

"That's right Mr. Hanway. She runs your computer section and believe me, I won't let anything happen to her boss." With that the nurses wheeled Joe into Operating Room number two.

CHAPTER IV

"IF THE IRON BECOMES DULL,
THOUGH AT FIRST HE MADE EASY PROGRESS,
HE MUST INCREASE HIS EFFORTS"

When Ted entered the OR suite, after his surgical scrub, he could see that Joe was sound asleep with the breathing tube (endotracheal tube) in place through his mouth into the windpipe. The anesthetic gases flowing through this tube would assure that he would remain unconscious for the duration of the operation and the percentage of oxygen in the mix would also assure adequate oxygenation to all the body tissues. Joe's body was rather contorted, his left flank and chest pointing upward at a 60-degree angle. His pelvis and legs were as flat as possible on the table, facing up. His left arm was elevated out of the way, bent at the elbow across his face, resting on a splint attached to the table. The circulating nurse had already prepped his skin with an antiseptic solution from the nipple line to his knees.

"Tom, how are things at the head of the table?"

"Rock stable, Ted. The wedge is still 13 and the oxygen saturation is ninety-two percent. Vital signs are fine and the EKG is normal."

Ted dropped the towel he had used to dry his hands into a hamper and turned to Helen Curry, the scrub nurse, pushing his arms into the proffered surgical gown. As Betty Felton, the circulating nurse, tied the gown in back, Helen pulled sterile latex gloves onto Ted's hands.

"Well, no one could ask for a better team than we have tonight. Right, Helen? We'll keep you busy for two and a half hours or so. Is the cell saver set to go?"

"Yes, Doctor. Which retractor system do you want?"

"The Buckwalter will do just fine. Betty, do you have appropriate music for tonight's performance?"

"I know you love Broadway but how about the latest in country."

"Sure, as long as it's not too hokey."

Ted and Dr. O'Leary rapidly draped the patient so the only portion of Joe's anatomy to be seen was his left lower rib cage, left flank, abdomen and both groins. A second, more junior, resident, scrubbed and gowned, had joined the group at the operating table. He took his place at Ted's left side opposite Joe's hip.

"Can we start, Tom?"

"Sure, Ted, anytime."

With that, Ted took the scalpel from Helen and made a long incision from the midline of the abdomen about five inches below the belly button obliquely upward to the left in a lazy S pattern ending at the lower margin of Joe's rib cage. Blood, oozing from the incision, was blotted away by Dr. O'Leary as Ted used an electrocautery to seal off each bleeding point. He then used the same cautery to divide the subcutaneous fat exposing the thick, fibrous fascia covering the muscle layers of the abdominal wall.

"Jack, for many years surgeons used a long midline abdominal incision to approach the aorta through the abdominal cavity. Exposure was good, but, if the patient had previous abdominal surgery, adhesions could make the dissection quite difficult. Post-operatively, because of its length and violation of the abdominal cavity, pain was a problem as well as delayed gastrointestinal function. With the patient's reluctance to breathe deeply and cough, collapse of lung segments or pneumonia were frequent complications. It's still a good approach when the aneurysm extends distally into the iliac system where an inverted Y graft would have to be used as a replacement with the distal anastamoses made within the pelvis.

"Joe's aneurysm involves the aorta only and ends above the bifurcation. He also had his gallbladder removed years ago and may very well have significant adhesions. Therefore, we're going to approach the aneurysm retroperitoneally behind the abdominal cavity from the left side. This will avoid any difficulty from adhesions and at the same time afford great exposure to control the aorta and place the graft. The common iliac arteries will have to be controlled below the aortic bifurcation, but so long as the dissection doesn't have to go more deeply in the pelvis, that shouldn't be a problem. This incision will be more comfortable post-op and has less GI and pulmonary complications."

"One thing I've been wondering about, Dr. O'Hara. Why are we doing an open procedure at all? There's been a good deal of literature about placing a graft over an expandable balloon within the aneurysm, gaining access by a catheter from the femoral artery in the groin. There would be no incision at all and the recovery period would be greatly shortened."

"If it were as good as you seem to imply, Jack, the answer to your question would indeed be, 'why?' However, with all the research done in the late 'nineties and early years of the new millennium, two problems remained. First, the graft, when deployed, depends on small hooks at either end to anchor itself to the normal arterial wall above and below the aneurysm. Sometimes, for whatever reason, they don't do their job and the graft can shift position. This can lead to continued arterial pressure in the aneurysm with the danger of rupture, or obstruction of the distal circulation should the graft hang up at the aortic bifurcation. Secondly the paired lumbar arteries, exiting the aorta from within the aneurysm continue to back bleed and could compress the graft or leave enough pressure within the aneurysm to still rupture it.

"Research was being done to solve these problems when, as you know, in 2004 the federal government took over the medical profession. It didn't take long for this procedure to be placed on the no-no list, not because of the problems I alluded to, but the expense was too great even though hospital time was decreased. Now you have to get special approval case by case, and it's limited to elective cases in patients judged too great an anesthetic risk. Indeed, it was just last year that the National Health Administration came out with the edict that we could not resect aneurysms on anyone over the age of seventy-five. Thank God, Joe's only sixty-five."

Ted was incising the muscles with the cautery when he turned to the junior resident and asked. "Sam, what layer am I going through now?"

"From the location and the direction of the muscle fibers I would say it's the external oblique."

"I'm impressed, Sam, but what happens here at the lower end where the muscular portion ends and the fascia continues medially over this strap-like muscle running vertically beneath it?"

"The fascia covering the external oblique joins with the fascia of the internal oblique to form the anterior rectus sheath and the muscle beneath it is the rectus abdominus."

"Hey, Jack, your protégé here sounds like an anatomic text. Bravo! But, unless I have to I'm not going to cut the rectus, just retract it out of the way."

Beneath the oblique muscles Ted came across a fibrous layer which laterally blended into the thin muscular sheet. "Okay, smart guy. What am I looking at now?"

"That's got to be the transversalus fascia blending into the transverses abdominus muscle laterally."

"Jack, I can't stump him."

With a gentle sweep of the cautery Ted was through this final layer overlying the peritoneum, a thin sheet lining the abdominal cavity. He then took his fingers and gently teased the shiny peritoneum away from the fat and muscular layers going deeper behind the abdominal organs and in front of the psoas and paraspinous muscles. In the upper part of the incision, the dissection plane brought him in front of the left kidney which he left in place.

"Helen, let's have the post for the Buckwalter."

Ted took the large metallic cylinder and with a scissor cut a hole in the paper drape above the upper end of the incision he had just completed. He passed the end of the post which had a large C clamp on it through the hole to Betty's waiting hands. She then anchored it to a rail on the side of the operating table. Ted then anchored a large metal ring to this post. The ring lay just above the incision and completely surrounded its periphery.

"Sam, one more try. What is this gizmo used for?"

"You finally got me, Dr. O'Hara. I can't imagine."

"Gotcha, huh? Well, that's okay, Sam. I didn't expect you to know. But you keep doing as well as you have and I won't mind Jack graduating next June. Sam, this apparatus is intended to save your ass. If we didn't have it, we would need both your hands and both feet to haul retractors and expose that aorta for us."

After he had draped damp cloths (lap tapes) over the wound edges and the dissected peritoneum, Ted turned to Helen, "Give us four of those intern savers." He placed two shallow bladed retractors over the left side of the incision and slipped their ratcheted handles through clips fastened on the metallic ring. Two deeper retractors were similarly placed on the right side of the ring, the blades pushing the peritoneum and its contained abdominal content out of the way.

Now Ted devoted his attention to a more meticulous dissection as he lifted the remaining peritoneum off the lateral sides of the bony vertebral bodies. He could see the pulsations as the aorta slowly came into view. During this phase, he identified the ureter passing downward from the kidney over the psoas muscle and over the left iliac artery as it disappeared into the pelvis. He placed a linen tape that looked like a shoestring around it to keep it out of harm's way.

As Ted grasped the stringy tissue overlying the aorta with a forceps, he would undermine bits of it with the tip of a clamp and then spread its jaws. Jack would then divide the offered tissue with the harmonic scalpel.

Finally, the entire abdominal aorta was exposed from the branching of the artery to the left kidney above to a point along the right and left common iliac arteries two inches below their origin at the bifurcation of the aorta. In front of the left renal artery (artery to the kidney) lay the left renal vein, a large vessel which passed from left to right in front of the aorta and then emptied into the inferior vena cava, a huge vein paralleling the right side of the aorta. One inch below the renal vein the aorta rapidly widened, in the shape of a football. Its wall became thinner and the pulsations more marked. At its widest point the bulge measured a little over three inches, and then just as rapidly it narrowed to join the normal segment of aorta just above its bifurcation.

"Sam, get your hand in here and feel what an aneurysm is like. Gently now – I don't want you to loosen up any plaques or clots to float downstream."

"Wow, Dr. O'Hara, that feel's awesome. It's so thin. You can feel the pulsation and flow of blood just under your finger."

"Okay, Jack, let's clean off the neck of this monster up here, just beneath the renal vein." Dr. O'Leary began to separate the fibrous tissue surrounding the aorta where the aneurysm was just beginning. He used a similar technique to that of Ted's and soon the adventitia was exposed.

"Sam, what are the layers in the wall of an artery?"

"The lining is called the intima, covered by the media, and finally the adventitia on the outside."

"The man is a walking encyclopedia. Right again, Sam. Perhaps you could tell me what goes wrong in the arterial wall to allow an aneurysm to form."

"Well, I'm not sure. Is it caused by hardening of the arteries (arteriosclerosis)? In the textbooks, there's something about a congenital weakness caused by an abnormality in the genes."

"Let's explore that a little further. What layer is involved in arteriosclerosis?"

"The thickening is due to cholesterol and fat deposited in the intima, forming plaques which can become calcified."

"I couldn't have said it better myself. Would the pathology you just described explain the bulge we see here?"

"It's hard to imagine."

"Right. The normal intima is only one cell thick and contributes almost nothing to the strength of the arterial wall. The media and adventitia are much stronger. So, what layer has to be defective to allow an aneurysm to form?"

"I'll guess it's the media since it's thicker than the adventitia."

"Well, you're right, but the adventitia, though thin, has fibrous tissue formed in bands which crisscross in all directions. In contrast, the media's fibers are arranged in a circumferential fashion only. Is the media the same in all arteries?"

"I've heard of muscular arteries and elastic arteries. Does that have something to do with the media?"

"Again, you're right. The larger arteries, particularly the aorta, have a relatively thinner media without muscle fibers, but a predominance of elastic fibers. As arteries get smaller the media contains more muscle fibers. Aneurysms are far more common in elastic arteries, and when they do occur in muscular arteries they tend to be saccular and arise from the crotch of a branching where a small gap in the medial muscle fibers can be found. Sam, you're on the right track. Something does happen to the elastic fibers either on a genetic basis or, as I more readily suspect, secondary to degeneration considering the age group where aneurysms are more likely found. Whatever the cause the aorta or other major artery loses elasticity, and thus strength, in its wall. Over a period of time, it enlarges and can eventually rupture. Arteriosclerosis is commonly seen within aneurysms, but then it is a common finding in a great number of people beyond the age of fifty. It is probably only a coincidental finding. Research as to why this occurs and what can be done to avoid it has been ongoing, but with the recent lack of financial backing from the federal government, the answer may be a long time in coming. In the meantime, we simple-minded surgeons will continue to do our thing."

"Jack, we have the neck pretty clean in the front, now let me get around the aorta so we can clamp it off later. The secret is to get in a plane right on the adventitia, particularly on the right to get between the aorta and the vena cava. If we get a hole in the cava we've got big time problems; Helen, let me have a kidney pedicle clamp."

Helen handed him a large clamp, the jaws of which were in the shape of a lazy semi-circle, and the tip of which was suitably blunt. He began pushing the tip into the tissue plane around the adventitia over the aorta, first gently push and then spread so as to progressively create a tunnel. He was quite careful to avoid pushing too hard if he felt significant resistance.

Having developed the space between the aorta and the vena cava, he placed his left index finger in it. Then using his right hand he maneuvered the clamp from the left side of the aorta gradually coaxing it behind the artery until he could feel the tip with his left index finger. Keeping his finger between the two vessels so as to protect the huge vein he ever so gingerly guided the clamp through its natural arc until the tip could be seen protruding anteriorly. He then spread the jaws to widen the tract as Jack placed the end of a linen tape in the jaws. Having grasped the tape with the tip of the clamp, Ted rotated the handle and pulled the tape behind the aorta. This maneuver was repeated so that the tape formed a loop around the artery. Traction on the ends of this tape could close the loop and compress the aorta as a precaution, should a vessel clamp slip when the aorta was open. Similar maneuvers were carried out around each common iliac artery.

"Tom, we're just about ready to cross-clamp the aorta. How is Joe doing?"

"Smooth as silk. Vital signs are fine. He made forty cc of urine in the past half hour and his wedge is still thirteen.

"Let's give him 5,000 units of aqueous heparin now and let me know when five minutes are up. Also give him a slug of mannitol." Up till now Ted wanted Joe's blood to clot normally during the dissection necessary to expose the aorta, but once it was open, with clamps above and below, he didn't want it to clot in the stagnant vessels beyond the clamps. Heparin is an anti-coagulant which has a short life span in the body and serves this purpose quite well.

Although the arteries to the kidneys branch from the aorta above the point where Ted intended to clamp, the hemodynamic changes precipitated by this clamping would place an extra stress on the kidneys. Mannitol is a diuretic which enables the kidneys to extract a greater volume of fluid from the blood to be excreted as urine. By thus increasing their efficiency, the kidneys would be afforded a greater degree of protection.

"Helen, let me have a Kelly clamp and a 25 mm sizing template to measure the aortic diameter." He placed the template in the jaws of the clamp and pressed the concave portion against the normal aortic wall. It was a perfect fit. "Okay, give me a 25 mm straight, thin walled, Gore-Tex graft. How about it, Tom, has it been five minutes?"

"Three and a half, Ted."

"Helen, I need two angled Pott's clamps." (A Pott's clamp is one of a variety of vascular instruments designed to temporarily occlude an artery without crushing its wall.)

"Five minutes, Ted."

"Tom, I'm going to occlude the iliacs first. When I clamp the aorta above the neck of the aneurysm I don't want any debris or clots traveling into the legs. Let me know if he drops his peripheral pressure or the wedge." He first clamped the right common iliac and then the left.

"Steady as a rock, Ted."

"Glad to hear it, Tom."

He took a large clamp which had semicircular jaws similar to the kidney pedicle clamp but with a curved handle which allowed the instrument to be out of the way when properly placed. Placing his left index finger in the tract he had created between the cava and the aorta, he rotated the tip of the clamp around the left side of the aorta until it abutted his finger. Again as before, he guided the tip anteriorly between the two vessels. He had done this maneuver with the jaws open and had guided only the posterior jaw through the tunnel, so that now he was able to slowly close it on the aorta until all pulsation ceased within the aneurysm.

"What about it, Tom? Any change?"

"The wedge is at eleven. Go ahead, Ted. Joe's tolerating it without a hitch. I'll bump up the IV fluid."

"Here we go, ladies and gents. Jack, get that cell saver ready to go."

Up to this point bleeding had been minimal and controlled with the harmonic scalpel or ligatures, but once the aneurysm was opened there would be a sudden gush of blood and the lumbar arteries opening in the back wall of the aneurysm would backbleed until they were controlled with sutures. Jack placed the sucker leading to the cell saver in Sam's hand.

"From here on, Sam, aspirate all the blood in the operative field. The cell saver will separate the red from the white cells, plasma, and any other debris. It will automatically wash the cells and enable us to give them back to Joe through his IV line. That way we may not have to transfuse him from the blood bank. Here, Jack, open up the aneurysm for me while I get ready to tackle these lumbars."

Jack took the scalpel from Helen and cut vertically through the front wall for a short distance. The blood trapped in the aneurysm rushed out and Sam diligently sucked it away. With a large scissor, he rapidly enlarged the opening to meet the normal aorta above and below. Inside, Ted could see laminated, gelatinous layers of old clot hugging the posterior wall. He scooped them out with his right hand and directed Sam to aspirate whatever was left. Beneath the clot the wall was thickened with arteriosclerotic plaques, many of them brittle with calcium. Bright red blood steadily oozed from the many orifices of the lumbar arteries scattered among the plaques.

"With all that calcium, it's going to be difficult to suture those openings shut. Helen, give me another Kelly."

He grasped each plaque with this simple clamp and one by one stripped them away from the back wall until he had exposed the softer media. Using one suture after another, he transfixed each lumbar aperture as Jack tied them until the backbleeding had ceased. On the left anterior wall near the lower end of the aneurysm, there was significant bleeding from the orifice of the inferior mesenteric artery. The bleeding was quite brisk, which encouraged Ted. This indicated to him that the circulation to the left side of the colon was adequate even though this artery were to be sacrificed.

"Shall we measure the pressure in the inferior mesenteric?" Jack asked as he turned to Helen to request the equipment.

"No, I don't think it will be necessary, with the briskness of that bleeding. One final suture stanched the flow. Had the circulation been inadequate it would be necessary to implant the end of that artery into the wall of the graft used to replace the aneurysm.

"Jack, Sam, take a look here on the back wall between two of the lumbars. See the ulcer where the wall has eroded. That shiny white surface at its base is the anterior spinous ligament. That's the nipple of dye we saw protruding posteriorly on the CT scan and the reason Joe was having back pain."

"Well, I'll be damned. I haven't seen that bit of pathology before." Jack leaned over to get a better view.

Sam could only say, "Cool!"

"Well, let's not admire it. We've got work to do"

Ted directed his attention to the neck of the aneurysm at the upper end of the aortic incision. He took a long scissor and cut transversely through the front wall, right and left. He continued the cut across the back wall until the entire aorta had been divided above the origin of the aneurysm. He took a clamp and remove the remainder of the plaques lining the cuff of aorta below the cross clamp he had previously placed before opening the artery.

"I'm going to make sure there are no loose pieces of plaque or intima caught by the clamp." He opened the clamp for several beats of the heart. Blood gushed into the operative field including several pieces of intimal debris. Ted quickly ratcheted the clamp shut once again, and Sam expertly suctioned the field thus donating another three hundred cc of blood to the cell saver.

"Let's have that Gore-Tex graft, Helen. Thanks, and that 3-0 prolene double-armed suture."

"Of course, Doctor. It's right here on your card."

"Jack, run that suture up the right side of the anastomosis and I'll do the same on the left."

Jack took the needle holder from the scrub nurse and passed one needle through the edge of the gortex graft. Then, grasping the needle on the other end of the suture, he passed it through the back wall of the aorta, where Ted had cut across it. Ted then tied the suture approximating the back wall of the graft to the aortic wall, leaving equal lengths of the suture, each end with a needle attached.

Jack grasped one in the jaws of the needle holder and, passing it through the graft and aorta in a continuous series of stitches, anchored the one to the other. Clucking in approval, Ted repeated the same procedure on the left. Jack completed the anastomosis by tying the two ends together on the front of the aorta.

"Helen, basin, please." Ted took the stainless steel container and placed the open end of the graft into it. "Sam, get that sucker in the basin. I want to save any blood we spill when I move the clamp off the aorta down onto the graft. I have to be sure the suture line is tight without leakage before we sew the lower anastomosis."

Jack placed a large vascular clamp across the graft one inch below the just completed anastomosis. He held it open, ready to close it on Ted's command. Ted then slowly opened the clamp on the aorta above. For several beats, blood rushed into the basin clearing any clots or debris from the anastomosis.

"Okay, Jack. Shut her down." Jack's fist reflexly closed the clamp stanching the flow. Sam dutifully aspirated the blood and the cell saver was again 300 cc richer.

"Sam, suck inside the graft here. We don't want any clots forming inside."

Ted left the aortic clamp in place, but open, and directed his attention to the suture line.

"Jack, do you see any leaks that could use an extra stitch?"

"Not on my side, Dr. O'Hara."

"Well, it will please you to know that my stitching was equally as good. There's just a slight ooze from a few suture holes on the back side here. Helen, give me some thrombin."

He took a fluffy bit of gel soaked in liquid thrombin and with the tip of the forceps placed it against the suture line, covering it with a gauze pad to exert pressure. The thrombin would provide the blood with the factors the heparin had deprived it of. Small clots formed rapidly, sealing the suture holes.

Ted picked up the free lower end of the graft and stretched it out within the aneurysm bringing it alongside the open end of the normal sized aorta below. At that point he marked it with a clamp and cut completely across the graft with a scissor, discarding the excess length. With the same technique he had used above, he transected the aortic wall where it had shrunken to its normal caliber.

"Okay, Jack, time for act two. Let's see if you can perform a reasonable encore."

With that Jack anchored the lower end of the graft to the back wall of the aorta with a double-armed suture similar to the one he had used on the proximal anastomosis, and repeated the running suture to approximate the right side of the graft to the aorta below. Ted began suturing the left wall of the graft to the aortic wall, but with a few bites remaining he stopped and asked the scrub nurse for a Fogarty catheter.

"Sam, you've had it easy for quite a while. So what am I doing now?"

"You've got me. I thought you would just finish the anastamosis and we'd be ready to close."

"Do you know what a Fogarty catheter is and what it's used for?"

"Sure. It's a catheter with a soft inflatable balloon at one end and it's used to remove clots from arteries or veins."

"I can't fool you, can I, Sam? Then why do I want to use it now?"

"I don't understand. The patient is anti-coagulated, so that his blood won't clot, and you're about to close the anastomosis to reopen the circulation."

"Okay, Sam, do you remember earlier that I clamped the iliac arteries before I clamped the aorta?"

"Sure, I think that's done to avoid dislodging any clot or debris from the aneurysm and having it go down into the legs."

"Bingo! But now is the time to be super-cautious and assume that, despite all the precautions, some debris or clot may have passed distally. Therefore, before I complete the lower anastamosis, I'll pass the Fogarty all the way down each leg and withdraw it with the balloon inflated just to make sure to remove any clots which might have slipped by."

While he was talking, Ted had threaded the catheter into the arterial system of the right lower extremity and upon retrieving it found no clot or debris. However, when he repeated the same maneuver in the left leg a 1.5-cm. clot popped out through the anastamosis.

"You see, Sam, an ounce of prevention is worth a pound of cure. It's a lot easier to get that out now than to return to the operating room later when the pulses are gone in a cold, mottled foot."

Ted finished the last few stitches on the left side of the anastamosis but left them loose while Jack released the clamps on both iliac arteries. Immediately, bright red blood welled up from below, filling the aorta and the graft. As he prepared to tie the sutures together and complete the anastamosis, air bubbles vacated the aorta through the suture line. The oozing of blood and bubbles ceased as he tied the knot.

"Tom, we're going to open momentarily, I'll release the clamp slowly, but keep an eye on those vitals."

Jack pulled up on the linen tapes around each iliac, as Ted unlatched the clamp across the proximal portion, of the graft and very slowly opened its' jaws. The graft began to pulsate and a few more air bubbles escaped between sutures along the lower anastamosis.

"Jack. Release the iliac tapes one at a time. Good. That's fine." At this time he had the cross clamp about a third open.

"Tom, how is he?"

"Blood pressure down,ten millimeters of mercury, wedge remains thirteen. I'm giving him a little more IV fluid. Everything's fine."

"Okay. Clamp off."

There was no significant oozing from the lower anastomosis and the graft pulsated with each beat of Joe's heart. Indeed the blood flow distally within the iliac symptom was fine.

"Is Joe still doing okay?"

Blood pressure back up to 130. Wedge is 13 and his urine output has been more than adequate."

"Probably due to all the beer he drinks."

Ted carefully removed the original aortic clamp which although open, had remained in position in case of leakage.

"Betty, how much blood have you processed in that cell saver?"

"About 800 cc."

"Well give it back to him. I don't want him whining for an extra stroke on the first tee because I made him anemic. Sam, it's your turn again. What are we going to do with the wall of this dearly departed aneurysm?"

"Remove it, I guess."

"I'll be danged. I finally got a wrong answer. Time for me to give a lecture. I won't go back to prehistoric Neanderthal times, sixty or seventy years ago, when surgeons would wrap aneurysms with various materials to hopefully prevent rupture or to fill them with wire and by heating the wire cause it to clot off. A British surgeon, Sir Ashley Cooper, in 1818 was the first to tie off the aorta above the aneurysm and have the patient actually survive. Needless to say, the results of all such procedures proved dismal. With advances in anesthesia, blood transfusion, the advent of antibiotics and most importantly the techniques developed by the early cardiac surgeons such as Blalock, Hufnagel, Gross, and Taussig, it remained for Dr. Charles Dubost to perform the first successful resection of an abdominal aortic aneurysm in 1951. He replaced the aneurysm with a homograft, a human aorta from a cadaver.

"This technique necessitated several hours of meticulous dissection including ligation and division of each branch of the aorta below the renals. With the availability of fresh donors rather limited, various techniques of freezing and treating the donor grafts with preservative solutions allowed the establishment of banks from which specimens could be taken when needed. However, it soon became apparent that the middle – and long-term results of this procedure were unsatisfactory with degeneration, rupture, or thrombosis. Hence a great deal of research began to find an artificial material that could be an adequate substitute for an arterial wall. But, rather than go through a litany of the various grafts which have evolved through the years, let's concentrate on that old aneurysmal wall and what to do with it."

"One problem that rapidly became apparent with the use of artificial grafts was, if you left the front wall of the graft in contact with the intestine or covered it with only a thin layer of peritoneum, the two could adhere one to the other, and over a period of time an opening could form, allowing lethal hemorrhage into the intestine.

"Since there isn't much tissue available, other than the peritoneum, to interpose between the two, surgeons had to become creative in placing something viable between the intestine and the graft. This complication was more frequent where the upper anastamosis lay directly behind the duodenum (the first part of the small intestine) with no intervening peritoneum. Innovative local muscle flaps or tongues of omentum from within the abdominal cavity promised some help; but were time consuming and poorly effective. It gradually dawned upon a few of our predecessors that two hours of dissection could be saved by leaving the aneurysm in place. One could open into it; place the graft within its walls; and close the anterior wall over the graft, effectively building a barrier to the intestines in front. So, Sam, someone over the age of fifty was actually smart enough to save operating time and at the same time almost eliminate a dreaded complication down the road."

"Truly amazing, Dr. O'Hara. Just imagine what the intelligence and imagination of my generation will contribute."

"I'm in your corner, son, but the generation you're referring to will have to somehow find its way out of the blind alley our profession finds itself trapped in today."

While the previous oratory was going on, Ted had closed the aneurysm wall over the graft having trimmed it to fit snugly. He also covered the area of the proximal anastamosis with available fibrofatty tissue and anchored all in place with several sutures.

"You will also notice, Sam, since we used the retroperitoneal approach there was no reason to open the peritoneum; and therefore no necessity to waste time in closing it."

"Jack, let's get all the hardware out of here and close. Betty, I'm getting kind of weary listening to country. Got a good Broadway CD, some good closing music? Jack had already removed the Buckwalter retracter system and all the lap tapes. Let's go Jack, interrupted O-vicryl on all the layers. Put them back together the same way the good Lord made them."

"I've got the score from *The Fantastics*, kind of old, but then so are you, Dr. O'Hara."

"No need to get smart, young lady, but you're right. Let's all reminisce a little. Get in here, Sam. Help Jack keep his sewing straight. Good practice, tying those knots."

El Gaillo's baritone filled the room: *"Try to remember the kind of September when life was slow and oh so mellow."* Nostalgia closed in on Ted. Indeed, the words rang true. In retrospect, his youth did seem slower, thought it probably wasn't; and certainly was oh so mellow.

"Try to remember the kind of September, when grass was green and grain was yellow." The words mesmerized him, gradually eliminating all external sensory stimuli. Even as the adrenaline level, occasioned by attention to the operation just completed, now ebbed from every tissue of his body, his mind became free to wander.

He was with Laura enjoying the electricity wherever they touched, wrapped in the cocoon of the hammock on their lanai oh so many years ago, too many years. Her sweet face was aglow with a kaleidoscope of flattering hues from a typical Hawaiian sunset as a gentle trade wind walked a few strands of golden hair across her tanned cheek.

"Try to remember when life was so tender, and love was an ember about to billow."

The immediacy and mutual fulfillment of their love drew no distinction between memories past and the delicious present; just as the ecstasy marking the culmination of their physical union differed only as to time and circumstance from the joy of a shared decision, or the simultaneous enjoyment of good food, music, or an artful theatrical performance. Ted and Laura, an exquisitely carved cameo, smiling its façade to the world amongst a treasure trove of remembrance. Their sum was truly greater than their parts. When Ted saw patients, lectured, or operated, Laura was ever present; chiding his temper; choosing his words; or showing him the road to understanding and compassion. And when Laura was chairing a meeting of her board of directors; discussing a new contract with her employees; or bidding for a new job, Ted was there reminding her to be firm when necessary, a good listener, and steadfast in her insistence on efficiency and personal responsibility.

"Deep in December, it's nice to remember without the hurt the heart is hollow."

"Careful, Ted. Don't be maudlin." Their connubial heart was far from "hollow," filled with the tears of many tragedies, which when pumped forth formed the cement which bound all the good times and shared memories together. It was just unthinkable to be without each other, the thought of which oddly disturbed him.

"Dr. O'Hara, we just have to glue the skin together and Mr. Hanway will be ready for the recovery room."

"Great, Jack. How about it, Tom? Is he ready to move?"

"Sure thing. Pressure's rock steady. His oxygen saturation is ninety-five percent, the wedge and the urine output are fine."

"Do you plan to extubate him right away (take the breathing tube out) or wait 'til morning to wean him?"

"I'd like to wait until morning when we'll have a better idea how stable he'll be and what kind of pain control we'll get from that epidural catheter."

"Sounds good to me, Tom. Jack, keep an eye on the hemoglobin and Swan-Ganz readings. Let me know immediately of any changes. I'm out of here to talk with his wife. Thanks, girls. You did a great job tonight and I genuinely appreciate your help. Put in your order for donuts tomorrow. To hell with the expense and your girlish figures."

CHAPTER V

"The wise man's understanding turns him to his right."

As Ted entered the waiting room, Vicky was on her feet in a trice anxiously trying to read his expression. He smiled broadly and crossed the room taking her into his widespread arms.

"Joe's just fine. He went through the surgery without a hitch. Right now he's in the recovery room starting to wake up. The aneurysm is gone and his circulation restored. In a few minutes I'll take you there, but be prepared to see a zillion tubes and monitoring machines. That's normal. One thing, though, he won't be able to talk to you. The anesthesiologist and I decided to keep the endotrachial tube in place until we're sure he remains stable and can adequately breathe on his own. Dr. Arthur also placed a catheter adjacent to the spinal cord and will periodically delivering a narcotic through it to control pain. I would anticipate using this for two or three days."

With a sudden massive exhalation, all the anxiety drained from Vicki and she collapsed into Ted. "I can't say how much Joe and I appreciate this. You and Laura have always been there for us. I can't express it in words, but I think you know what I mean. You're the best and I'm honored to be counted a friend."

"That's enough Vicky. Joe's my friend and if I happen to have the ability to help him through a tough time, I'm there. That's what friends do. Laura and I love that guy and we love you. Being selfish there's no way I was going to let him get away from us."

As Vicky regained her balance she dabbed at her eyes with a tissue and turned to embrace Laura who had been standing behind her, a reassuring hand on her shoulder.

"Laura, you tell this lug how good he really is. Forgive me, I'm at a loss and I'm quite sure you can think of a special way of doing it."

"I refuse to give him a swelled head, but I might know a way to show him how much he's appreciated. There are a few tricks I haven't shown him yet."

"Well, now, if my fee is to be paid with such delightful debauchery, I may just bring Joe back to the OR and do it all over again." With that remark he gently patted Laura's posterior which earned him a playful push. "But listen. I'm famished. How about the three of us stopping for a burger at Chili's. My treat."

"I don't know, Ted. I want to stay near Joe tonight."

"He's going to be mostly asleep with a lot of busy nurses and residents hovering about. I know where you're coming from, but after your brief visit there's nothing you can do to help him. You can help yourself by getting some food and a good night's rest. Now, doctor's orders. Let's go see him and then my treat."

"Don't fight the inevitable, Vicky. He's getting into his superior, better-than-thou routine." This time it was Laura who patted Ted's posterior.

∽

It was midnight before Laura and Ted arrived home. Their brief visit to Joe in the recovery room had confirmed Vicki's belief in the success of the operation. Joe was alert enough to respond to her kiss delivered on his sweaty cheek, and the pressure of their clasped hands communicated a lifetime of union and caring. Though still somewhat groggy and befuddled, his eyes reflected a silent gratitude to Ted from a depth of emotion more akin to brothers than friends. Afterward, even Vicki had to recognize the burger and fries filled a void which none of them were previously willing to admit existed. Sated, at peace with themselves and each other, they had parted, each anticipating the escape and regeneration of a good night's sleep.

Laura stood at the bedside talking to Ted who was already ensconced beneath the sheets. He could envision nothing in this world more beautiful, as she stood motionless in a clinging black negligee. All traces of makeup were gone which only served to heighten the stirrings in Ted's now adrenaline-depleted body. Masked by her exquisitely applied cosmetics she was a singular Aphrodite to the business world she excelled in, and an affable, sympathetic paragon to their circle of friends and acquaintances. The face she gave to the world was all of that and more; but without these harlequin accoutrements this was the vision only he knew, forever imprinted in passion and gratitude on every vestige of his being.

Engulfed in these feelings, he looked up into her eyes which were radiant with understanding and admiration. All the while she searched his to seek out the return on her investment. Indeed, if it is true that the eyes are the windows to the soul, she immediately sensed the depth of his concern and protection. In that incandescent instant they experienced a union of their souls bereft of time and place and therefore without their limitations, wherein they did not think, but knew; did not imagine, but became aware. This is what poets refer to as love, the one portion of our existence which dares to touch upon eternity renewed within the confines of this all-too-mortal world.

"Sweetheart, after all these years, you're simply irresistible. My resistance is nonexistent. So, hop in here and take advantage of me."

"Just hold your horses, Romeo. How do I know you didn't leave it all in the operating room?"

"Well, I could give you the scientific explanation or I could just show you. You call it."

Laura had slipped into her side of the bed and as they turned to each other she playfully held his face away.

"Hmmm! Not much of a choice. Score or bore! Well, macho man, why don't you give me the scientific lecture."

"Okay, Juliet." Ted drew her to him and they kissed passionately while each began to tenderly explore familiar topography. "Now let's see. I want to be sure you understand fully why what's already beginning to happen does happen."

"Amazing. You're absolutely right. It is happening."

He gently nibbled at her ear while caressing the turgid nipples surmounting her warm breasts.

"How can I explain this if you keep distracting me, Laura?"

"I think you mean distracting your mind. Everything else seems to be right on line. Kiss me like that again."

"Are you going to let me explain? So, during all that surgery my adrenaline level was sky high. This improved my vision, fine-tuned muscular coordination and got the cobwebs out of my brain, but literally put a mutual friend of ours to sleep, and I'm not referring to Joe."

"Oh! Poor baby. Our mutual friend missed all the fun."

"That's not his idea of fun, so, he enjoyed the nap. Then, by the time I was talking to you and Vicki, that same adrenaline was escaping like air out of punctured balloon. Right now, it's at subnormal levels providing the perfect environment for our friend to waken and be record-breaking sensitive to appropriate stimulation. If only my brain can stay awake to appreciate his performance."

"Oh, Rhett. You do know how to turn my head. That was a beautiful story and don't you fret one bit. I won't let the rest of you fall asleep while super-friend and I enjoy the party. Now, come here and don't you dare ever leave me."

"Frankly, my dear, you need never fear."

CHAPTER VI

"SHOULD THE ANGER OF THE RULER BURST
UPON YOU FORSAKE NOT YOUR PLACE;"

I t was a week and a half later. Joe's postoperative course had been quite benign and he had been home for the past five days. Ted had started the day with a short case in the operating room and was well into his office hours when Sally burst in with an expression of utter disbelief on her face.

"Doctor! Lieutenant Anthony D'Amato of the Westbury Police Department is outside insisting that he see you with a warrant for your arrest."

"Well, it's always a pleasure to see Tony but did I hear you correctly? A warrant for my arrest? It sounds so preposterous my curiosity is up. Show him in, Sally."

"Doctor, I don't know. What's going on here?"

"Sally, we can't find out unless you show him in."

"Yes, Doctor, right away."

Sally led a tall, athletic detective into Ted's chamber. He was balding with close-cropped hair and wore a light-colored sports jacket over a yellow shirt opened at the neck.

"Tony, somehow I don't think you're here to tell me about a stomachache or hemorrhoids."

"Right, Doc. I do have the latter but they go with the territory. When this warrant came through I couldn't believe it. Doc, I don't make the laws but I am sworn to uphold them. Sometimes that's not very pleasant and this is one of those times. I've known you long enough that I owe it to you to deliver this myself."

"So, Tony, what have I done? Am I double-parked outside?"

"Not so simple, Doc. The Feds are after you. I have to inform you that the people of the United States accuse you of having breached the intent of Public Law 548, Section X, Paragraph III, in so far as you performed major surgery upon Joseph Hanway on the twenty-fifth of August 2005, in the city of Westbury, Connecticut. Said patient was not assigned to your patient list. Under the statute, the offense is a felony – punishable by a fine not to exceed $100,000 and incarceration in a Federal penitentiary for a period from three to five years.

"The Constitution requires that I inform you of your rights: You have a right to remain silent. If you talk to any police officer, everything you say can and will be used against you in court. You have a right to consult with a lawyer before you are questioned, and may have him with you during questioning. If you cannot afford a lawyer, one will be appointed for you. If you wish to answer questions you have the right to stop answering at any time and talk to a lawyer. You then may have him with you during any further questioning. Do you understand these rights?"

"Yes."

"Are you willing to waive these rights and answer my questions?"

"I don't think so, Tony."

"Well, Ted. I'm ashamed to say I've done my duty. I assume you'll have an attorney present when you talk to the Feds."

"Woah! Did I hear correctly? I'm under arrest for doing surgery on my best friend? Ever since my profession was socialized a year ago, I've tried, though sometimes reluctantly, to live within the bureaucratic regulations forced upon us, including patient assignment. But to make it a felony to go outside that list? And for a friend?"

"You won't get an argument from me, Ted. How can I get on your list? I went to the judge and, due to the nature of the offense, got his agreement not to book you today provided you promise to appear before him tomorrow at 10 A.M. I would recommend you have a lawyer with you."

"Tony, I appreciate the way you've handled this. As you might imagine, I'm a bit taken aback, but thanks again."

"Would to God I wasn't here as the messenger. By the way, I haven't had a chance to ask. How's Joe doing?"

"There's the single bright spot in what has become a depressing day. I saw him this morning and he's doing just fine. I'll tell him you said hello, or better still, you can call him yourself. I'm sure he'd appreciate your stopping by in a few days."

"Thanks. I will. Again. Sorry, Doc. If I can be of any help getting you through the formalities, let me know. By the way, I have to leave this warrant with you."

⤙

Sally stood silent, her face a reflection of shock and disbelief. She had been Ted's secretary for many years; had seen his practice grow; seen the respect rendered to him by many grateful patients and relatives. She was proud to have contributed her share of experience to his success. She had entered the lists on his behalf to argue her way through the recently departed era of HMO's and Managed Care Associations, and more recently used this experience in maintaining a modicum of sanity vis-à-vis the National Health Administration. A glint of fire inbred from her Irish heritage flashed from her eyes as she turned to Dr. O'Hara. "How dare they!"

"They dare, Sally. Now, how many patients are left? When I've seen the last, get Attorney Holleran on the phone, okay?"

"Okay? Those vermin that I deal with every day, those ignoramuses who haven't a clue as to what their decisions lead to, who don't know the difference between a bypass and a tie-clasp, they want your hide as an offering to Big Brother? And you say, okay? I wouldn't wipe my shoes on them."

"I've got plenty of that Irish temper too, but it won't help to keep my hide where it is. Pat Holleran can. Sally, track him down for me, will you?"

❧

As the last patient left. Ted dropped wearily into the chair behind his desk, picked up the phone, and dialed Laura's office.

"Kean Manufacturing Company, Irene speaking."

"Hi! Is the universe's most beautiful, alluring and sexy CEO there?"

"Doc, cut that out. You're going to make me mad at my Roy. He never says things like that."

"Not to worry. I know from a reliable source that you have no grounds for complaint in that department."

"You can say that again, Doc. Hold a minute. I'll get Laura for you." Seconds later Laura was on the line.

"Hi, hon. What's up?"

"*Vas ist nicht eine gebunden ist los.*"

"Now stop it. I've heard your old chestnut too many times. 'What is not up is down.' Seriously, why the call?"

"Serious is right. I've got some bad news."

"Now, you didn't interrupt my sales meeting to tell me you're going to be late for the dance tonight?"

"No, and there's no good way to say this. I've been arrested."

"You've been what?"

"I've been served a warrant for performing surgery on Joe. It seems he was not on my patient list, and under the new law it has become a felony to do so. I've told you about some of the idiotic rules the federal government has imposed."

"So, it is idiotic. Pay the fine and this weekend we'll laugh and have a drink with Vicki and Joe."

"Not so simple, lovebug. I could do hard time in jail. There's going to be a trial."

"Oh, Ted, no! I can't believe this. I'll come right over. Are you still at the office?"

"Yes, but I've got a call in to Pat Holleran. I want to meet with him and show him the warrant. Don't you think he'd be the best choice to defend me? I do."

"Of course, sweetheart. Look, when you finish briefing him, I insist the both of you come home and fill me in."

"Consider it done. I apologize for disturbing your meeting, but I had to tell you as soon as I could."

"Darling, are you kidding? I love you far too much. Now, you hurry home. Laura will take good care of you. We're going to beat this."

"Love you back. We will beat this."

⤸

"Dr. O'Hara, I have Attorney Holleran on the line."

"Thanks, Sally. Pat, it's Ted. I hope I didn't take you away from something important?"

"Just a gin game. I had the afternoon off and played eighteen with Frank. Right now I'm trying to win back what I lost to him on the golf course, and not doing too well, I don't mind saying."

"Well, I hope your luck is better for what I need you for. Can you get over to my office within the hour? It's important. I'll fill you in when you get here."

"Sure, Ted. But what's going on? Can't you tell me now?"

"I'd rather go over everything when you get here."

Roger, Ted. I'll be there in half an hour."

⤸

Pat was still attired in a short-sleeved polo shirt and light tan slacks when Sally ushered him into Ted's consulting room. Ted came around his desk to shake hands with his good friend of many years.

"Thanks for coming so promptly, Pat. Please sit down. Can I get you something? Coffee?"

"Do you have some of that great Irish whiskey?"

"Sure thing. Tulamore Dew? On the rocks?"

"Fine. Will you join me?"

"Sally, three glasses with ice. After this afternoon, I'm sure you could use one too."

Ted picked up the warrant from the blotter on his desk and tossed it into Pat's lap. "Tony dropped in today to serve me with that warrant. It seems I'm facing felony charges for operating on Joe. Under the new laws socializing medicine, I can't provide medical care to anyone not on my patient list, and Joe wasn't."

"Ted, are you up to one of your practical jokes? If you are, I'm not laughing."

"No joke, Pat. Read it and weep."

Pat quickly scanned the warrant noting that it was issued by Judge Harold Cummings of the Second Federal District Court, and called for arraignment at ten in the morning on the following day. "You say Tony delivered this?"

"Right. When he saw it in the hopper, he went to the judge and arranged for me to remain free on my own recognizance until the hearing tomorrow morning."

Sally came in with the glasses and set them on the desk. Ted opened the credenza behind his desk and extracted the bottle of Tulamore Dew. Depositing a healthy slug in each glass, he passed them around.

"I can use this right now and I suspect both of you could also. Pat, I want you to represent me in this – all the way."

Pat let out a low whistle, took a generous portion of his drink, and stretched further into his chair. "I love you like a brother but I would be less than frank if I didn't advise you to get someone who routinely pleads cases in the federal system, from Boston, or New York City – I can give you a few names."

"I appreciate that, Pat, but you're stuck with me. I know you and can talk freely. I don't know them. Will you do it?"

"Okay, okay. But I hope you can afford me. I'm going to need a constant supply of that whiskey and Sally for at least four hours a day to fill me in on all the regulations and directives you've received here in the office since the law was passed. I can read the law but I need Sally to interpret all the nuances applied to it by the National Health Administration. Okay with you, Sally?"

"When do we start, Mr. Holleran? As far as I'm concerned, the government just declared war, but they neglected to check on who's in the other army. That's their fatal error."

"Tomorrow, after the hearing."

"I'll have everything ready." She took a final large gulp from her drink, smiled at Ted, and excused herself.

"Ted, let's talk about what happens tomorrow at ten o'clock."

"Hold up a second. One more favor. Laura's waiting at home for both of us to show up. She wants in on all the details and there's no sense repeating them; if I'm not mistaken she should have some more of that Celtic ambrosia, ready and waiting."

CHAPTER VII

*"MORE WEIGHTY THAN WISDOM OR WEALTH IS
A LITTLE FOLLY."*

I t was ten minutes of ten the
following morning and they
were sitting at a table to the right front of the elevated desk belonging
to Judge Harold Cummings. The judge had not entered as yet and
there were only a few law clerks and interested bystanders in the benches
behind the railing which bisected the room. Ted and Pat were
appropriately attired in dark suits with quiet ties. On the surface they
appeared quite calm although Ted seemed somewhat withdrawn and
preoccupied. Pat was engrossed in reading from the legal pad on the
table in front of him, occasionally making notations with his pen.

The rear door opened and two determined-looking men entered, one
middle-aged with a shock of graying hair, and the other in his thirties with
an athletic build. Both were dressed in medium gray suits, as if in uniform,
and carried bulky briefcases. They were busily conversing but nodded to
Pat as they passed through the gate in the center of the railing and took
their place to the left front of the judge's desk.

Pat leaned toward Ted to whisper in his ear: "My friend, you must have seriously pissed off some grand Pooh-Bah with your surgical derring-do. Do you know who the Hollywood type with the graying temples is?"

"Haven't got the foggiest. Am I supposed to? He's not from Westbury."

"That's Richard Sterling, former Senator from the Commonwealth of Pennsylvania and presently the head of the criminal division of the Department of Justice, the right hand of the Attorney General of the United States. When you do something, you do it big."

"Are you saying the government is swatting a fly with a sledgehammer?"

"No, but I suspect they want to make an example of you to the other physicians throughout the country."

"Who's the All-American quarterback type with him?"

"I'll have to research that but he's probably a blossoming star in the same department."

"All rise. The Second Federal District Court is now in session, Judge Harold Cummings presiding."

Everyone stood in response to the bailiff's request as Judge Cummings swept into the courtroom and gaining the position immediately behind his desk, banged the gavel, and took his seat.

"Bailiff, what case is before the court?"

"The people of the United States versus Theodore O'Hara, M.D."

"Who represents the people?"

"Your honor, may I introduce myself, the honorable Richard Sterling, director of the Criminal Division of the United States Department of Justice."

"And what is the nature of the peoples' charge against Dr. O'Hara?"

"That he willfully and knowingly ignored the specifications of Section X Paragraph III of Public Law 548 passed in Congress on the twentieth of September in the year of our Lord two thousand and four. He did so by performing a surgical procedure upon one Joseph Hanway, an individual not assigned to Dr. O'Hara's patient list, on the twenty-fifth of August of this year at St. Lucy's Hospital in the city of Westbury in Connecticut."

"And who represents the accused?"

"Your honor, may I introduce myself. I am Patrick Holleran, a practicing attorney before the bar here in the city of Westbury in the State of Connecticut."

"Dr. O'Hara has engaged your service in his defense?"

"He has, your honor."

"May I assume that neither of the parties objects to my allowing Dr. O'Hara to remain free on his own recognizance, without bail, until a plea date?"

Mr. Sterling stood up. "I have no objection, your honor, but I would request that Dr. O'Hara's license to practice medicine be suspended until this matter is settled, in so far as the people of these United States are his employers."

"Objection, your honor?" Pat's voice resonated clearly throughout the courtroom.

"Sustained. Mr. Sterling need I remind you that Dr. O'Hara remains innocent until the people prove him guilty beyond a reasonable doubt? In so far as the people are his employer, decisions that could be interpreted as based upon a conflict of interest should be scrupulously avoided. The people during this trial must remain further from reproach than Caesar's wife. Is there any further business to discuss before I set a plea date?"

"If it pleases the court." Again, Pat stood to address Judge Cummings, at the same time reaching into his briefcase to retrieve a document. "In the interest of my client, I wish to file a brief challenging the constitutionality of Section X, Paragraph III of Public Law 548 and respectfully request your honor set a date to consider the matter when both parties may be better prepared." He stepped forward, placing the document in the judge's hand.

Mr. Sterling perceptibly reddened but was instantly on his feet. "Objection, the law in question was passed with a majority vote in Congress and duly signed by the President."

"Overruled. I am not aware of any precedent to date concerning this particular law. Dr. O'Hara is within his rights to challenge." At that point he consulted his calendar and turned to both counsels. "Three weeks should provide ample time to prepare your arguments. I will consider them at 10 A.M. on the third of October. Court is adjourned."

The bailiff rose and again intoned the familiar phrase. "All rise – ."

‿

Richard Sterling was sipping a Glenlivet on the rocks while sitting in the First Class section on his flight back to Washington. Next to him was the quarterback type whose name was Robert Giorgio. Indeed, he was a rising star in the Justice Department having been Law Revue at Harvard and subsequently clerked for the Chief Justice of the Supreme Court. Recently, he had successfully prosecuted a series of drug dealers in the Southern States. Both had their briefcases open with a sheaf of papers on their laps. They were discussing the morning's activities.

Sterling spoke first. "Did you say Judge Cummings had been appointed to the bench during the older Bush's administration? He certainly seems to know the law."

"He's a no-nonsense judge. Runs his courtroom by the book."

"Well, whatever his motivation or beliefs, he's given us a good deal of extra work. I'll concentrate on the trial itself. I want you to research and write the brief upholding the constitutionality of the law. What are your thoughts?"

"Before I get into that, what about Dr. O'Hara's lawyer, Pat Holleran? My first impression was of a typical general practitioner, but within the space of five minute he placed us on notice as to extra-curricular activities and has embroiled us in a defense of the law under which we are prosecuting the good doctor."

"I'm not sure I agree. He got the judge to slap our wrist about Dr. O'Hara continuing his job, but he's in over his head on the constitutional question. Check him out, but in the end it's one guy against the entire Justice Department. Remember, both the President and the Director of the National Health Administration want this fellow hung out to dry. There have been rumblings about this particular aspect of the law and without it the entire package could unravel. What's your estimate as to how he's going to argue the brief?"

"If I were doing it, it would be first amendment all the way. He has to equate freedom of choice of one's doctor to freedom of speech. Without checking I can think of two or three precedents against that position. Anyway, I'll get started tomorrow and have the brief on your desk at least one week before the deadline."

~

Laura served a great dinner, smoked salmon with chopped onion, capers, and Bernaise sauce over toast points, followed by stuffed sole with wild rice and sautéed snow peas. Pat and Ted were relaxing over coffee as Laura entered from the kitchen. (Laura was the first to speak.)

"So, Pat, how did we do in round one?"

"I would call it a draw."

"But you got the judge to allow Ted to continue working. Not only that, he warned them about any other dirty tricks which could be construed as a conflict of interest."

"Peanuts, Laura. It changes nothing about the charge or the possible penalties, if convicted. Frankly, our best defense is to avoid a trial. This is a new law which to date has never been challenged. One way to do this is to convince a federal judge to place a stay on it, forcing the Supreme Court to render a decision as to its constitutionality. I did surprise the opposition with this one but don't get your hopes up. I've got a lot of work ahead of me in preparing that brief. Remember, we're going up against all the facilities of the United States government."

It was Ted's turn now, "Are you saying that if we can convince Judge Cummings to place a stay on the law the Supreme Court has to render an opinion before, or even if I can be prosecuted."

"That's right, Ted. But again, there's only a slim chance of that happening."

"How do you intend arguing that point in your brief?"

"The obvious avenue open to us is the first amendment. If a citizen has the right to freedom of speech and association, he should have the right to choose his own doctor. To you and I that seems obvious, but in a legal argument the issues become blurred and there are precedents out there which could be detrimental to such an argument. I personally feel we have a better chance along the lines of restraint of trade. There are many laws, both Federal and State, protecting freedom of trade. If we argue that medicine in its present milieu is a business and not a profession, we may be able to convince this one federal judge to give us our day in the Supreme Court."

"I knew my country lawyer is sharper than any big-city mouthpiece."

"Look, Ted. This country lawyer did surprise them today, but they'll be more than ready in three weeks. Sterling will be the mouthpiece but his sidekick, whose name by the way is Robert Giorgio, is the one to look out for. He's brilliant: Harvard Law Review, Supreme Court clerkship, photographic mind, and a prosecuting record reminiscent of Sherman's march to the sea. I'll wager he already has computer printouts of every first amendment case in the history of the Republic."

"Pat, both Ted and I are aware of the danger he's in and we're deeply appreciative of your efforts. Just tell us what to do and we'll do it."

"Thanks for the confidence, Laura, but I hope I've made it clear they're out to make an example of you. The big guys are rolling the dice on this one. Everything we can do to gain sympathy prior to the trial we should do. Which brings to mind step number one. The last thing Sterling and company want before the trial is publicity. After conviction they'll shout it from the housetops. Now don't you agree that a constitutional challenge to a new law which concerns every citizen and their doctors should be properly advertised?"

"Absolutely."

"Ted, I already reported today's proceedings to Sam Vicario over at the *Westbury Gazette*. He has assured me the story will go out over the AP wire tonight. So, prepare yourselves for the onslaught of the fourth estate. If I don't miss my guess, in three weeks, that courtroom will be overflowing with reporters from every newspaper and TV network worthy of the name."

"How should we react? Should we talk to the press?"

"It's going to be difficult but the answer is no. Let me do the talking for you. Now, Ted, let's assume the judge or the Supreme Court shoots us down. Judge Cummings will then set a plea date."

"What does that involve?"

"You either plead guilty or not guilty to the charge. Don't misunderstand me but now I'm really going to play the part of a lawyer. Correct me if I'm wrong but to the best of my knowledge, you did operate on Joe at his request and with the knowledge that he was not on your assigned list of patients?"

"That's right."

"Now hear me. If it is your intent to plead guilty, I will approach the Justice Department to work out a plea bargain, which could result in a reduction or suspension of a sentence or fine. There would be no trial. It's my opinion that their purpose is to set a precedent by finding you guilty. Whether that is by your plea or by a trial is immaterial and for that matter so is the punishment. Should you plead not guilty a trial date will be set, giving both sides ample time to prepare. I want you to think about your options. You have plenty of time to make your decision since the hearing on the briefs has to be settled first."

"I can tell you right now, Pat."

"Please don't. I meant it when I said, 'think about it.' Besides, for the next three weeks, I'll have enough on my mind."

CHAPTER VIII

"THE END OF HIS TALK IS UTTER MADNESS."

A week had passed and the lights in the surgical office on Phoenix Avenue had just been turned on to accommodate the opalescent twilight engulfing the familiar rooftops and spires of an Autumnal Westbury. Rush hour traffic had subsided and the pastel hues of the fading sunset accented the few remaining cars in the adjacent parking lot like somber haystacks similarly scattered in an oil painting by Monet. Inside, the frenetic daylight activity had been supplanted by an eerie silence disturbed only by the occasional whirr-clack-buzz of an incoming fax or the ratcheta-ratcheta of a computer printout of the latest email.

Pat Holleran leaned back, shirt sleeves rolled up and glasses precariously perched at the very tip of his nose. He wearily glanced above their horn-rimmed frames to isolate Sally with a haggard stare of frustration, as she busily stacked an olio of papers scattered in disarray on the desktop between them.

"Lord, save us. I hope that's it. I thought I'd seen it all, but this bureaucratese is something else again. In spite of your help, I can't make head nor tail of it. Ever since the Feds took over, they've been flooding your office with monthly mounds of gerbalese. Most of it amounts to the tinkling of brass, signifying nothing, or God knows what."

"More pity for us poor secretaries who have to read all that garbage. You don't think Dr. O'Hara does? Do you?"

"To be sure, after a few months of wasting my time, I wouldn't, either. I haven't found a word which could possibly help me to defend Ted. But we had to look and thanks for your help. I know you have been a delightful fixture in this office for many years. How long have you been Ted's secretary?"

"From the early 'seventies when he came to Westbury from New York. One year ago, when the government took over the medical profession, they bought this building, enlarged the office, and moved in three other surgeons to form a coverage group. Fortunately I was kept on as one of the secretaries."

"Then you must know Ted as well as anyone?"

"Almost."

She picked up a thin pamphlet, handing it to Pat. "How about the paragraph I underlined on the second page of this one? I read it as saying that any surgeon can provide care in an emergency."

"I saw that, but it specifically states that it must be a life-threatening emergency. Sterling would never let us get away with that one considering there was no evidence Joe's aneurysm had already ruptured. Help me, Sally! As you may or may not know, Ted and I have been friends for a long time. We grew up together, in Queens, where our parents were neighbors; went to the same grammar school, high school, even college. After graduation, we didn't see each other much, what with his going off to Boston for medical school and my staying in the city to learn the law. Internship and residency took him further away while I tried my hand before the bar in Manhattan. Then in 1970 the army took us both. I spent two years in the Judge Advocate's corps on a grand tour through Europe while stationed in Munich. Poor Ted found himself in the jungles of Vietnam. I met him again during Christmas of 1972, after we both had been mustered out. I didn't recognize him. He was a totally changed person. Whereas I had always known him to be an outgoing 'king of the hill' personality, he had become silent, and withdrawn with none of the spontaneity or camaraderie which had previously identified his character. Of course, we remained the best of friends, but he would never voluntarily talk about his service in 'Nam, nor could I or anyone else prompt him to do so. He began working at the Emergency Room in Roosevelt Hospital, hardly what he had been trained for, but would take off on an occasional free weekend to Connecticut. I finally got out of him that he was visiting Westbury to see a good friend whom he had met in Southeast Asia, our own Joe Hanway. Gradually, I noticed traces of his old self returning. One Sunday, after watching a Giants football game at the old Polo Grounds, Ted announced he would be moving to Westbury to open his practice. An unaccustomed smile lit up his face as he invited me to join him the following weekend to introduce me to a girl he was dating there. Nothing could have kept me away. That's when I met Laura and immediately understood the magic that was transforming my buddy to his former self."

"She brought along her classmate and best friend, Mary. If one believes in love at first sight, that was it. When we drove through the countryside the following afternoon, enjoying all the antique New England villages throughout the valleys of the Litchfield hills, I fell in love for the second time in two days. Pursuit of a corporate law career in New York City soon paled in comparison to being my own boss in Westbury. I also met Joe, who was simply Joe: sarcastic, amusing, quite obviously intelligent, and a tiger of a friend. He too was cloaked in that convenient "full metal jacket" which protected so many Vietnam veterans. In all the years that have since passed, other than the acknowledgment that they first met it the jungle, I haven't once been able to delve into the details of their Vietnam experience, which brings me to the question I must now ask you."

A puzzled expression overtook Sally's countenance, masking an unspoken query as Pat continued.

"I can fully understand why in normal times friendship would be the assumed basis for Ted's performing the surgery on Joe. But these are not normal times. A $100,000 fine and five years in jail are definitely abnormal. My lawyer's curiosity is killing me. There has to be something light-years ahead of just friendship to explain Ted's quixotic behavior. I believe that something lies in the mystery which has eluded me all these years. If you know, help me save your boss. What happened to the two of them in Vietnam?"

"I had assumed you already knew or I would have said something sooner. If it can help Dr. O'Hara in this upcoming trial, I'm quite sure he wouldn't mind my telling you."

"Perhaps it would help me understand the facts I can plan a defense on."

"I could just say that Mr. Hanway saved Dr. O'Hara's life but the story deserves a better benediction than that. Dr. O'Hara was assigned to a MASH unit, which saw almost constant combat service in the year and a half he was in Vietnam. The obscenity of the carnage he dealt with on a daily basis rapidly destroyed his idealism to the point that, beyond mechanically caring for his patients, he became introverted and struggled only for survival. Despondent, he even began to experiment with drugs to dull the edge of fear he lived with twenty-four hours a day. God knows they were as plentiful as the putrid water inundating the rice paddies which seemingly engulfed them all. Then, with only a month left 'in country' a North Vietnamese offensive overran the leading regiment of the marine division they were supporting. Casualties filled the MASH to overflowing when the sounds of the surrounding battle came audibly closer. Headquarters ordered evacuation of his unit and arrangements were made to helicopter out all of the wounded, as well as the medical personnel. Unfortunately, a dozen wounded were too critical to be transported and Dr. O'Hara was in the midst of salvaging a patient with a lacerated liver and spleen. As the others left, he remained at the operating table with the anesthesiologist and several corpsmen who volunteered to replace the OR nurses.

"Just as they finished, a platoon of North Vietnamese swept into the compound. After ensuring there was no armed resistance, and aware their prisoners were medical personnel, their leader placed the business end of his automatic rifle to Dr. O'Hara's temple and indicated that he was to take care of their own casualties. While Dr. O'Hara and his team proceeded to do so, the Viet Cong massacred the injured Americans, including the young soldier whose life had just been spared by Dr. O'Hara's surgery."

"Go on, Sally."

"When they had finished with the enemy wounded, the Americans were lashed together with hands tied behind their backs. A squad of Viet Cong was detailed to carry the stretchers and escort their prisoners to the enemies' rear. Dusk descended an hour later and the leader called a halt. The prisoners were huddled together near the tiny path where the group had entered what optimistically could be called a clearing. A single soldier with an AK 47 was assigned to guard them and scouts were dispatched front, rear, and to the flanks, twenty yards deep into the forbidding jungle. The balance of the squad gathered at the opposite end of the clearing where, murmuring in muffled tones, they placed their weapons nearby so as to be retrievable in an instant, and opened their packs to get at food and water.

"Despairing of ever leaving this hated jungle alive, Dr. O'Hara lost all interest in resting and thus was surprised by a muffled cry to his left, almost indiscernible amongst the constant background noise of the oppressive forest surrounding them. Apparently, the Viet Cong had not heard it, since no one reacted. However, several seconds later, a gunshot reverberated from the dense growth forward of the clearing followed by a sharp cry in Vietnamese. The enemy group at the opposite end of the clearing quickly reached for their weapons and the prisoners' guard turned, pointing the muzzle of his automatic rifle at Dr. O'Hara. As he was squeezing the trigger, a dark shadow erupted from the jungle's edge, driving the guard into the ground as the bullet from his rifle rattled harmlessly through the trees. The thrust of a bayonet, held in the right hand of the intruder, killed the guard instantly. Simultaneously a series of well-aimed shots from the undergrowth removed any threat from the remaining enemy soldiers. Sgt. 1st Class Joe Hanway of C Company, 1st Battalion, 3rd Marines introduced himself as he rapidly freed the prisoners' hands. 'You didn't think the old man was going to leave you strays out here to fend for yourselves? Did you?'"

"So that's it. It wasn't just friendship. Ted was repaying a debt – a debt of honor."

"When the warrant was served last week in the office, I had guessed as much." From that day Dr. O'Hara and Joe have been like two peas in a pod, brothers from the same fabric. They helped each other overcome the Vietnam syndrome so firmly fixed in the souls of too many survivors of that ill-starred conflict. But it was something only between the two of them. They felt no one else could possibly understand. Correction! I'm sure Laura knows, and knew from the start of their relationship. That beautiful lady deserves a medal for completing Dr. O'Hara's rehabilitation and much more. The love they share makes anything possible. I only became privy to the story one afternoon about twenty years ago. Dr. O'Hara was stewing about some slurs he had heard about Joe's race and background that had emanated from a few of his competitors in business. That day I was just a sounding board as he proved what kind of a person and friend Joe really was."

"That explains the why but there is something about the doctor-patient assignment list that I haven't grasped as yet. The documents only confuse me more. Help me. How about a quick course in futility?"

"Well, within two months of socialized medicine becoming the law of the land, a veritable tome arrived from the National Health Administration. Among 2,000 pages of regulations, there was one chapter dealing with the subject of doctor – patient lists. The lists are totally computerized. Individual patient information can be printed out but, because of a computer block, a doctor's entire list of patients cannot. Each surgeon in our office is provided with a password allowing him to access his list of patients but not the entire physician referral database. The National Health Administration maintains a system containing the entire database, which can be accessed from hospitals and other medical institutions throughout the country, again through appropriate passwords unique to each institution. A backup system, designated solely to the same database, is available at the headquarters of the National Health Administration in their Washington office, but for safety's sake it cannot be entered from outside that office. Unfortunately, that office is closed each day from 5:00 P.M. to 8:00 A.M. the following morning."

"Do you mean that no one can enter it from a distant computer?"

"Correct. You have to telephone the office and offer them proper identification before they will do it for you."

"Okay. I follow so far. Anything else that might help me out?"

"I mentioned before that surgeons cover each other in groups of four, since no one individual can be available 365 days a year. On the computer, following a given doctor's name and address, a distinctive icon or symbol can be seen. When you click on that marker, the names of the other three covering surgeons will come on the screen. That doesn't mean you can then enter their patient files, but whatever institutions needs the information may at least check locally which one of the surgeons is covering. The reason for the system remaining computerized is the unwieldiness of the numbers involved. Each primary physician in the Westbury area is assigned 3,000 patients, each surgeon, 8,000, since their services are less utilized on a percentage basis. That's it in a nutshell."

"Okay. Then check this out for me. Access to the entire physician referral database is available twenty-four hours a day through the computer system shared by the National Health Administration hospitals and other medical institutions, but not individual doctors. Is that right?"

"Yes. A computer in a doctor's office has the potential to access the entire database but the individual physician doesn't have the code to do so. He can obtain his own list of patients only."

"Let's keep it going. If the hospital's computer is down, a call can be placed to the Washington Office of the National Health Administration and with proper identification they can enter the database on their back-up computer, but not between five in the evening and eight the following morning Eastern time. Is that correct?"

"Yes."

"Then, let's pose this problem. It's after 5:00 P.M. Eastern time, and an ER physician is seeing a patient and needs a surgical consultation. He accesses the hospital computer but finds it to be totally out of whack, in other words, 'down.' The patient, for whatever reason, names a surgeon he wants to be seen by. The surgeon arrives and after examination recommends an operation to be done that night. Is there any way to determine whether or not that surgeon is the one assigned to that patient?"

"If the surgeon uses his own computer, he can rapidly see if he is the appropriate one. If he is not, it would be impossible through this avenue to determine who is. Of course, in order to do this he would have to have a laptop with him or go to the computer in his office. There is another route if the patient's primary physician were available and willing to get to his office computer to enter his patient list."

"Hmm! Sally, you've just given me something to work on. The combination of circumstances we've just been through may very well give us the basis for a reasonable defense. Its success would depend on three things. Firstly: Did Joe at any time that evening mention the name of a surgeon to Ted, even if he didn't know whether that particular surgeon performed vascular procedures? If he did mention a name, Ted would have been aware of that surgeon's expertise. Secondly, Was Joe's primary physician on call that night and if so, why wasn't he called? Lastly, will the prosecution pick up on these details and be able to bring them out through testimony by Dr. Curtin or Joe during the trial? If they don't, I've got ample justification for Ted's behavior. If they do, I better damn well have a backup defense to explore. It's past my bedtime. Let's call it a day and thanks. You've been a great help. Be sure and let me know if you can think of anything else."

"I'll do anything to help Dr. O'Hara. Having the government run medicine stinks. The whole system stinks; and his indictment stinks. I'll be in touch until we celebrate a victory or hell freezes over."

"It might be the latter, Sally. It might be the latter."

CHAPTER IX

"BUT THE FOOL'S LIES CONSUME HIM."

T ed emerged from the pool only to race for the towel draped over the back of his lounge chair. September on the Cape is routinely a beautiful month, which this day was amply proving. But albeit sun-drenched there can be a slight nip to its caress, particularly when one's skin is soaking wet and the breeze is stirring. Rare excuses for clouds allowed the sun to make a picture postcard of Stage Harbor. The incoming tide lapped at the sugar sand scant feet below their idyllic perch beside the pool. Beyond the dock, Lilliputian white caps teased the slick hulls of the class J boats as, one by one, they leaned far to windward when rounding the half-way buoy – dipping their billowy alabaster triangles in the iridescent spray, ritual homage to the gods of the sea.

He loved this acre of land, the gabled house, the pool, the dock and the harbor. Sometimes it seemed that everything else in their lives served only to prepare them for time spent here in Chatham. A close friend on the Cape had once told him that when he crossed the canal at the Bourne Bridge all concerns and cares were erased from his mind and dropped beneath the bridge, only to be picked up again when he crossed back to the mainland. Ted had found this to be universally true until this weekend. There just wasn't enough space beneath that bridge to accommodate all that was preying on his mind. As he was toweling off, Laura peeked from beneath the brim of a large straw hat, which shielded her face as she lay soaking up the sun on the adjacent lounge.

"Penny for your thoughts, hunk. Come over here. I feel neglected."

She wore a revealing black swimsuit tantalizingly provocative to Ted in his preoccupied state. As Ted bent over, he kissed the warm skin above her bodice.

"Sorry, Scarlett, but my mind's not blanking out the way it should."

"That felt nice, but you're blocking the sun."

"Blocking the sun! Well, excuse me!" Ted playfully lifted her, knocking the hat from her head, as he walked toward the edge of the pool.

"Don't you dare!"

With Laura in his arms, he jumped into the deep end. Her scream was interrupted by the bubbly splash. Once underwater they embraced and kissed, gently floating to the surface only to be interrupted by a female voice.

"Nice to know your parents are still in love. Hi, Mom. Hi, Pop."

"Beautifully timed, honey, but aren't you a little early?"

"I finished rounds in a hurry and since it was such a beautiful day, I called Dan; grabbed the kids; and got an early start."

This time they both ran for their towels and, after properly assuring their warmth, greeted their daughter as Ricky and Morgan burst through the patio door.

"Grandma! Grandpa!"

Many hugs and kisses later, wet bathing suits notwithstanding, Dan and the kids excused themselves to change and enjoy the pool before the sun dipped too low on the horizon.

"Dad, what have you gotten yourself into this time? It's all over the TV and newspapers. Everyone at the hospital is talking about it."

"Actually I was just doing what I've been trained to do. Apparently the federal government has taken exception to it."

Laura interrupted. "That's enough of that, you two. Let's enjoy the rest of this fabulous afternoon; have a delicious cookout; and, after the children are in bed, we can relax and discuss how David here is going to slay Goliath."

"I keep telling you my name is Rhett. Annie, here comes Dan with the kids. Why don't you change and join in the fun?"

During the balance of the afternoon, the cookout, and between playing with grandchildren and passing pleasantries with those he loved, Ted mused about his daughter, now forty years of age. Anne had inherited Laura's beauty as evidenced by her willowy figure, a sculpted face alive with intelligence, a hint of deviltry, all crowned with a thick kresh of chestnut hair coifed short to complement but not distract from the symmetry of the whole. She had made a late decision, four years out of college, to enter medical school. Ted had tried to dissuade her knowing at that time the direction in which his beloved profession was inexorably slipping. But, when she persisted he was consoled by the conviction that at least she had made the decision fully aware of what lay ahead of her.

As the years passed, Laura was apt to point out what their daughter inherited from Ted, namely a position near the top of her class, acceptance into a renowned residency program in internal medicine, the kudos and praise won from her teachers, peers, and patients. She learned; she applied; she cared. She knew the intricacies of diagnosis, the limitations of treatment, and the compassion which legitimized both. Ted had long since realized how futile and off base his litany of discouragement had been. He was extremely proud of her accomplishments and had come to revel in a singular relationship shared by only a fortunate few, the pleasure of conversing with one's own blood sharing the mutual language earned within their Hippocratic fraternity. Indeed, since her clinical years in medical school, whenever they spoke either by phone or in person, each felt free to discuss their most interesting patient, frequently to their mutual benefit. Ted remained acutely aware he had tried to throw that away before he was even aware of its existence.

During her senior year she had met, fallen deeply in love with, and married Dan, whose complementary personality had formed a union to rival his own with Laura. On occasion Laura would tease him by claiming it perhaps was slightly better. Oh, the delicious challenges she could come up with! They were a perfect couple for the new millennium. Both pursued their own careers while sharing the upbringing of the children, Ricky and Morgan, now age ten and six, respectively. Dan could just as expertly cook a dinner or do the wash as he could design an intricate software package to fit the needs of a client in his computer-consulting firm.

In another era, Laura had been happy and fulfilled remaining home while Annie and her brother, Tim, advanced through their fledgling years. However, her education and abilities had never for one moment been squandered or neglected in this arrangement, a fact which had obviously been confirmed at the time of her father's death. She was an only child and there was no one to take over the family business, Kean Manufacturing Company. Not to worry, Laura announced to her mother that she could do it and the rest was history. After several years of learning, filled with long hours and hard work, under her guidance, the business had thrived to the point her cosmetic products were considered among the best in the industry. Ted's respect, engendered by her fantastic performance, not surprisingly, as in alchemy of old, converted into a deepening of his love for this remarkable woman who long ago had promised to be his and his alone for life.

"So, Dad. I'll ask again. What crazy thing have you done now?"

Annie's voice brought him back to reality. The kids in bed, the four of them were enjoying the last of the sunset from the deck outside the sunroom overlooking the harbor.

"I'm sorry. I probably seem a bit distracted to you. Can I get anyone an after-dinner drink?"

"Ted, for heaven's sake. What's this in my hand? Chopped liver? Dan has his cognac, Annie her Grande Manier. We figured if you're going to tell all we'd best shut you off."

"Forgive my nagging wife, Dan, but she has many other attributes which make up for her rudeness. Please forgive mine."

"My curiosity has gotten more than the better of me." Dan leaned forward as he sipped the cognac. "Just last night your name was all over the major network news, something about an upcoming constitutional question?"

"Well, that was my lawyer's doing, steps number one and two: question the constitutionality of the law I have been accused of flouting and then invite the media to share in the fun. If any of this is going to make any sense, I've got to start at the beginning, some forty years ago.

"Oh Dad, what does that mean? You're just going to make it more complicated than it is."

"Annie, honey, do you remember my tale of woe when I tried to discourage you from going to medical school? For many reasons, which have nothing to do with the subject we're now discussing, I'm forever grateful you paid no heed. But, the points I made then were true and what has happened to our profession since then confirms their validity.

"First of all, we're all familiar with Medicare which came along in the early 'sixties. At that time, doctors enjoyed a freedom in their practice they have never experienced since. Regulation came not from the government or insurance carriers but from their own organizations and the hospitals in which they practiced. Advertising was forbidden. Indeed, announcements in the press were restricted to simple notices of opening or moving an office. Photographs were not allowed, nor anything other than name, specialty, and phone number.

"In return for the granting of privileges hospitals required attendance at various meetings, teaching obligations to residents and medical students, coverage for the clinics and inpatient admissions for the indigent population. Recompense for these services came from their fees in private practice, which in turn were paid by the patients themselves, or by private non-profit insurance companies, predominantly the Blues. Most physicians and surgeons expected twenty to twenty-five percent of their time and expertise to be written off, but only in a financial sense. Indeed, more than a few of my most interesting and professionally rewarding patients fell into this category.

"Insurance was truly that, the recurrent payment of a premium which would protect one against the financial burden of illness, a risk which was open to actuarial calculation. Insurance companies invested the premiums and charged a reasonable administrative fee. Beyond that, they were for the most part non-profit.

"Then, as I said, along came Medicare, the first step in a long progression of governmental involvement. Originally, Medicare was a non-profit insurance company managed by the federal government which paid a fee for service to medical providers for the age group sixty-five and over. Premiums were acquired through social security taxes paid by active workers. One exception was Part B, which covered doctor fees, for which each beneficiary paid a monthly premium out of pocket.

"At this point, two things began to happen. First, we entered an inflationary period whence twenty years later the dollar was worth about fifteen percent from where it started. Secondly, medicine itself underwent an explosion in research and technologic development, most of which rapidly became practical in the everyday diagnosis and treatment of disease. There was a tremendous demand in the market place for the sale and ownership of these state-of-the-art products. Dan, you're well aware that this was only possible because of the computerization of our society. All phases of production, sales, social intercourse, even family relationships, have been influenced by these advances. As a result the cost of medical care shot through the ceiling, easily outstripping inflation alone. I should also mention that during this same period state sponsorship of welfare programs began to flourish. Medicaid became the byword for this way of life. Again, federal and state taxes paid the freight.

"As the programs became more expensive, during the 'seventies, the Feds became concerned as to what they got for their money and began to regulate accountability. The entire country was divided into Health Service Areas. Actually, the governors of each state were charged with this task. In Connecticut, Westbury fell into HSA-V, encompassing New Haven and Litchfield counties. Committees with representation from the federal bureaucracy, local hospitals, and physicians met to establish guidelines or health service indicators to evaluate treatment outcomes in their particular areas. Directions from Washington were rather sketchy and nothing serious in the way of regulation was forthcoming. But the administrative network had been established. I'll refer to that again later.

"We doctors paid no heed and continued as before, jealously guarding our ability to manage our own lives. The 'eighties saw the fruition of double-digit inflation. Whereas the average citizen did not object to paying twenty-five thousand dollars for a car which cost him four thousand in 1965, he did object to paying five hundred dollars a day for a hospital room which cost sixty dollars in that same distant year. I should say his insurance carrier, be it private or governmental, objected for him. Tremendous pressure to cut costs was applied to the medical profession. Length of stay for hospital in-patients was lowered; many procedures and treatment programs were converted to an outpatient venue; and restrictions were placed on the type and number of tests ordered by physicians. By and large the profession responded and significant savings were made. Hospitals downsized and laid off nursing and supportive personnel. Doctors, however, continued to charge fee for service and adhered to their ancient patterns of practice and referral, although group practice became increasingly popular with its sharing of office overhead and increasing personal time."

"Dad, all that seems quite reasonable. Do the best you can to hold prices down without changing the quality of the care. We both know there were excessive hospital stays and questionable tests ordered, particularly in light of the malpractice explosion."

"Reasonable, yes. But now several factors came to bear. First, by the late 'eighties inflation came under control and we had emerged from a banking crisis bloodied but still standing. Interest rates fell and corporate America anticipated a bullish time in our economic fortunes. They were the ones paying most of the cost for medical care in premium dollars. They and the insurance companies were quick to see how well the profession had responded to pressure thus far and just as quickly realized that further cost containment had to involve changes in the way medical care was delivered. The era of HMO's, PPO's and managed care had been born. Medicine entered a corporative milieu and profit was to be made, not by providing care, but by lowering overhead, defining risk pools, restricting benefits, and discounting charges by hospitals and doctors. Medicine ceased being a profession and became a business where profit was king. Insurance companies became stock corporations with the bottom line being financial reward to their executives and investors. They were bought; they were sold; they merged. Hospital chains were formed, surgi-centers, laboratories. Patients, hospitals, and doctors had to live by the rules they – the insurance companies – established which rewarded those who did not refer, did not hospitalize and did not order lab tests."

Dan broke in. "Business, I understand, but that doesn't explain how things came to the crisis you're faced with."

"Patience, son, and all will be revealed. I've described the corporatization of medicine, now behold its politicization. Recall how the government had orchestrated pressure for cost savings in the 'eighties. By the end of that decade, they were realizing diminishing returns and shifted their emphasis to direct reduction of fees paid to hospitals, doctors, and other providers. Medicare published a fee schedule in January of 1992, which paid doctors forty-five cents on a 1992 dollar. The same decreased percentage was paid to hospitals under the DRG system (diagnostic related categories)."

"I was in medical school at the time and my classmates and I were in a quandary why most of the attendings were always grousing about fees." Anne was talking. "I must confess that in our idealism we didn't understand, but to a certain extent I do now."

"Let me explain. At the time Medicare, upon request, provided me with their fees for all the CPT codes for general and peripheral vascular surgical procedures. When I read them I was flabbergasted to say the least. Now, I have to go back to when I first came to Westbury fresh from the Army in 1974. I didn't have a clue what to charge for my services, but after asking around I found out what other surgeons' fees were. For the sake of argument, let's take just two fees, one relatively straightforward and the other more complicated. The going rate for repair of an inguinal hernia was $295 and $1200 for resection of an abdominal aortic aneurysm, neither of which figures were exorbitant.

"You will also recall that over the next twenty years, the dollar decreased to fifteen percent of its former value. By 1992 my customary fee for hernia repair had risen to $990, and $4000 for excision of the aneurysm. Please note that represents a rate increase only half that of inflation. Now, can you guess what Medicare offered for these procedures in their 1992 schedule?"

"Obviously you wouldn't be telling us if it weren't less. So, I'll say $700 and $3,000." This time it was Laura who spoke.

"If you can believe it the answer is: $367 for the hernia and $1,800 for the aneurysm. To further put it in perspective, in 1974, I paid a premium of $500 for malpractice insurance as opposed to $28,000 in 1992. Office rent had gone from $150 to $960."

"Sounds like a prescription for going broke." Dan's tone was one of absolute conviction.

"No question, and add to that just a few of the dogmatic regulations that went with it. If you became a participating provider in Medicare you agreed to accept their fee as payment in full for your services. You could not bill for the difference between your customary fee and Medicare's. Indeed, if you chose not to be a participating provider, you could not balance bill the patient more than ten percent over what Medicare allowed in their schedule. In 1997, even that ten percent differential was abolished. And this was true whether your patient was a billionaire or a pauper.

"So much for those who could afford your usual fee. What about those who didn't have two nickels to rub together? Medicare paid eighty percent of their fee and the patient was obliged to pay the balance. If the doctor knew the patient could not afford to pay and decided to write the debt off, he could not do so. By bureaucratic fiat he had to bill the patients or face a significant fine for his negligence although there was no corresponding penalty for the patient who chose to ignore the bill. The net result was that if a doctor did the same amount of work in 1992 as he did the year previously, and forty percent of his practice dealt with Medicare, he experienced a thirty-percent drop in income. And this at a time when his overhead costs were increasing at a steady rate year in and year out."

"Dad, you're painting a very bleak picture, but, you did mention politicization. What do you mean by that?"

"Well, honey, if you recall, a significant part of the rhetoric during the presidential campaign of 1992 had to do with the cost of medical care and how to provide it. Clinton and the Democrats ran on a platform of centralizing authority and control within the federal government while the Republicans opted for some form of privatization of Medicare. When Clinton won the election, before half of his first term had elapsed, he appointed a commission headed by his wife, Hillary. They met in secret to research recommendations for legislative action, the gist of which was to expand federal control not only over those above the age sixty-five but also over the rest of the population through further regulation of the private insurance carriers. Several themes were paramount and constantly broadcast through the media. First, the cost of Medicare had continued to rise in excess of inflation each year and would soon be intolerable. Secondly, the Social Security Trust and Medicare in particular would soon be bankrupt. I would defy anyone to recall a single politician who mentioned a word about the cost saving measures the profession had already taken or for that matter, the fifty five percent cut in fees foisted upon medicine by Medicare in 1992. If legitimate audit figures were made available, there could not have been a steady rise in the yearly percentage of the Gross National Product spent on medical care. If there were the explanation would have to be on the one hand, increased administrative overhead experienced by both the Feds and the private insurance carriers as a result of their mutual efforts of regulatory control, and on the other, in the case of private medical corporations, the increase in executive salaries and profit to investors. Perhaps that's why no legitimate audit has ever been presented to the public. Concerning social security taxes and, since 1991, a special Medicare tax, has the public ever been made aware how much is collected so that a true comparison can be made between income and outgo? Of course not! Both taxes go into the general fund and expenses of the Medicare program are paid out of the same fund. They become a statistic only in the overall picture of running the government. For all we know the program could have been running at a substantial profit."

"Ted, this is all very interesting, but do I have to remind you how wordy you can get? Wrap it up, Rhett."

"Touché, Scarlett. I'll get off my soapbox in a few moments. By early 1994 Clinton's attempt to further federalize the control of medical care had obviously failed and, with the election of Republican majorities in both the House and Senate, no further effort of the Administration to propose a grandiose governmental scheme was forthcoming. However, what was not possible by fiat could be gradually accomplished surreptitiously. For example, witness this regulation bureaucratically promulgated through the Federal Register. Should a Medicare patient of independent means, for whatever reason, choose to pay a doctor his usual and customary fee and not use his Medicare policy, the physician could provide that service but only if he were willing to sacrifice treating all other Medicare patients for a period of two years. If anyone thought that ever increasing progression to socialized medicine would allow for the coexistence of a purely private sector, such as existed in England, this regulation was proof of the obvious.

"Another initiative taken by the Administration in 1998 was to widen coverage under Medicare to age fifty-five ostensibly to provide a reasonably priced coverage to a segment of our society experiencing increasing difficulty in obtaining it in the private sector. It did no such thing. In reality it was a measure to increase the size of the Medicare risk pool with a statistically healthier portion of the population so as to reduce payments as opposed to income.

"Also by 1998, corporate insurance carriers were beginning to experience financial difficulties. Witness the Oxford Health Plan for one. They lost several hundred million dollars in 1997 and were four to six months in arrears to hospitals and doctors. Faced with these problems, they reorganized and fired the CEO, but not before giving him a golden handshake worth nine million dollars. One wonders what he would have gotten had he run a profitable enterprise. All of the HMO's and managed-care companies had to face the fact that even with good investments of premium dollars in a bull market payouts exceeded income. In the hope of survival their choices were few: 1) Increase premiums; which would not be tolerated by the rest of corporate America who were paying eighty percent of the freight by then; 2) decrease services; which patients and doctors would no longer tolerate; 3) increase co-payments; which patients would say no to; or 4) further discount fees; which hospitals and physicians by this time would laugh at. Smaller firms, facing bankruptcy, were sold to larger conglomerates with the expectation that increasing the risk pool could forestall the inevitable.

"Throughout this period corporate medicine continued to milk every dollar they could from our profession in spite of the growing problems I have already alluded to. We doctors slavishly provided our services as best we could complaining more each day but putting greater effort into accommodating to the status quo than uniting and working with hospitals to make our own assessments and recommendations for the future of healthcare in this country. Whatever muted voice we mustered was drowned in the cacophony of patronage and lobbyists infesting the walls of Jericho on the shores of the Potomac.

"Meanwhile, the national election in the fall of the millennium loomed large. In a hard-fought contest over issues, not the least of which was how to provide and finance healthcare, the Republicans won a squeaker not only for the presidency but maintained control of Congress. However, as we all know, within a year a Republican senator switched political allegiance and the Democrats had a majority in that cliquish Country Club. At the same time the economy took a turn South. Over the next two years, it gradually spiraled downward and was a prime focus during the Congressional elections in the fall of 2002 when the Republicans surprisingly regained control of the entire Congress but by a very narrow margin. In spite of efforts from the administration to bolster business and the market, the economy continued to sputter along without significant improvement. The situation was worsened by the worry and expense involved with our commitment against world-wide terrorism following the disastrous attacks on the twin towers of the World Trade Center in New York City.

"Then in August of 2004 the unforeseen happened. What took twelve years of a burgeoning economy to create disappeared in one Wall Street working day. On the tenth of the month, the Dow dropped below three thousand to its lowest point in two decades, and the world entered a depression that promised to rival that of the nineteen thirties. Were it not for the safeguards built into the system, perhaps it would have. An extremely slow recovery began within the month but it was too late for those companies whose losses over the preceding years had placed them on the fringe of vulnerability. This included all the HMO's who closed their doors and left patients, hospitals, and physicians like yesterday's garbage. When society needed medical advocacy more than ever before, our profession had none to offer. In this vacuum, Congress proposed legislation to alleviate the suffering and confusion. Enough Republican Congressman and Senators crossed the aisle to assure its passage. President Bush vetoed the bill but the coalition which enacted the law had the votes to override it. By early October, Socialized Medicine became the *sine qua non* throughout the country. For the brief time left before the presidential election of 2004, Bush ran on a plan to restore medicine to the private sector, but lost to the Democratic nominee who again had a Democratic Congress to back him up. The law, thus confirmed, established the National Health Administration which was authorized to purchase all existing medical facilities, including physicians' offices, with no down payment at a price set by the value of the dollar at the Market's closing on the tenth of August, the day of the crash. Such purchases would be amortized over thirty years. Any losses to banks and lending institutions were compensated by tax credits over the life of the mortgages. All health care providers became employees of the government. 'The Department of Health Education and Welfare' lost the 'health' part but provided the new bureaucracy with the framework of the old Health Service Areas from the middle 'seventies. With a few adjustments, they provided convenient bases from which to administer the new behemoth. Thus Westbury again became a part of HSA-V. Budgetary concerns were met with a combination of a separate medical payroll tax on individuals and an increase in corporate taxes that exceeded by half what they had paid in premiums to private carriers in the past. The balance of the laws two thousand pages dealt with the regulations necessary to make the entire system work. Among these was section X, paragraph 3, which established the restriction to provide medical or surgical care only to assigned patients, the violation of which constituted a felony punishable by a fine not to exceed one hundred thousand dollars and confinement in a federal prison for a period not to exceed three to five years. Apparently, I violated that rule."

"Mommy, I'm scared. There's a monster on the wall in my room." Morgan stood in the doorway wearing her PJs and clutching Freddy, her teddy bear and constant bedtime companion. Her eyes were glazed with sleep, and her tousled hair fell helter skelter about her shoulders.

"Oh, honey! There's no monster in your room." Annie swept Morgan into her arms giving her a tender hug. "I'll bet you were dreaming and when you woke up saw the shadow of a tree on the wall. The moon is bright tonight. See it shining on the water by the boats out there? Come on, Mommy will go down to the room with you. Now say goodnight to everyone."

"G'night, Daddy, Nana, Poppy."

"G'night honey. Sleep tight and we'll go swimming in the morning."

"Dad, I'll be back in a minute and we can talk more about that monster who devoured our profession."

"His appetite is never sated, but Laura, since you saw fit to cut me off before I embarked upon this soliloquy, now that I'm finished I think I deserve some of that Tulamore Dew. On the rocks with a splash of water and a twist."

⌒

"Sweetheart, your dinner was fabulous. Glad I was able to contribute the grilled swordfish from the barbeque. I was ready with burgers and dogs for the kids but both of them wolfed down that endangered species like true Cape Coders. And how about Morgan? Wasn't she cute, coming upstairs with her teddy, all uptight about a monster in her bedroom?"

"I just wanted to hug her to death," Laura answered. She had just entered their bedroom from the open door of the bathroom. The slider was ajar allowing the harbor breeze to modify the humidity within the room to maximum comfort. Rhythmically rotating like a giant cyclopic eye, the searing candle power of the Chatham Lighthouse intermittently complimented a full moon in transfiguring the assorted seacraft anchored to their moorings throughout the harbor. The equable silence of midnight accented the gentle lapping of the incoming tide on the sandy shore below, as Laura traced the few steps necessary to gain the sanctuary of Ted's arms. Both of them turned to assimilate this unique and familiar site as he remarked:

"That makes two of us. Call it bragging, if you will, but Annie sure knows how to handle those kids. Must have inherited it from me."

"Excuse me! Inherited it from whom? Since when has a bedside manner been your forte? Without boasting I'll take credit for our daughter's knack with her children, if you don't mind."

"Well, I do mind. Haven't heard any complaints about my performance either in or at the side of the bed."

"There you go – " Her rebuttal was stifled in mid-sentence by Ted's kiss. As their lips parted, she leaned further into him. "Let's call it a draw. So both of us raised our daughter right."

"Sounds good to me, but all kidding aside, did I get my points across with that diatribe about the history of medicine for the past forty years?"

"It was a bit wordy, but yes I would agree you did."

"Have I been correct in assuming you know why I chose to operate on Joe, why I didn't entertain the thought of anyone else doing it?"

"Need you ask? Were I in your place I couldn't have done otherwise. Joe saved your life in Vietnam and now you've returned the favor, your debt of honor. I love that in you."

"Thanks for understanding, but I'm still facing a real dilemma. You heard Pat the other night. I have the option of avoiding a trial, with all its uncertainties, by copping a plea. Admit my guilt and the government's ecstatic, probably to the extent of voiding a fine and reducing any sentence to a few months of community service. Thus can I repent my sins. It's certainly an easy way out. Should I take it?"

"No question, it's the easy way but I can already read the signs. Your back is up. The last thing you want is to admit to any wrongdoing when you're convinced it was the best thing you've ever done. Forget about repaying a debt to Joe. I suspect your decision will have a lot to do with your mother and thirty-five years devoted to your profession."

"What do you mean? My mother?"

"Don't play games with me. You didn't talk about it at the time probably because of your frustration for being so helpless. But Sally told me all about the number of calls you made to New York. Even about your final decision to operate yourself, a decision which tragically came hours too late."

"Sally told you all that?"

"Yes, darling."

Ted audibly exhaled, overtaken by the same crushing sense of guilt he had experienced at his mother's funeral one year previously. The room began to spin as he became nauseated. Gagging and reeling, he stumbled to the foot of the bed where he flopped on the cover for fear of falling. Satan's embrace could not be worse than the gut-wrenching vise that gripped his abdomen. Struggling to regain his composure, he sat up to face Laura and, rubbing unaccustomed tears from his eyes, blurted out a response.

"And I thought I hid it so well."

"Sweetheart, I wanted nothing more than to share the agony with you, but I had to respect your silence. I knew the time would come for you to tell me." She rushed to his side to cover his face with the repetitive warmth of her lips for an eternity that lasted several moments. Emotionally spent, they collapsed on the bed beside each other as Ted was first to break the silence.

"Sally didn't know the whole story."

"Nor do I. I want to hear it from you."

"Okay! Okay! One year ago, my mother was eighty-seven, hale and hearty, sharp as a tack. She was one of the lucky few having enjoyed a long life exempt from serious illness. After my father's death, she continued to live independently in her house in Queens. Remember how we enjoyed holidays there. She was a great cook and how she so entranced her great-grandchildren. One evening she called to tell me she had experienced three or four episodes of temporary blindness in her left eye. Each dim-out lasted twenty to thirty seconds with normal restoration of her sight afterwards. She saw her doctor who heard a bruit (rushing sound) in the left side of her neck. An ultrasound indicated that she had a very tight stenosis (narrowing) at the origin of the left internal carotid artery.

"I telephoned him the next day to confirm what my mother had told me and asked him who her vascular surgeon would be. I was so upset that I failed to reflect on what I already knew. He was quick to remind me that it made no difference who her surgeon was since the National Health Administration had stipulated that no one over the age of eighty could undergo the surgery necessary to alleviate her symptoms and prevent a major stroke. Bits of plaque or clot from the narrowed area in the carotid artery could break loose at any time and travel upstream to the left side of her brain where, depending on their size and final location, could cause anything from slight paralysis to a major stroke and death. Should the plaque not be removed, the incidence of a major stroke would be twelve to fifteen percent per year.

"Her internist started anticoagulation (thinning out her blood) but I was furious that she couldn't have the surgery she so desperately needed. My repeated calls and challenges to her assigned vascular surgeon were futile. He sympathized but his hands were tied. He would not risk the same penalty as I face now. In desperation, I called several other surgeons in New York, friends whom I had known for many years. The answer was always the same. Friendship was not sufficient excuse for the gamble. Even though it was one of my core beliefs that I could not ethically operate on my own mother I reluctantly decided that I would have to do so. Before I completed the arrangements my sister called. Mom had been taken to Columbia Presbyterian in coma with total paralysis of her right side. Within days she developed a raging pneumonia, went into septic shock, and quietly passed on.

"Cursing the system that trapped me, wallowing in self-pity and utter frustration, my soul cried for justice from the depths of a stygian darkness I had not experienced since Vietnam. I wanted to reach out to you, Laura. I wanted to quiet the demons devouring whatever remained of my sanity but I couldn't. Rage though I might, at the end of the day, during sleepless nights, it was the numbing guilt, the paralyzing realization that I had failed her. I should have acted sooner. I could have saved my own mother."

"Darling! Your mother lives in every expression of your being. Even as you bared your anguish to me just now, the bitter words became gentle with the love she has for you. Forgiveness is a stranger where it's not needed."

"Honey, literally I cannot live without you. I know I should have come to you sooner with this. Perhaps that's where the only forgiveness is necessary."

"You're forgiven, hunk." Laura's radiant smile signified Ted's absolution and their subsequent embrace a playful penance to eliminate his imagined guilt.

"Beauty saves the beast once again. Thanks, but perhaps I can redirect the anger that's still consuming me in a different direction. Damn it, Laura, it's my job to decide when to treat and when not to. I've devoted my entire adult life honing the skills to make that choice. The edicts from the charlatans in Washington have made a mockery of my entire career. My surgical judgment, the marrow of my very existence, is denied me while obsequious sycophants in the government tell me what I can or cannot do with my abilities. What a disgraceful substitution for what was once a revered profession! Honey, I know I'm risking being without you and I can't abide the thought of losing you for five years, but – "

"Don't you dare even think of backing down on this one. Never mind being away from me for five years, I won't speak to you for five years if you plead guilty. Now it's my turn to pay back. There's absolutely no way I can lose you when you're fighting for what's right. I could lose the Ted I know in my heart if you were to cop a plea. I'm just as angry as you; end of discussion. Now squeeze me and tell me again how much you love me."

"It could get nasty. Are you quite sure?"

"The only thing I regret is that you're still talking. C'mon, Romeo, a little less gab and a lot more action."

CHAPTER X

"I HAVE SEEN UNDER THE SUN ANOTHER EVIL,
LIKE A MISTAKE THAT PROCEEDS FROM
THE RULER. "

"Good evening, this is Richard Donlevy with the ABC evening news. Our lead story tonight concerns the presentation of briefs before the second Federal District Court in Westbury, Connecticut. This is the latest in our continuing coverage of the United States versus Dr. Theodore O'Hara. You will recall that Dr. O'Hara has been indicted for performing surgery on an individual not assigned to his practice. This activity is forbidden under the law passed last year effectively socializing medicine in this country."

It was the evening of the third of October and Ted, with Laura, Vicky, Joe, Pat and Mary were gathered before the TV in the O'Haras' den, eagerly awaiting what spin would be given to the day's happenings.

"Dr. O'Hara's attorney, Patrick Holleran, had filed a brief with the presiding judge challenging the constitutionality of that particular section of the law. Today, Judge Cummings listened to arguments from both sides. Our man on the scene is Raul Ramirez. Raul, can you hear me?"

"Yes Richard. It's evening and I'm standing in front of the Federal building in downtown Westbury. The Second District Court is on the second floor and just a few hours ago was a beehive of activity as lawyers from both sides in the U.S. vs. O'Hara presented arguments based upon those briefs which you mentioned had been submitted to Judge Cummings earlier today. A large crowd of interested citizens and a huge media entourage spilled into the corridor and surrounding sidewalk, some of whom, as you can see, are still here."

"Were you inside the courtroom itself during the presentations? Can you give us a first-hand description of what transpired?"

"Yes, I was. The hearing was open to the public although TV cameras were not allowed inside the courtroom."

"Can you give us the gist of the arguments put forth?"

"Richard Sterling, the Director of the Criminal Division of the Department of Justice representing the people, argued against the unfettered right of anyone to choose their physician, or, for that matter, a physician to choose his patient. According to him, the relationship between a doctor and a patient is a contract either explicit or implied, and that all contracts are subject to many conditions and variables some of which may legitimately encroach upon a carte blanche choice of physician or patient. For example, a condition to such a contract may define payment for services rendered, in this case the responsibility of the federal government. Thus the Government as a third party to the contract has its own right to regulate choice so as to promote efficiency and lower costs. Although a citizen has the right to free speech he does not have that right to the detriment of the general good. Thus he cannot yell, "fire," in a crowded theater when no fire exists. Since the taxpayers are footing the bill for all medical care, the people – that is the government – can legitimately restrict access or choice for the general good of efficiency and savings."

"What did the defendant's lawyer have to say?"

"Attorney Holleran was brief but made some cogent points. Under the law, he maintained that there is not one contract between a doctor and a patient, but rather three separate contracts. There is the one between the Government and the doctor whereby he provides services for salaried compensation. A second contract exists between the government and the patient wherein the Government agrees to provide medical services for payment of specific taxes. The final contract exists between the doctor and the patient. Traditionally, in English law, this contract is based upon mutual acceptance after an interview process. After the initial contact either party can walk his separate way before the establishment of a contract, and even after affirmation the contract can be broken upon proper notification and establishment of continuity of care. Therefore the basic choice stems from an innate right and not from the verbiage of the contract. Indeed he addressed the point that in the past a patient who felt that his physician had not lived up to their contract, in so far as his services had been rendered below the community standard, the patient could sue him for malpractice. Now, since medical providers are salaried employees their employer, namely the federal government, is responsible for the quality of that service. Just six months ago Congress passed a Tort Reform Act restricting the amount of malpractice awards and totally eliminating consideration of recompense for pain and suffering as a cost containment measure."

"It seems Judge Cummings will have no shortage of homework navigating the labyrinth of first amendment rights and contract law. Were there any surprises?"

"Well, Attorney Holleran seemed to disturb Mr. Sterling when he detailed yet another argument for the defense."

"What was that, Raul?"

"Citing the recent history of the medical profession with its rough passage through the waters of corporative insurance and now its complete socialization, he argued that it was no longer a profession but a business and should be dealt with as such legally. He enumerated a number of recent court decisions involved with restraint of trade by various corporative and labor groups. A comparison was then drawn between restraint of trade and interference with a doctor's free choice of patient. In conclusion, he maintained that, the cornerstone of free choice of doctor by the patient resided in the protection of the first amendment while choice of patient by the doctor was best defined in trade law."

"How long will it be before we can expect a decision by Judge Cummings?"

"Ordinarily, it would take up to three months. However, he promised that a decision would be forthcoming in three weeks. Richard, I have some brief footage of interviews with both attorneys as they exited the courtroom a few hours ago."

⤿

Richard Sterling was smiling as he waved to the crowd gathered at the entrance to the federal building. His handsome features betrayed no hint of concern as Raul interrupted his exit by thrusting a microphone in front of his face. Raul became the representative of the media dragon belching fiery questions at the prosecuting attorney.

"Mr. Sterling, are you pleased with the way things went in there?"

"Yes, I am. Mr. Giorgio and I have done our homework and presented the correct arguments to settle this matter and get the upcoming case on the docket. We were extremely pleased to hear Judge Cummings say that his decision will be forthcoming in only three weeks. I would only wish that all trials and judicial hearings were so propitious."

"Do you have any comment about Mr. Holleran and his defensive tactics?"

"It would be improper for me to say anything further than what I said in court. I admire Mr. Holleran. He is an intelligent and thorough opponent. Thank you, but that's all I can say for now."

The screen then filled with the image of Pat exiting from the same doorway as the media's chaotic foreplay repeated itself. "Mr. Holleran, how would you say it went for your side today?"

"That's impossible to predict. We made our points. Whether they score or not depends on Judge Cummings. But let me say I wasn't only speaking on Dr. O'Hara's behalf but for every citizen of this country. It's not just his freedom which is in jeopardy but everyone's. All of us will be the safer for it when my client wins his case. If we can do this by raising a constitutional question, we all win. If it goes to trial and he loses we all lose. There is no compromise, or middle ground. Either a citizen in this constitutional democracy is free or he isn't."

"Should this case go to trial, that will mean a Federal Appeals Court will have found the law constitutional. How, then, will you present a defense?"

"We'll take it one step at a time. The trial itself could establish an important precedent should the jury vote for acquittal. A guilty verdict would engender an appeal which could go all the way to the Supreme Court and provide the opportunity for a more pertinent and detailed debate of the law's legitimacy."

"But what of your defense strategy?"

"All in good time, my friend, all in good time. The first quarter ends in three weeks. Thank you."

"Back to you, Richard."

Joe smiled in admiration as he poked his friend in jest. "Whew, Pat, I knew you can play a decent game of golf; make out wills; and handle real estate deals. But I'm impressed. What a performance!"

"I can whip your black ass anytime Joe, even with that sandbagger's handicap. Ted, I wanted to turn you down when you asked me to represent you because I didn't think I was right for this. Now I confess, as a lawyer, I'm beginning to enjoy it. It gets the juices flowing rather like you doing the aneurysm resection on Joe while teaching the residents at the same time. But I'm also concerned for you as my client. There are so many possible pitfalls along the way and there are no life jackets on board. If the boat sinks, we've got to swim on our own."

This time Vicky chimed in. "Joe's black ass looks just fine to me."

"Now, honey, don't give away any trade secrets. I get your meaning, Pat. I feel the same when business is already hot and then out of a clear sky I land a sweetheart of a contract. We like to think we work to relax but the truth is without the challenge we're lost sheep."

Ted uncharacteristically seemed annoyed. "Before the dirty jokes start can I please find out how we stand? Pat, I heard what you said to the media. Now tell me how it really went."

"Look, Ted, I didn't feel it necessary to quote the Declaration of Independence or the Gettysburg Address, but I got my points across. I spent hours and days editing the legal points each one weighted and positioned to have maximum effect. The oral presentation was just an outline which reflected the detail of the written brief. My remarks to the press were just as programmed. Ted, that's step number two. Now that we have the publicity, let's take advantage. Get every citizen to put himself in your place. Make them think seriously about what's at stake, not just for you but for them too. If I'm going to save your white ass, you be Don Quixote but let me be Machiavelli. That's my job, pal. I think I can do it well. Now, how about a refill from your Irish still?"

"Scarlett, he's not a blue-belly, after all. He's a Johnny Reb. Fill up his glass, honey."

⌒

They were on the seventh tee at the Country Club of Westbury. Ted and Joe were playing a five-dollar Nassau against Pat and Tony D'Amato. As Ted teed up his ball he turned to speak. "Joe, we managed to win the last hole but these turkeys still have us two down. I didn't do all that surgery so you could get a higher handicap. Let's get with it. You stroke here along with Pat. I'll play my man. You play yours."

"Nag, nag, nag! I get enough of that at home. You want to win. Treat me right."

"Hey Pat, we've got them talking to each other. Win this hole and they'll be so confused the rest will be a cake walk."

"Well smartass, five dollars says I win the hole."

"Okay, Ted, show us your stuff."

With that Ted uncorked a wild swing which dribbled his ball thirty yards ahead to the ladies tee. The guffaws lasted a full minute. "What were you saying, Ted?"

"Never mind. Just play your man, Joe. I'll play mine."

The other three all got reasonable drives in the fairway and it was Ted's turn again. He addressed his ball with a three wood as it lay on the grass between the ladies markers. Pat roared with laughter. "Joe, I sure wish I had a camera. Imagine, Ted teeing off between the red markers. Who would believe it? We need proof."

"He who laughs last. Make that five a ten. I get par and beat all of you."

"Ho, ho. This I have to see. You're on. You still have three hundred and sixty yards to go. No way!"

Ted struck the ball cleanly following its arching path through a blue sky two hundred and ten yards, bisecting the fairway as it ran downhill, nestling on the green carpet to the left of a fairway trap one hundred and fifty yards from the flagstick.

"Take that me buckoes!" Ted exclaimed as he dropped the club into his bag; sat behind the wheel; and started down the cart path.

It was a "ten best" day in late October. The air was crisp and clear, the trees set aflame by an arabesque sun hanging low on the horizon to the Southwest. The russets, browns, and gold of the departing foliage framed the lush green of the manicured fairway and accented the rock-bound hills and valleys of this bit of central Connecticut sculpted by a glacier millennia before the footprint of a man, much less the divot of a five-iron, had intruded upon its pristine perfection. The celestial architect whose magnificent design, basking before them, delighting their every sense, must have been extremely pleased when, with a whimsical wink, he dispatched the soul of Donald to far away Scotland into the womb of Mrs. Ross. He knew full well that someday He would lead him to this very glen to work the magic of his Celtic ancestors in the midst of an old New England mill town. The other three had struck their second shots, none landing on the green, when Ted decided on a six iron for his third shot. "Hey, Pat, how about sweetening the pot? Dinner at Marco's?"

"I'll stick with the sawbuck. After all, I lie two in that trap to your right."

"Okay, Byron. If you thought my three wood was a good shot, just watch this one." Ted struck the ball firmly taking a moderate divot just in front of the spot from whence his ball had just departed on it's high arching course on line to a yellow-flagged pin beckoning to the left rear of a deceptively rolling green. Joe expressed his admiration with a low whistle as the ball struck the middle of the green, bounced once, came to a skidding halt a mere two feet directly below the hole.

"Is that a gimme, Pat? Or do I have to go through the formality of putting it?"

"Great shot, Ted, but remember that's only half the bet. You got your par but you haven't won the hole yet."

Five minutes later, Ted recorded Pat's double bogey and Tony's bogey on the scorecard. He paused momentarily to pocket a ten-dollar bill in his wallet. "I'll save that to help pay your fee. God knows I have no idea how much that's going to be."

"That'll be my surprise when this is all over. Seriously, I still can't believe how you played that hole, much less calling it after that miserable drive. Fantastic! But speaking of fees the clock starts running again tomorrow. Before I came over here my office received word that the Judge wants us all in court tomorrow at ten. He's kept his word and made his decision within three weeks. I had my secretary call Sam Vicario over at *The Gazette* to alert the press."

"It's a relief to hear it. I have to confess what I hate most is the waiting. If we could get this whole matter settled tomorrow, it wouldn't be soon enough for me. Do you want me there? I have a hernia scheduled at seven forty-five but I'll be finished long before ten."

"Yes, I do. It's time the American public makes your acquaintance and hopefully begin to identify with you."

"You got it, pal, quarter of ten in your office, okay? Joe, let's get with it. We're still one down and if I'm going to pay this lecher's bill, I need every penny I can get."

∽

"Attorney Holleran, Raul Ramirez of *ABC News* here. Do you have any comment on Judge Cummings' decision upholding the constitutionality of the law your client is accused of violating?" Again the scene was a busy and confused one on the steps outside the federal building. Pat was smiling as he approached the proffered microphone.

"Dr. O'Hara and I are understandably disappointed, but this afternoon my office will file an appeal in the Federal Circuit Court in upstate New York. Hopefully they will also extend the courtesy of an early decision. Again, I would emphasize how deeply I feel that I represent not only my client but also every citizen of this great country of ours. Thank you."

As Pat departed the view of the camera and Raul began making his comments into the microphone, he grabbed Ted by the elbow and steered him around the corner to the parking lot where his car awaited. "Ted, I know how disappointing today's decision must be to you. I must confess that without any test cases to go on I really didn't think Judge Cummings would unilaterally find the law unconstitutional."

"To be honest, I'm not surprised either. I don't know the legal profession, but if I were in his shoes, I would have made the same decision."

"On the bright side, there's the continued press coverage and publicity. I'm quite serious in using every opportunity to encourage John Q. Public to think about the issues at stake and identify with you. That's why we're appealing the decision. I don't anticipate the Circuit Court will be any different in their judgment. At least the public will get one more reminder. The honorable Mr. Sterling must be fuming at all this show and delay, but he's powerless to stop it."

"I don't tell you often enough but Laura and I deeply appreciate all your efforts. Our fate is in your more than capable hands. What can I do?"

"Nothing for now, but I'll let you in on one secret. Judge Cummings has assured me that the Circuit Court will cooperate and render an early decision. As I told you I expect their decision to be the same. Between you and me, I have no intentions of further appealing to the Supreme Court. We have the media coverage and, I assume, the attention of enough of the citizenry to go to trial, should you choose to do so. Any appeal to the Supreme Court would have for more consequence after a trial when all the arguments have been publicly dissected. Of course, this would only be necessary should the verdict go against you. Ted, early on I asked you to delay any decision as to your plea of guilty or not guilty. Under the present scenario a plea date will be set within days of the Circuit Court's decision. Now I must know how you wish to plead. The real decision is do you want to go to trial or not?"

"I haven't changed my mind. Let's go all the way. Not guilty."

"Okay, that's it. So far I've invested my time in writing legal briefs. Now I've got to start gathering details, listing our defense witnesses and preparing them for their testimony. I'll begin tomorrow with Joe. Now get out of here. I've got to make a few phone calls."

"Joe, Pat Holleran here. How are things going? I couldn't get over how you and Ted came back from three down after five holes to win the Nassau on the eighteenth green. Never mind Ted's miracle at the seventh. You carried him the rest of the way and administered the coups de grace with that forty-foot putt on the eighteenth. If an operation by Ted can improve one's golf game that much, I'd better get in line and book myself for his bloodthirsty ministrations, but something a bit more simple. Say a hernia. What's the theory behind it? No pain, no gain?"

"Ha! Between you and me, it wasn't his surgery but all those *Golf Digests* and *Bobby Jones* "how to" books I read when my ass was in a sling post-op. The blowhard can take all the credit he wants but it was really my own research and disciplined application which turned the trick."

"Hey, Joe, my lips are sealed. Seriously, I know you must have heard of Judge Cummings' decision?"

"Right, and also that you're appealing it."

"We should be hearing from the Circuit in three weeks. Meanwhile, I have to anticipate a negative reply and start getting ready for a trial. I'm sure you'll be called as a witness by the prosecution and the defense will need you in the same capacity. We need to get together to talk about your testimony and what to expect when you're on the witness stand. Ted tells me you haven't returned to work as yet and I'd like to make this as convenient as possible. Could we get together at your house some afternoon or evening?"

"Sure thing. Why don't you and your lovely bride come over for dinner and afterward, while the ladies gossip, we'll retire to the den and talk about whatever you want. If I can help Ted in any way, I will. How about Friday?"

"I'll check with Mary and have her call Vicky. The timing is great with me. Thanks, Joe."

CHAPTER XI

"THE WISE MAN'S UNDERSTANDING TURNS HIM TO HIS RIGHT."

Mary and Vicky had retired to the kitchen to clean up after what had been an outstanding dinner. Joe showed Pat into the den off the living room. "With such great culinary skills, Vicky should open a restaurant. What a meal!"

"Thanks, I'll tell her. Now you know why Ted complained about my girth. Can I offer you some brandy?"

"Did you ever hear me refuse? Are you going to join me?"

"Absolutely. I've got to get ready for some tough questions. Don't I?"

"Not really. I'm just going to validate what transpired the night of your operation and fill you in on what to expect when you testify at the trial. Have you ever been a witness before?"

Standing beside a trolley Joe had removed the stopper from a crystal cruet and was gently pouring Courvoisier into the heart of a large snifter in his left hand. Offering it to his good friend, he answered: "No, I've never had the pleasure."

Pat caressed the bottom of the glass in the palm of his hand, slowly warming the golden nectar within. Simultaneously, he lifted the glass beneath his nostrils allowing the liquid's sensuous aroma to tingle the olfactory receptors in his nasal passages. Delighted to be the messengers, these same sentinels emailed his cerebrum where the message was received with a phantasmagora of exploding rocketry in an ebon sky. Reflexly a motor message inspired his hand to angle the glass to his waiting lips, flooding countless taste buds with rivulets of the tantalizing distillate. A golden surge warmed his entire chest as he swallowed and seated himself in a comfortable leather recliner. "Lordy, that was perfect. Here's to you, Joe."

"My pleasure, now how can I help you?"

"First of all, I want to review the sequence of events on the date of your operation." Pat opened his briefcase and removed a copy of Joe's hospital chart." I'll go over the facts recorded by Ted and I want you to stop me at any time if your recollection differs in any way."

"Sure thing."

Pat then read from the chart as Joe listened attentively, occasionally nodding his head in approval. As he finished, Pat put the chart down and, removing his glasses, looked at Joe for affirmation. "You got it, pal. I agree with every syllable. Is there anything I can add so long as it can help Ted? I can't tell you how badly I feel that I'm the cause of his problems. Don't get me wrong. I won't apologize for requesting Ted after Dr. Curtin examined me in the emergency room. At that time I didn't know what was wrong but I knew instinctively that, whatever it was, it was serious. If treatment required surgery there was only one person I wanted to do it."

"Did you know that you were not on Ted's patient list?"

"Yes, I did. For general surgery I'm on a Dr. Burton's list. I've never met the man and have no idea who he is or, for that matter, what his training and experience are."

"I was going to ask you about that. How was it that the hospital didn't pick up the discrepancy? They did so on the following day and by regulation had to report the error to HSA-V. You know what happened from there."

"I don't know all the details, but Dr. Curtin mentioned that the computers were down that evening and he had no reference from which to call the appropriate surgeon. All I know was that Ted was the only surgeon I wanted, so I mentioned his name. I thought the worst scenario would be some sort of a fine. What the hell! I'd have paid it for him."

"I'll verify that with Ted and the hospital. Now let's talk about your testimony. You'll be under oath and a court reporter will be typing everything you say as a permanent record. Both Mr. Sterling and I plan on calling you as a witness, but no matter who is asking the questions just answer truthfully and briefly. Never volunteer information not even with me. There is one occasion when I won't be there. As I understand it after the Circuit Court has done its thing, the prosecution plans to call witnesses before a grand jury to further legitimize their indictment. You will be one of these witnesses and I won't be privy to what you say. However, the same rule applies, namely the truth, the whole truth, and nothing but the truth. Actually, the circumstances surrounding that day's activities seem quite straightforward so your testimony shouldn't be prolonged."

"I'll behave, but I must confess to being more than pissed off about this whole deal. How the hell did we ever arrive at this point? A great surgeon and human being faces up to five years in prison for successfully operating on his best friend?"

"I don't have an answer for you, Joe, but I do have a confession to make. At the moment I'm at a loss as to how to defend Ted. Oh, I know we've had more than our share of excellent publicity about first amendment rights and restraint of trade. All of it is quite emotional but when all is said and done they're legalistic jive, and without an existing precedent the Appeals Court is not going to overturn the law. Once the trial starts, if I bring up the same arguments, the prosecution will object and the judge will sustain. So where do I go from here? According to what you just affirmed the fact is that Ted did knowingly operate on you when you were not on his list. Ted is going to plead not guilty and I have to agree with him. Now I've got to look for legitimate extenuating circumstances. Up to now I haven't found any."

"I don't envy you your job, Pat. This whole deal reminds me of one of my ancestors, the first of my clan to come to this country."

"What do you mean, Joe?"

"He was befriended, not by someone he knew well, but a total stranger. His benefactor's good Samaritan act was also rewarded with an indictment by the federal government. It all led to a situation just as outrageous as this one."

"Sounds intriguing, Joe. That ancestor wouldn't be the man whose portrait is in the frame on top of your desk, would it? The eyes in the picture hypnotize one and seem to follow everywhere as one goes about the room."

Joe chuckled as he picked up the sepia-toned venerable daguerreotype. Indeed the dark pools of the eyes in the photograph did fixate one's attention but not at the expense of appreciating the overall symmetry of a flat, prominent brow, broad nose, and full lips engaged in a slight frown. An ill-fitting suit jacket and obviously unfamiliar wing collar with bow tie completed the portrait of an intelligent black man more accustomed to hard physical labor than the milieu suggested by his studio attire.

"Pat, meet my great, great, great-great-grandfather. He was brought here from Africa sometime around 1845. Upon arrival, he was bought by a Mr. Gorsuch, who owned a plantation in Maryland where my ancestor worked relentlessly, all the while chafing under the loss of his freedom. In Africa, he had been the son of a chieftain of the Wasabi tribe and to him this life of servitude in the New World was anathema."

"I assume that after the Civil War he gained his freedom and eventually came North."

"His story was a good deal more interesting than that. In 1851 he escaped and was aided by the underground railway in his flight northward. He and other runaways were at a waystop in Christiana, Pennsylvania when his owner showed up with a warrant for his arrest authorized by the Fugitive Slave Act enacted the year before in 1850. In the confrontation that followed, the slaves were supported by a bystander who happened upon the scene, a Mr. Hanway. Mr. Gorsuch showed the warrant to Mr. Hanway and requested his help in retrieving his property. Under the same Fugitive Slave Law, Mr. Hanway was obliged to do so under penalty of a significant fine and incarceration. However, he refused his help and advised the slave owner to desist since the slaves were armed. In the fight that followed Mr. Gorsuch was killed and his son wounded. My ancestor escaped eventually to Canada but Mr. Hanway was indicted not under the Fugitive Slave Law, but rather for treason since there had been armed resistance."

"Hold on, Joe. You're saying the federal government indicted Mr. Hanway for treason just because there were gunshots and one death? Treason involves organized armed rebellion, conspiracy to rebellion, or aiding and giving comfort to a known enemy in an armed conflict. Conviction is essentially unknown except in time of war. From what you've told me, that's a huge stretch. You are aware that the penalty for treason is death?" Joe walked over to the bookshelves on the wall opposite his desk and removed a thin, manila-bound volume from its upper tier.

"You lawyers are all alike. I can see your hackles standing on end out of curiosity. Here's the entire story recorded by my grandmother back in the 'forties. You'll find a transcript of the trial with all the legal conflict you lawyers seem to love. I won't tell you the outcome but the rest of the document deals with the further adventures of my ancestor until his death during the Civil War."

"Thanks, Joe. I'm extremely curious. I'll get it back to you next week."

"No problem, keep it as long as you like. I'm sure you've observed that Mr. Hanway's name matches mine."

"A very interesting observation and one that need's an explanation should you care to volunteer it."

"Not at all. My ancestor was so grateful to his benefactor that he adopted his name when he became a free man in Canada. It was almost the rule that former slaves took the names of their masters, a particular white man whom they admired, or one who had helped them in some way. Interestingly, our Christian name of Hanway did not become legal until my father read his mother's treatise after returning from Army service in World War II. After a bit of research, he traced Mr. Hanway's descendants still in Lancaster County. He met with them and, upon showing them this document, gained their permission to legally adopt the Hanway name. I was seven at the time and, though born a Hanway, technically it was not legal until 1947."

"What a fascinating story. I can't wait to fill out the details for myself. Do you have any other family secrets?"

"None that I would tell you. There are some things that should be interred with everyone's bones."

"Okay, okay! Let's get back to the girls!"

CHAPTER XII

"THE CRAFTSMAN HAS THE ADVANTAGE OF HIS SKILL"

"Pat, I've said before that I'm grateful for all your efforts on my behalf. You had me well prepared for the rejection you anticipated from the Appeals Court. Now that it's a reality it doesn't bother me; but I'm sticking by my decision to plead not guilty." Once more they were in Judge Cummings' courtroom. It was a cool day in November with a slate-gray sky foreboding rain or snow depending on the fickleness of the temperature during the afternoon. The Appellate decision had been announced two days previously and had received such rapid attention from the media that Pat's call to alert Ted had scarcely beaten its pronouncement on the national TV and radio. "You're timetable has been impeccable, particularly when you predicted Judge Cummings would have us here for a plea hearing within two days of the decision."

"Okay, I'll accept your kudos but listen up. I also told you this session would be very brief. Once you enter your plea the judge will set a trial date and if my scheduling remains correct, it will be about a month from now. That month will be a busy one. I want to meet you at three o'clock this afternoon in my office. We have to go over everything that happened on that day in August, what Joe told you, what you did to make a diagnosis; why you decided the surgery had to be done that night; and why the hospital didn't pick up on the fact that Joe wasn't on your list." He looked across at Richard Sterling and Robert Giorgio who were patiently waiting for Judge Cumming's appearance.

"From here on in things get tough. I'm out of tricks to win the public over or delay the trial. Furthermore, any defense based upon restraint of trade or first amendment rights is now out the window. I'm looking for extenuating circumstances and friendship isn't one of them. I'll do my best to defend you but frankly right now I'm not sure how to do that. So help me as best you can."

"All rise. The Second District Court is now in session, Judge Harold Cummings presiding."

"Please be seated." The judge opened a loose-leaf binder in front of him and gazed over the rims of his glasses at the attorneys seated below him. "Mr. Holleran, has your client decided upon a plea?"

Pat and Ted both stood. "He has, your honor."

"And how does he plead?"

"Not guilty, your honor."

There was an immediate commotion behind the railing as reporters made haste to vacate the room and communicate with TV crews waiting outside or their editors in offices throughout the country.

"Order, order in the courtroom!" Judge Cummings pounded the gavel while staring down the perpetrators of the disturbance. "Thank you, Mr. Holleran. Trial is set for the fourth of January at 9 A.M. Do you have anything to add?"

"No, your honor."

"Mr. Sterling?"

"Not at the present time, your honor."

"Court is dismissed."

"All rise."

Richard crossed to their bench. Pat had noted during the brief exchange that the prosecutor had betrayed no look of surprise or for that matter resignation. His features were inscrutable.

"Mr. Holleran. May I call you Pat?"

"That's fine with me, Richard."

"I assumed your client would be pleading not guilty since you had not contacted me regarding a plea bargain. I'm sure you're aware that it would have been quite generous."

"Undoubtedly, but, I must abide by my client's wishes."

"Your office should have received notification of a grand jury hearing next week. I will be calling all the witnesses I listed for the trial beginning on the fourth. Based upon the evidence, I would expect confirmation of the indictment."

"I assume you have received my list of witnesses also?"

"I have, but I'm a bit puzzled. I can understand why you won't be calling Dr. O'Hara. But why only one witness, Joe Hanway?"

"Chalk it up to inexperience, counselor."

"Interesting. My best wishes, Mr. Holleran. See you in court."

"My pleasure, Richard."

～

The telephone rang three times before a female voice answered.

"Hanway Metal Products. May I direct your call?"

"Is Mr. Hanway there? Pat Holleran calling."

"One moment, please." Joe answered within seconds. "Hey, Pat. What's up?"

"Remember when I spoke to you about your testimony before the grand jury? I told you not to volunteer any information. Right?"

"Yes, I do. Just answer the questions."

"Well, listen up. I do want you to volunteer one bit of information."

～

It was one week later and Joe had just seated himself in the witness box. He was the last witness of the day and the jury members were restless, reflecting the fatigue the majority of them were experiencing. Even the court recorder, Mrs. Robinson, seemed flustered as she fussed with her recorder which had run out of paper. Attorney Giorgio was the first to speak. "All set to go, Mrs. Robinson?"

She nodded assent as the bailiff intoned the time-honored oath: "Mr. Hanway, would you raise your right hand. Do you swear to tell the truth, the whole truth and, nothing but the truth so help you God."

"So help me God."

"Please state your age, and address for the record."

"Joseph Hanway, age sixty-five, er . . . perhaps I should clarify that. The name, Joseph Hanway, was on my birth certificate but it was not legal until I was seven years old in 1947."

This time the question came from the presiding judge. "I don't understand. What are you saying? Your name is Joseph Hanway?"

CHAPTER XIII

"First Night"

The band was playing an older rock tune from the 'seventies, an accommodation to the age spectrum vibrating on the dance floor. Strobe lights intermittently illuminated the dancers, their limbs akimbo, gyrating to the frenetic beat like so many Kens and Barbies dressed to the nines on a marionette stage. It was 11:45 P.M. on New Year's Eve and the revelers, anticipating the magic of midnight, were progressively losing their inhibitions in a Bacchanalian mixture of food, wine, and music. Outside, a moonlit silence reverenced the hoary crust of new fallen snow garnishing the salad hills of the Mattatuck National Golf Club. After a busy holiday season highlighted by Christmas rituals and a visit from Santa, the O'Hara clan had gathered in Chatham primarily to relax. Ted had reserved a table for the annual New Year's Eve bash at the club. Their party included Annie and her husband Dan as well as their son, Tim, with his wife, Alice.

As the orchestra gratefully ended its latest marathon, Laura feigned collapse into Ted's arms.

"Whew! Another minute at that pace and this torture bra would just have to go."

"Now, Scarlett, some of your charms are not meant for the general public, if you get my drift."

"Rhett, don't you pay any mind to what others might imagine. These charms are meant only for you."

Laura was breathtaking in a strapless emerald gown with gossamer wisps seductively draped about her shoulders and tucked into a silk bodice barely concealing the charms so playfully referred to.

"Before you change you mind, let's sit the next one out."

"I'm just putty in your hands, Rhett."

Everyone returned to the table at the same time. "I didn't know you and Dad still had it in you, Mom. I'm just amazed. You were the best couple out there." Tim's voice had just a hint of irony in it.

"Your father and I had a lot of practice, but mind your manners, Tim. I detect a slight note of sarcasm."

"Not me. I thought Allie and I were pretty good but we can only step back in admiration."

"Your mother and I accept your compliment, son, but we're whipped. Why don't you and Allie get back up there?"

"Thanks, Dad, but we'll pass."

"Suit yourselves but your mother and I want tonight to be something special. Before we get into the haggling of a trial, with all its uncertainties, we wanted to just be a family again; to enjoy each other's company. I must admit it has been succeeding beautifully."

"Oh, Dad! We're with you everyday, all twenty-four hours worth. If love could win this, we wouldn't even be going to court. If it can't there's still an ocean of it available at this table." This time it was Annie speaking having enfolded one of her father's hands in both of hers from across the table.

"Thanks, sweetheart. I'll swim in that ocean any day. Wouldn't even mind drowning in it."

Dan broke in. "So, what's the schedule? When does the main event start?"

"Next Monday, nine o'clock sharp – we start picking jurors. Pat tells me there shouldn't be too many challenges. He thinks we'll be getting serious by the end of the week."

"Well, Dan and I are planning to take a few weeks off and come to Connecticut for moral support."

"You'll do no such thing. You're welcome to take a vacation but make it just that, a vacation. Besides, aren't the kids back in school? Just take good care of them and your patients. Dan, isn't January one of your busiest months coming as it does so soon after the holidays? We'd love to see you on weekends but otherwise having Scarlett here is more than recompense for me, and I don't expect her to take time off from work either."

"Rhett, there you go again, being so masterful in organizing any situation complimenting li'l ole me at the same time. My fathers! He leaves me breathless."

Allie, who had been listening intently, chimed in. "Dad, you're not going to lock the doors against Tim and I, are you? After all, we're only a half mile away."

"So long as Tim continues to emulate his mother at work and you tend to that beautiful baby, your advice and support are always welcome, even on weekdays."

It was Dan again: "Understood, but what worries me is the lack of notoriety in the press ever since the decision by the Appeals Court over a month ago. It's almost as if everyone has forgotten the entire process."

"Only the calm before the storm, son. Every major network and newspaper have hotel reservations in Westbury ready for daily coverage of the trial. I would be quite willing to make a substantial wager there hasn't been a day you haven't personally heard some discussion about the principle in question."

"True. Annie is your greatest advocate. She never misses an opportunity to bring up the topic at work, cocktail parties, or even the grocery store. More importantly, she has a distinct problem in finding any opposition. Mysteriously, as you know, various polls show opinion to be more evenly divided making one wonder where these so called polls come from."

"Polls won't be deciding this trial, Dan. A jury of twelve tried and true will, even if they don't want to."

Allie jumped in again. "So, what has been going on since the decision by the Appeals Court?"

Ted interrupted a sip of Merlot to answer his daughter-in-law. "Allie, honey, the prosecution set up shop in an anteroom on the third floor of the federal building and brought half the population of Westbury before a grand jury; at least the half that were working at St. Lucy's the night I operated on Joe. Even Joe had his turn. On the basis of the testimony, the grand jury agreed there was sufficient cause to go forward with the trial." At that point a group of three couples resplendent in their finery arrived at their table, interrupting the conversation. As Ted stood to greet the newcomers, he shook hands with the tall gentleman who appeared to be their spokesman. "Frank, Happy New Year! Mary, you're ravishing tonight. All of you Harry, Sylvia, Rosemary, and you too, Mike. What a fashion parade!"

By now Laura was also on her feet, greeting each of their friends in turn. "I'm sure all of you know our Annie and her husband, Dan, and say hello to Tim and his wife, Allie." Frank was the CEO of a large manufacturing firm outside of Boston as were Henry and Mike, although in different areas of the business world. What they mutually shared with the O'Hara's was the love and enjoyment of this seaside corner of Massachusetts, in particular the congenial premises they graced this evening.

"It seems rather inane to wish you a Happy New Year. So I won't. I'm sure you're well aware that everyone here tonight are numbered among your friends. We're sort of a self-appointed committee to express our concern and good wishes. All of us have followed the media coverage of your upcoming trial and are convinced that, in a real sense, we will share your fate whatever the verdict is. That lawyer you have has guaranteed that one way or another each of us has to think about what's at stake and identify with the outcome. But more than that we individually represent concerns shared by business in general. We inherently despise the waste and inefficiency of huge governmental bureaucracies managing areas of the economy better served by private enterprise. In the past few years, our collective voice, as that of your profession, has fallen upon deaf ears in Washington. Minus that voice, or the hope of its being listened to by the bastards on the Potomac, change can only come from some small glitch conceivably leading to a complete unraveling of the cocoon choking your profession. Ted, you could provide that glitch, that spark. So for those selfish reasons and the most selfish of all, our friendship, I drink to your acquittal."

"Here, here!"

"If there's anything we can do to help, let me know; and I'm quite serious about that, Ted, anything. I've already made a tee time for nine in the morning on the fifteenth of March; the first day the course here at Mattatuck National will be open. We don't want to be a threesome; so be there."

"Frank, I can't tell you how much I appreciated that toast. Don't get me wrong. I'm not a martyr or a hero. I'm more interested in showing up for that tee time than I am in unraveling anything. If I show up that morning, and by the way that is a date, it will mean that Danbury Federal Prison will not be my address in the foreseeable future. That's my selfish motivation. Now let's continue this great evening. It's almost midnight, so grab your gals and get out on that dance floor. By the way, I've already booked our reservation for First Night next year here at the club. Can I add six to that reservation?"

"You sure can, Ted. If we don't talk sooner, I want to have a long discussion with you, after your acquittal. Okay?"

"Sure, Frank, Happy New Year."

The band had returned from its break and struck up a slow foxtrot.

"At last a danceable tune. Come on, Scarlett. Let's show the younger generation how it's really done."

⌒

Later, in bed, Laura sensed something different in Ted's embrace, perhaps just a hint of immediacy in the pressure he applied to bring their bodies together. "Ted, what a wonderful evening. The kids were great and wasn't it sweet? Frank and the gang really went overboard with the well-wishing."

"Right, hon. It was great. But forget the hero stuff. All I want is the freedom to grow older in your arms and no interruptions, please!"

"Is that why I noticed a little extra squeeze a moment ago?"

"Perhaps, but then you were extra beautiful tonight."

"Keep talking, Romeo."

"I noticed a few moments ago, you were quite correct earlier this evening."

"How so?"

"That bra you were wearing was a torture device. The marks it left on those gorgeous breasts will require the best of my medical ministrations for a least the next half-hour."

"Good try, but at the moment I'm more interested in what's bothering you."

"Other than your breasts?"

"Do you want me to wear that bra all night?"

"Touché! I'll behave." After a further embrace and a prolonged kiss, Ted rolled on his back bringing Laura on her side within the protective arch of his right arm. "Do you remember what a great time we had New Year's Eve at the Millennium?"

"Do I? I was sore for a week."

"No, I meant before that, at the party."

"Okay, darling, I'll try to be just as serious as you now appear to be."

"It's just that when we were with our friends that night sharing the champagne you had hoarded a year in advance, anticipating what proved to be a real shortage, all of us entered into a certain spirit of hope, a feeling of wiping the slate clean and starting afresh."

"Yes, and you drank more than your share of that champagne."

"As it turned out, I didn't have enough. With what's happened since, the new millennium hasn't lived up to its revues. But, before you became so sore, do you remember what we envisioned for ourselves in the years to come?"

"Every ever-loving sweet word of it. We were a unique team, a union which had known the best. We anticipated that the years left to us would be invested in keeping it that way. We weren't looking to improving anything. We talked for hours about our hopes for the kids and the bogeyman of retirement but decided that love would conquer all. I haven't changed my mind. Have you?"

"No way. Time out for proof?"

"Oh Rhett, you say the sweetest things."

Twenty minutes and a great deal of energy later, totally spent in each other's arms, Ted croaked, "Time in?"

"I think I'm going to be just as sore as at the Millennium."

"Condolences. I'll prescribe something. A long time ago, earlier tonight, you asked what was bothering me."

"I seem to recall."

"Well, I'm scared and afraid I may lose the trial and have to live without you, even if only for a few years. Any time is too long."

"Oh, Ted, even if I have to hand-wrestle Sterling and Giorgio, *mano-a-mano*, I just won't let that happen."

"Those carpetbaggers see it differently."

"Well, Scarlett won't let it happen."

"Then, I pity the blue-bellies. Goodnight, Scarlett."

CHAPTER XIV

"THE FOOL'S UNDERSTANDING TURNS HIM TO HIS LEFT."

"The state will prove beyond any reasonable doubt that, on the evening in question, the accused made no effort to determine if Joseph Hanway was on his patient list. We will also conclusively show that Joseph Hanway not only knew his name was not on that list, but he was aware which surgeon's list he was on. Further testimony will confirm that he volunteered this information to Dr. O'Hara but not to any other responsible person at the hospital. You will hear the motive for such an omission from Mr. Hanway's own sworn statement."

Judge Cummings appeared relaxed and attentive as he surveyed the courtroom from his accustomed position dominating the scene unfolding beneath him. Richard Sterling, pacing in front of the jury, was about to conclude his opening remarks. Ted and Pat sat behind the table for the defense, Ted obviously intent, but Pat curiously somewhat distracted. At the prosecutors' table, Robert Giorgio was reading a sheaf of legal papers, occasionally making marginal notes. It was 11 A.M. on the first Thursday in January, the fourth day of the trial, the first three days of which had been invested in selecting and swearing in jurors. As Pat had predicted most of the challenges had come from the prosecution and were relatively few in number. The final makeup was seven females and five males; five Blacks, three Latinos, and four Caucasians. Most of the females were black or Latino and all four Caucasian were elderly and retired. Attorney Sterling was well pleased with the selections justifiably feeling that the majority's sympathy would be on the side of government-controlled medicine. He reasoned that the retirees and the three on welfare fit that scenario and, of the remainder, all had limited income and were of an age mainly concerned with the economic burden of raising and educating their children. What concerned him was why Pat had not used his challenges to object to any of those presently sitting in the jury box. Indeed, time and again he had not bothered to question them when the opportunity presented itself. Most mysterious was his single use of a challenge to dismiss a forty-two year-old Caucasian male businessman from Danbury. He was the sales manager of a large metallurgic firm and on the face of it would be just the type of juror Pat should want. Instead, he had dismissed him without cause. It was almost as if the defense wanted the same jury he did and that was truly baffling.

Pat was listening to Richard but his eyes were on the jury noting each of their reactions in turn as the prosecutor embellished upon his arguments. Thus far, he had not regretted his strategy of tacit approval for the jury the prosecution had selected. Sterling and Giorgio had to be confused as to why, particularly with the preemptory challenge he did make use of. In truth, he wanted no part of a juror who would resent every moment he sat in that jury box. The young fellow was obviously a comer in the business world and could better use his time in furthering his career than spend it deliberating on the fate of a doctor who should have known better than to break the rules. Besides, although Sterling couldn't possibly know, he did get the exact jury he wanted, but for reasons only he was privy to.

"And so ladies and gentlemen of the jury, I would again remind you of the duty Judge Cummings placed upon your shoulders when he swore you in as the panel to dispense justice in the case before us. You have obligated yourselves to pay close attention to all the evidence; to impartially consider that evidence; and to render judgment without prejudice, rancor, or any influence beyond that generated by the evidence itself. My colleague and I have complete faith in your ability to so comport yourself. Thank you for your attention."

In response to a ruffle of conversation within the courtroom the judge rapped his gavel. "Mr. Holleran, you may proceed with your remarks."

"I have none at this time, your honor."

The prosecutor had yet to gain his seat when he stopped in mid-stride, aghast! The judge's subsequent words struck him unprepared.

"Mr. Sterling, you may call your first witness." His first witness? The emergency room physician, Dr. Curtin, wasn't even in the courtroom. Indeed, he had told him to be ready after the lunch break when the defense's opening discourse would have been finished. Will this provincial lawyer ever cease to surprise him?

"Your honor, I beg your indulgence. My first witness will not be available until one o'clock this afternoon. Perhaps, your honor could declare a recess until then."

"Mr. Sterling, I would remind you that in my courtroom, I expect attorneys to be prepared to argue their case with appropriate awareness and flexibility. The hour is approaching eleven. Court is recessed until one o'clock." The judge concluded by rapping the gavel and exited rapidly with an expression on his face which could not be misinterpreted by Richard.

"All rise."

⟿

Ted, confused by the rapid exchange just completed, turned to his lawyer, looking for an answer. All he got was a quizzical grin. "Pat, what's going on here? I thought all you guys love nothing better than hearing your own voice. I didn't know what you were going to say but I was prepared to bear it for at least an hour."

"I'm going to come as clean as I can. In one important way, you're a perfect client."

"I'm not sure I'm ready for this, what with the games you play; but okay, How so?"

"You seem to have complete faith in my advocacy for you, as a result of which you don't bombard me with a thousand questions about my defense strategy. For that I'm grateful. First of all because that plan, up to now, is not etched in cement. Secondly, the plan I have in mind requires me to be rather secretive. So a lot of things during the trial are going to come as a surprise to you and I want it that way. I don't want the jury thinking for an instant that your reactions to what happens here are rehearsed or any less genuine than their own."

"Okay, I'll buy that. But what happened here this morning? Don't you think the jury wanted to hear something from our side?"

"Well, I did have a few remarks prepared and they weren't bad. Here, read them if you like." As he was speaking Pat removed a folded piece of paper from the breast pocket of his suit and handed it to Ted. "But three things happened while Richard was waxing so eloquent. Number one I've grown to appreciate that Judge Cummings is an eminently fair but a no-nonsense courtroom arbitrator. Secondly, I knew that Brian was to be his first witness and that he was not present in the courtroom. More importantly, I got all the answers I needed this morning by observing the jurors' reactions to Richard's remarks. I would not have gained anything further from their reactions to mine. So I had a little fun at Sterling's expense. I wish I could be a crumb on the tablecloth when the prosecutors lunch together today. I've succeeded in confusing them again and I've got to maintain my ability to do so. Sterling's the one who can't abide surprises but Giorgio's the one I've got to keep confused until it's too late. So that means total secrecy. Deal?"

"Deal! But when will I get it?"

"When they get it. Hey, I'm not saying this will work or that you'll get home free. I could even change my mind along the way. Just trust me."

"Let's get some lunch, pal."

⌐

"Raise your right hand. Do you swear to tell the truth, the whole truth, and nothing but the truth, so help you God?"

"I do."

"Please state your full name."

"Brian Daniel Curtin."

Richard Sterling's voice was friendly but cryptic. "Dr. Curtin, could you briefly outline your professional background?"

"Certainly. I received an M.D. degree from Tufts University Medical School in 1988 and completed a residency in Emergency Medicine at New England Medical Center in 1992. Since then I've been employed full time at St. Lucy's Hospital, in their Emergency Department where I've been the Assistant Chief for the past three years."

"Are you board certified in your specialty?"

"Yes, in 1993."

"Were you on duty in the Emergency Room at St. Lucy's on the evening of August twenty-fifth last year?"

"I was."

"And did you treat a patient by the name of Joseph Hanway during the course of that evening?"

"I did not treat him. However, I did examine him and try to sort out a diagnosis."

"Thank you for that correction, Doctor. Could you tell the jury at what time you first saw him and what he was complaining of?

"Yes. I first examined Mr. Hanway shortly after four in the afternoon. He complained of a backache which had awakened him that morning and which had persisted all day without relief."

"Can you describe what you did then?"

"He stated he felt fine when he went to bed the night before and that he had never had a similar pain. He informed me that, years before, Dr. O'Hara had removed his gallbladder. The only thing he had was the pain, no nausea, vomiting, diarrhea, or other GI or GU symptoms."

"What do you mean by GI or GU? The jury may not understand."

"Excuse me. I meant symptoms that could be referred to the stomach or intestines, or the urinary tract, er, that is the kidney or bladder."

"I see, and what did your physical examination show?"

"Not very much. The only abnormality I noted was fullness with localized tenderness in the upper mid-abdomen. No fever. His pulse and blood pressure were normal."

"Did you perform any laboratory tests?"

"Yes, I did."

"And what were they?"

"A complete blood count, serum electrolytes, liver function tests, blood urea nitrogen, serum creatinine, blood sugar, a chest X-ray, plain X-rays of the abdomen and an electrocardiogram."

"Without getting into a great deal of detail, what were the results of these tests?"

"There were all normal and didn't help make a diagnosis."

"So, what was next?"

"I suggested a CT of the abdomen."

"What do you mean, a CT?"

"Computerized tomography. A special X-ray machine takes multiple films of the abdomen at various levels and a computer reconstructs these images to demonstrate all the abdominal organs."

"What happened then?"

"Mr. Hanway requested that I call Dr. O'Hara in consultation before any further tests were done."

"Why Dr. O'Hara?"

"Mr. Hanway told me that he was a close friend and you will recall he had operated on him in the past."

"Did you check to see if Dr. O'Hara was on Mr. Hanway's approved list of specialists under the rules of the National Health Administration?"

"I had the clerk put a call into Dr. O'Hara's service and then checked the computer for the list. It was then I discovered the hospital computers were down."

"Does your hospital have a backup for checking these lists?"

"Not after five in the afternoon and it was after five by then."

"Did you ask Mr. Hanway if he knew who his assigned surgeon was?"

"It's been my experience that, with the large number of specialists on any individual patient's list, in order to cover a variety of medical or surgical problems, a patient in the ER, particularly one in distress, could not possibly be expected to remember this information. Consequently, it has been my policy not to ask. I didn't ask Mr. Hanway."

"All right. How long did it take for Dr. O'Hara to arrive?"

"No more than fifteen minutes. I caught him in his car going home on I-84."

"Briefly, what happened then?"

"Dr. O'Hara examined Mr. Hanway and agreed that a CT should be done. He suspected an aneurysm of the abdominal aorta, a perforated peptic ulcer with a localized abscess, or a tumor of the stomach,"

"Did the CT give you the diagnosis?"

"Yes, Mr. Hanway had a large aneurysm with an ulceration on its back wall to explain the pain he was feeling."

"Did you agree with Dr. O'Hara that, although Mr. Hanway was quite stable, an emergency operation was necessary that night?"

"I'm not a surgeon, but I respect Ted's, excuse me, Dr.O'Hara's opinion more than any surgeon I've ever known. He recognized the ulceration for what it was, a friendly but dangerous warning. He didn't want to run the risk of imminent rupture by delaying. I cannot and would not disagree with that assessment."

"I appreciate your opinion of Dr. O'Hara. It seems to be shared by many in the community; but I'm not here to dispute his competence or reputation. Tell me, did you ask Dr. O'Hara if he knew whether or not Mr. Hanway was on his patient list?"

"From the moment he entered the Emergency Room that night our involvement was entirely professional. Our mutual desire to arrive at a proper diagnosis and render appropriate treatment riveted our attention. I didn't even think of it."

"Thank you, Dr. Curtin. Your witness, Mr. Holleran."

"I have no questions." As Sterling again reacted in surprise, Giorgio was on his feet and saved the prosecutor from further embarrassment. "The State calls Helen Curry as their next witness."

Pat nodded to Ted who smiled in return as the bailiff intoned: "Raise your right hand. Do you swear to tell the truth, the whole truth and nothing but the truth, so help you God."

"I do."

"Please state your name."

"Helen Curry."

"Ms. Curry, may I call you Helen?" Richard had regained his composure and almost seemed unctuous as he addressed the comely young women before him.

"You may."

"Helen, can you recount your professional training and current employment for the benefit of the jury?" What followed was a detailed description of the surgery performed on Joe colored by the admiration of this obviously competent nurse for the care and skill of Dr. O'Hara.

"Thank you, Helen. Your witness."

"No questions, your honor."

And so it went with the circulating nurse, Betty Felton, the only difference being her confirmation that the hospital computer system had been down that night. "Could you tell us, Betty? Did you have computer access that evening to record the details of the operation done on Mr. Hanway?"

"No, sir. The computer was not working. However, the next morning it was okay and I entered the details then."

"Did these details include who should have been Mr. Hanway's surgeon?"

"No, sir. That's not my job. Since we didn't have the information beforehand, I left it blank and trusted in the record room."

"Thank you, Betty. Your witness."

"No questions, your honor."

This time it was the judge who covered up for Sterling. "Court is adjourned until 9 A.M. tomorrow."

"All rise."

CHAPTER XV

*"WHEN THE FOOL WALKS THROUGH
THE STREET IN HIS LACK OF UNDERSTANDING,
HE CALLS EVERYTHING FOOLISH."*

G iorgio was seated with his collar open and sleeves rolled up. A laptop computer was in front of him as he exhaled the dregs of a half-smoked cigarette. "Why can't I find the answer? He's got us on the edge, a clue here, a clue there, but nothing that makes any sense."

Sterling was pacing in front of the desk, suit jacket in place with only his tie loosened. He was obviously nervous and his sagging features betrayed an underlying anxiety. He was unaccustomed to being jerked about like a yo-yo on a string. "What's he up to? What can he hope to accomplish by his silence?"

"Calm down, Richard. Look at the positive side. We have the jury we wanted and are well on the way to establishing that Dr. O'Hara knew damn well he wasn't supposed to be the one operating that night."

"It's not what we know that bothers me. It's what we don't know. His clues are non-clues. Why didn't he object to our jury selection? Why does he accept all the evidence we present without rebuttal? I'll tell you why. He wants to distract us, to blind us. There's a huge surprise coming our way when it's his turn. Bob, I can't let it bug me if for no other reason than it obviously does. You've got to find the answer before the defense has its turn. I don't care how you do it. Just do it. What about all the background stuff you dug up on our Mr. Holleran? Anything there?"

"A veritable boy scout. Graduated from Fordham Law in 1968; passed the New York bar on his first try; started to work his way up a large corporate law firm in the city but didn't like it; moved to Westbury in 1974 and has his own practice since. He does general stuff, no criminal law or liability cases, nothing at all to suggest he's as clever as you seem to think he is."

"For Christ's sake, Bob! He's dragged us through a brief in the Federal District Court and an appellate review in the Circuit, all before the trial had a chance to start. I never know what he's thinking."

"I didn't say he wasn't smart, but, I think we're a helluva lot smarter. Just leave it to me, I'll figure it out. So far I suspect it's got something to do with that jury. For some reason he likes them as much as we do. And why has he provided us with the name of only one person on his list of defense witnesses?"

For the next three days the prosecutor quizzed one witness after another; the two surgical residents, the radiologist who read the X-rays and the CT scan, the administrator responsible for maintaining the computer system at St. Lucy's and the clerk from the record room who had picked up on the fact Joe was assigned to a different surgeon. At the conclusion of each bit of testimony, Pat had been given the opportunity to cross-examine, each of which he declined. The pace of the trial had become so predictable that the spectators, the media analysts and, perhaps most importantly, the jurors were becoming bored. Sterling never had the chance to get into a stimulating argument or take a swing at anyone or anything. Even he became tedious in the repetitive questions he asked each witness. Giorgio felt his time was being wasted and by Tuesday had isolated himself in the office made available to the prosecution where for the most part he stared at a few legal pads and law texts in disarray on the desk in front him. He was lost in such deep thought that someone coming upon the scene might be frightened into calling 911 for a patient in coma.

He had never been this intellectually challenged. In a peculiar sense, he enjoyed that. Pat Holleran would become his equal, if not more, unless he solved the riddle echoing and reechoing in his brain. For the hundredth time he started again from what he knew. First Holleran had granted the validity of the facts in this case, else why no cross-examination? Second, he had no opening remarks. Ergo, he refuses to wear his defense on his sleeve. "A trap awaits us but what trap? If he's not going to argue the facts then he's going to argue the law. But he did that before the trial and up to now has lost. He knows if he brings up the same arguments now we will object and we both know the judge will sustain. Are there any other arguments that apply to this law? Ever since he hit us with the restraint of trade charade, I've gone back and had our staff research every possibe avenue of approach and we came up with nothing. Besides, he knows that Cummings would not tolerate another legal donnybrook until the trial is over when it would take place in the Appellate Court, not his. What's left? Jury nullification? Could he be planning to roll the dice on convincing them to overlook the law and make their decision on what they feel is right or wrong? This band of twelve has more interest in continuing socialized care than unraveling it. If he wanted that kind of jury, he should have fought for twelve junior Rockefellers like the one from Danbury he dismissed out of hand. When push comes to shove, these twelve have a vested interest in the status quo. But he does like this jury. Why? The answer's there. I know it, but where? What?"

For the umpteenth time that day, he closed his eyes only to visualize the same gray, monotonous wall in front of him, having no top for him to see over or side to dart around. The answer he wanted was beyond that wall and he had to have it before Pat Holleran provided it. It would be too late then.

Again, he opened his eyes, rubbed them awake as he stood, stretched, and began to pace the room. As he returned to the desk, he picked up the fax he had received from his staff in Washington not more than a half-hour ago. The previous afternoon he had requested a computer search of all documented instances of jury nullification in the past hundred years, trying to come up with something to match the circumstances of this trial. Nothing reasonable had surfaced. Granted the pre-trial notoriety had provoked heated debates, not only on the Sunday talk shows, but also among the general populace. In spite of a fifty-fifty split of the polls on this issue, he never believed them. His own assessment was that the gentry favored free choice between doctor and patient. But, again, if Holleran wanted to exploit that he would have to resurrect the brief once more, which would not be permitted by the judge. Indeed, in his charge to the jury, he will emphasize that the verdict must be based on the law, not on one's own beliefs." What am I saying? He's got the All-American wrong jury for nullification."

"Well, he's calling one witness, Joe Hanway. Joe's due on the docket as our witness tomorrow. So why did the defense list him as their only witness? He must be planning to pass again on cross-examination and we'll be obligated to treat him as a hostile witness even though he's the key to our argument. Why? I fully understand why he won't be calling upon Dr, O'Hara. If he does so he knows we'll have the opportunity to cross and pin him down as to whether he was aware, at the time he did the surgery, he was wrong in doing so. Either that or he'll take the fifth. God knows he doesn't need him on the stand to add to the sainthood our witnesses have already elevated him to. Is he going to play the black card? Joe's black, but he's not on trial. He's Dr. O'Hara's best friend but that will never hold up as an excuse for his operating on him. Old Cummings will make sure of that in his instructions to the jury. No, it's something else. Something I'm close to but can't fathom. This puzzle is driving me nuts. Old 'smoke and mirrors' Holleran can't be that good."

His thoughts were interrupted by a messenger from the courtroom who, after introducing himself, handed him a folded piece of paper. "Mr. Sterling told me to get this message to you right away."

"Did he say anything else?"

"Only that he hoped you could make something of it." Closing the door, he opened the single sheet to read the following: "Richard, just wanted to let you know I won't be calling any defense witnesses. Best regards, Pat."

◠

The courtroom door fairly flew open causing a discernable commotion among the spectators as Bob Giorgio rushed to his seat all the while trying to attract Richard's attention as he was completing his questioning of Mrs. Merriweather, a clerk in the record room at St. Lucy's Hospital.

"Order! Order in the court!" Judge Cummings, aroused from his sonorous state, pounded the gavel as rapidly as he could. "Mr. Sterling, I need not warn you about any further such outbursts from your associate."

"Begging your indulgence, Your Honor, but I would appreciate a brief recess to ascertain what provoked my associate's breach of behavior."

"Court is recessed for ten minutes."

"All rise."

◠

"Bob, what got into you? You were assigned to me on your reputation of being unflappable and the smartest the Attorney General has. What gives?"

"It's that note you sent me. Somehow you've got to delay putting Joe Hanway on the stand tomorrow. I don't know what it is but I need extra time to figure it out. If we hear it from the defense counsel it will be too late."

"Jesus Christ, Bob! How can I do that? Joe's the last witness we have after I finish the next five minutes with Mrs. Merriweather. Pat's not going to cross-examine and Cummings will adjourn for the night. First thing in the morning Joe's on the stand. God knows I'm getting bored. I can't stand to hear my own voice. Two of the jurors had to be nudged awake a few moments ago. What possible excuse can I manufacture to convince the judge to postpone anything tomorrow? Pat just cancelled him as his own witness."

"Don't you get it? He's going to cross-examine Joe. Had he kept him as his own witness he would have passed again. Now all we're going to get is redirect."

"So what? He can only cross-examine on the facts Joe testifies to. He'll lose the opportunity to bring up anything else he might have if Joe were also his witness. I can't think of anything in his testimony which could be tampered with on cross."

"Neither can I, but there's got to be something – something that will turn these proceedings upside down. I need more time to figure that out."

"Look, pal. You've run out of time. There's no way I can delay Joe's testimony. If you strike gold tonight, call me at any hour but you'd better be back in your seat tomorrow morning. Son of a bitch – are you the best the department can offer?"

From across the room, Pat seemed totally relaxed and was smiling broadly. He didn't have to hear the conversation across the room to know exactly what was being said. For his part, Ted could only stare from the opposition to his mentor and shrug his shoulders in confusion. Whatever was going on his best clue was the smile on Pat's face as opposed to the obvious anger across the room.

༄

Half an hour later court was adjourned. Ted was in Pat's office sitting across from his lawyer friend who was quite relaxed behind his desk. They were in the sunset of a gin game, which had been going all Pat's way. "If you can stop looking like the cat that swallowed the canary maybe you could deal the cards shyster."

"Now Ted, don't get testy. After today, it's only right the cards are going my way."

"Okay, it's the ace of spades, gin double. At least, if I win I can get halfway back in this debacle. I can't use the ace."

"Neither can I. Take a card. What debacle are you referring to?"

"Stop being cute. What happened today?"

"Not much. Pretty boring. Wasn't it?"

"Yeah, until the boy scout quarterback had a seizure. I expected him to foam at the mouth at any moment."

"Now, now, don't be too harsh on him. He only heard something he didn't want to hear."

"And what might that have been, Macchiavelli?"

"What's the knock card? Oh, that's right. It's double gin."

"Come on, Pat. I know I'm not supposed to ask questions but Giorgio looked pale as a sheet and twice as nervous while the senator was obviously mad as hell, all at a time the rest of us were going to sleep, including Judge Cummings."

"Okay, Ted. Just this once. All I did was pass a note to the opposition that I wouldn't be calling Joe as a witness."

"Whoa, hold up a sec. He was going to be our only witness. I figured you were going to renege on cross-examination of Joe's prosecution testimony just as you have with all of the other witnesses, but at least you could introduce your strategy through his testimony as a defense witness."

"That's just what I wanted them to think and they obviously did. But that would have opened Joe to their cross-examination on any evidence I elicited from him."

"So what? Aw, forget it. I don't even know what that testimony was going to be."

"You'll know tomorrow. I'm going to cross-examine Joe."

"Well, hallelujah! My lawyer's going to do a little talking for once. Look's like I'll have to get my wallet out."

"You can do that right now! Gin!" Pat laid his winning hand on the desktop.

"Damn! I assume you're out in all three streets?"

"That's right, friend. I get a long cross-examination and all they get is a short redirect if they want it. How many over?"

"Thirty, you thief. But hold on. I still don't get it. All you can quiz Joe about are the facts he testifies to."

"That's right, my friend. Everything he testifies to. That will be thirty dollars, please."

〜

"Hi, Joe. Pat here. I hope I didn't interrupt anything." It was the same evening and Pat had just turned the TV off in preparation of retiring for the night.

"No, I was just reviewing some notes for my testimony tomorrow."

"Don't tell me any details. All will be revealed tomorrow. Do you remember everything we talked about when you became a defense witness?"

"Sure"

"Well, forget about it. I've decided not to call any witnesses."

"You what?"

"I've decided against calling any defense witnesses, but that doesn't get you off the hook."

"What do you mean? I don't understand."

"I'm going to stop taking the fifth. When Sterling is finished with you tomorrow I'm going to cross-examine you."

"Pat, I sure hope you know what you're doing."

"I do, Joe. Initially there's going to be a furor, but when everything quiets down, just answer all my questions honestly and directly. I can assure you the jury will be all ears. See you tomorrow."

"Sure, Pat."

CHAPTER XVI

"WHEN THE FOOL WALKS THROUGH
THE STREET, IN HIS LACK OF UNDERSTANDING,
HE CALLS EVERYTHING FOOLISH."
THE CRAFTSMAN HAS THE ADVANTAGE OF
HIS SKILL."

(Reprise)

Bob Giorgio was in his hotel room at the Marriott. The dinner he had finished hours ago sat like a lead weight in his stomach as he was preparing himself for a second consecutive sleepless night. Popping a chewable Xantax into his mouth, he settled himself on the couch in as comfortable a position as possible; picked up the fax report from his staff in Washington; and began reading it for the fifth time. He was sure he had missed something and was convinced something would click if he just read it often enough. Dozens of nullification cases were cited, the most famous of which had to be the O.J. Simpson murder trial. After nine months of testimony, the jury didn't review the evidence at all and within three hours came out with a unanimous vote for acquittal.

Also included was Clinton's impeachment trial before the Senate back in early 1999. In this case the jurors, namely the Senators, paid little heed to the evidence provided by the House of Representatives nor did they call witnesses, but rapidly proceeded to a vote which, lacking the two thirds necessary for dismissal from office, acquitted the president.

"In the first instance, the race card had certainly been played by O.J.'s lawyer; O.J., of course, was black and the majority of the jury matched. Little wonder that his attorneys spent a good deal of effort in assailing the Los Angeles Police Department for their supposed bigotry as motivation to frame their client. He had considered this many times before but asked himself again: Could Pat Holleran be planning a similar strategy? Again the answer was no. Joe Hanway's black but not on trial. His only connection to Dr. O'Hara is friendship. Cummings is a no-nonsense judge as opposed to Judge Ito. In his courtroom, if friendship is brought up, our objection will immediately be sustained.

"Let's analyze the Clinton fiasco. Here the jury was totally swayed by a combination of party loyalty and the fickle barometer of opinion polls. Granted our esteemed opponent has opened a Pandora's box of raging bulls and stampeding stallions in the corral of public opinion. God knows I can't even go to my favorite bar for a quiet drink without overhearing several heated discussions relative to the genesis of this trial. But two major roadblocks would be in his way. How can he get such evidence in front of the jury? We spent three months in pre-trial going down that road and to resurrect it now would be inadmissible. Besides he's got the wrong jury for it.

"So, what am I looking for? Somewhere here, there's got to be an answer." As he turned the page, his eyes encountered one of the most ambiguous decisions ever handed down by a court in the history of jurisprudence. In 1997, the Court of Appeals for the Second Circuit, Judge Guillermo Rodriguez presiding, overturned the conviction in a drug-dealing case. One member of the jury, for what appeared to be racial motivation, had stated to other jurors that no matter what the evidence he felt the accused had a right to deal in drugs. After questioning the juror, the judge dismissed him, whereupon the remaining jurors convicted the accused.

On the one hand, the Appellate Court overturned the conviction on the grounds the judge had not acted prudently in his dismissal of the errant juror. In their opinion there was not sufficient evidence to prove that the juror would have disregarded the law. On the other hand, Judge Rodriguez took the occasion to diametrically take a strong stand against jury nullification. He noted that, historically, its use had been both beneficial and detrimental. Prior to the Civil War it protected runaway slaves from being returned to the South in so far as northern juries would not convict for violations of the Fugitive Slave Law. On the opposite side of the coin were many instances where murder and lynching were sanctioned. One such notable case was the hung jury in the trial of Benjamin De La Beckwith, indicted in Mississippi for the murder of Medgar Evers.

Richard Nowell, a law professor at New York University was quoted: "It's become a two-edged sword. We can't live with it and we can't live without it. We acknowledge that jury nullification can be the ultimate defense against government oppression, but we also fear it because it's corrosive of the rule of law."

"Suspecting and then proving jury nullification places a heavy burden on judges to make a solid case that a juror, or jury, intends to disregard the law. Even beginning to question jurors about their intentions would mean invading the historic secrecy of the deliberative process. A presiding judge faced with anything but unambiguous evidence that a juror refuses to apply the law as instructed need go no further in his investigation of alleged nullification. Such a juror could not be dismissed."

Giorgio chuckled as he mused: "Damned if you do and damned if you don't." The secret to nullification is the jury and getting to them. Usually the defense counsel attacks the prosecution in a biased manner, a bias which individual jurors would share or identify with. The prejudice could be ethnic, racial, economic, social, any number of things. Such bias could be reinforced by testimony from defense witnesses. What have we here? The counsel for the defense has not presented an opening argument; cross examined the prosecution's witnesses, and, as of today, has canceled any defense witnesses. If nullification is his game, everything centers upon the one remaining witness for the prosecution, Joe Hanway.

"What about Joe Hanway? He's in his sixties, Black; intelligent, a self-made man, well-off, no history of particular political activity. And the jury? Lower income America, four retired people, more women than men, a predominance of blacks, not exactly crusaders to dismantle government health care. Holleran knows that and yet he wanted this jury as much as we do. God, how many times have I said that? The only common thread is blackness. That's got to be it: but where does that lead me? Wait a minute. There was something in that decision by the Appeals Court for the Second Circuit, back a few pages, h'mm, yes, here it is! Prior to the Civil War it (jury nullification) protected runaway slaves from being returned to the South in so far as Northern juries would not convict." Roused from his introspection, he literally ran to the phone rapidly dialing the home number for Richard Sterling's chief of staff in Washington. After eight or ten rings, a sleepy voice answered.

"Hello, Mike Rawlings speaking."

"Mike this is Bob Giorgio."

"Bob who?"

"Giorgio, Richard's assistant. I got your fax about jury nullification, but I need you to do some further research for me."

"Do you know what time it is?"

"Sure, it's after midnight, but I need your help now."

"Okay, okay, what is it?"

"We didn't go back far enough. We have to look for a case prior to the Civil War."

"You've got to be kidding. We'll be extremely lucky to find anything from that long ago. It certainly won't be in a computer. What do we have to go on?"

"Cross reference trials under the Fugitive Slave Law and the name, Hanway. I don't know his first name."

"Okay, I got it. But it'll have to wait until morning. I've got to go into the old files at the Library of Congress and it doesn't open until nine."

"All right, but get back to me as soon as you find anything. I'll be in court at nine. You've got the office number up here. Help me, Mike. Tomorrow may be too late."

"State your full name, please."

"Joseph Hanway."

The Friday morning session had opened without incident. At breakfast, the prosecutors had reported their overnight research to each other. Sterling had gone over Joe's anticipated responses from the witness stand. Quite honestly, he didn't find anything that Holleran could us as a wedge for jury nullification. For his part, Giorgio opined that the nullification defense would somehow stem from Joe's racial background and he was awaiting the results of Mike's search in Washington. In a better mood than the previous afternoon, Richard apologized for his rude behavior. Together they could find no justification to delay Joe's testimony.

"Bob, I agree with you. Holleran is going to cross-examine Joe so keep your ears open. Make an objection whenever we have an opportunity to delay or prevent whatever he has in mind. Maybe by lunchtime we'll have some welcome news from Washington"

⌐

Sterling approached the witness stand. "Mr. Hanway, on the twenty-fifth of August last year, you were examined by Dr. Brian Curtin in the Emergency Room of St. Lucy's Hospital. "Is that correct?"

"Yes."

"And what brought you there?"

"I had awakened that morning with a gnawing pain in the middle of my back. I took some Advil but it just wouldn't go away. My wife and I became concerned so we went to the Emergency Room."

"After Dr. Curtin had examined you and done a number of tests, what did he say to you?

"That the tests were negative and the only abnormality he found was tenderness and fullness in the upper abdomen,

"Did he recommend anything further at that point in time?"

"Yes, something called a CT Scan."

"And what was your response?"

"I knew instinctively something serious was going on and before any further tests I wanted Dr. O'Hara to be consulted."

"Why Dr. O'Hara?"

"He was not only the surgeon who had removed my gallbladder but also my best friend. Should whatever was wrong with me require surgery, I wanted him to be calling the shots and doing it."

"Were you aware at that time that under the law creating the National Health Administration you are assigned to a specific surgeon for such purposes?"

"I was."

"Did you know to which surgeon you are assigned?"

"There are many. I've never seen a complete list nor do I carry one with me. It depends on what area of the body needs surgery. I guess that decision would have been made once the diagnosis had been established. The only specific name I'm aware of is that of a general surgeon."

"And who is that?"

"Dr. Alfonso Burton, but I've never met the gentleman nor do I have any knowledge as to his training or experience."

"Is he the surgeon who should have resected your aneurysm?"

"I can't tell you that. I'm not familiar with his areas of expertise. I don't know if he does vascular surgery."

"Did you inform Dr. Curtin that Dr. Burton was the general surgeon responsible for your care?"

"No."

"Why not?"

"Dr. Curtin placed a call to Dr. O'Hara's service and when he returned he told me he had tried to ascertain who my surgeon was but, unfortunately, the hospital computers were down. I didn't want anyone but Ted, excuse me I mean Dr. O'Hara, operating on me, so I kept my mouth shut."

"And then what happened?"

"Dr. O'Hara arrived and examined me. He ordered the CT and eventually arranged for the surgery once the diagnosis of an aneurysm was made."

"Did Dr. O'Hara talk to you about the diagnosis and the surgery?"

"In too much detail. I was hurting but he made me listen to a nauseating list of everything that could go wrong, to the point when I told him to shut up and just operate."

"Did he mention anything to you about patient-doctor assignment lists?"

"Somewhere along the line he did bring it up. He told me that Brian, er, Dr. Curtin, had told him the computers were down and he had no idea whether he was the proper surgeon or not."

"Did he ask you if you knew?"

"I don't remember but I did tell him that my general surgeon was Dr. Burton, probably after the CT had been done and we were talking about the operation. I also told him that the only surgeon I needed or wanted was him."

"Did Dr. O'Hara tell you that it was necessary to do surgery that night?"

"He did."

"What reason did he give."

"He told me the aneurysm had not ruptured, but the back wall had ulcerated causing the back pain. He felt I was lucky to be so warned because the aneurysm could bleed at any time. Risking the increased morbidity and mortality of rupture by delaying surgery, even for a day, or two, was unwarranted. I had not eaten in almost twenty-four hours so he booked the Operating Room right away."

"Thank you. No further questions. Your witness."

Pat rose from his chair, came around the defense table, and, standing in front of it, crossed his arms while leaning back to rest his buttocks on its front edge. There was a murmur throughout the courtroom requiring Judge Cumming's attention.

"Order in the court. Mr. Holleran, you intend to cross examine?"

"I do, Your Honor."

"Proceed." The prosecutors were briefly lost in a vigorous discussion only to look up as Pat began.

"Mr. Hanway, what's your legal name?"

"Joseph Hanway."

"Was that always your name?"

"I was given that name at birth but it was not legally mine until the age of seven."

"Objection your Honor!" Robert Giorgio had leapt from his seat and nearly bounded over the table as he darted around its nearest corner to stand before the judge. The court erupted into an undecipherable cacophony of exclamations and questions.

Order in the court! Order in the court! Will counsels come forward?"

By now Richard Sterling had joined his cohort and all three attorneys rubbed shoulders within whispering distance of the judge's bench. Bob Giorgio was first to speak.

"Your Honor, cross examination is limited to the facts testified to by the witness. Mr. Holleran is out of order."

"Mr. Holleran?"

"Begging the courts indulgence, I fully intend to properly restrict my cross-examination. However, if in this trial Mr. Hanway has given contradictory or incomplete testimony relative to what he testified to before the Grand Jury, I am entitled to have such evidence admitted and it would be my right to cross examine the witness relative to its content."

"That's true, Mr. Holleran, but I, like you, have no direct knowledge of Mr. Hanway's testimony before the Grand Jury since only the prosecutor was present and would be privy to such information. May I ask you how you would come by the knowledge of what he did or did not testify to?"

"Your Honor, originally I had submitted Mr. Hanway's name as a witness for the defense in this trial. During my pre-trial interviews with him, subsequent to his Grand Jury testimony, he mentioned having clarified the origin of his name to the presiding judge."

Sterling was next to chime in. "Your Honor, this is not sworn testimony. It's merely an administrative clarification."

"If, as I would expect, the Grand Jury followed protocol, the first words out of Mr. Hanway's mouth would have been an affirmation to tell the truth the whole truth, and nothing but the truth. The very next would have been his swearing to the validity of his given name which to him required an explanation."

"Your honor, this is ridiculous."

"Perhaps, Mr. Sterling, perhaps. Do you have a transcript of Mr. Hanway's grand jury testimony? I'm sure we would all like to see it, a least the first part of it."

"I have it in my briefcase, but is this really necessary?"

"I would like to see it now, Mr. Sterling." Bob Giorgio fetched the proper folder from the briefcase and handed it to Richard. "Please read the opening portion of Mr. Hanway's testimony?"

"Yes, your honor."

Bailiff – "Mr. Hanway would you raise your right hand. Do you swear to tell the truth the whole truth, and nothing but the truth so help you God?

Mr. Hanway – "So help me God."

Bailiff – "Please state your name, age, and address.

Mr. Hanway – "Joseph Hanway age sixty-six, er, perhaps I should clarify that. The name Joseph Hanway was on my birth certificate but it was not legally mine until I was seven years old."

Judge Billings – "Just a moment. I don't understand. What are you saying? Your name is Joseph Hanway?"

Mr. Hanway – "Yes, your honor. Let me explain. My ancestor was a slave prior to the civil war and when he was freed he abandoned his African name and adopted an English one. As I am sure you are aware most former slaves adopted the name of their masters particularly if they had not been mistreated, or that of another Caucasian whom they admired or had helped them in some manner. My ancestor adopted the name Hanway from a gentleman who befriended him. In 1945, my grandmother wrote a short history of our family dating back to those times and, when my father returned from service in World War II, he read the document and was quite impressed, particularly with the part having to do with Mr. Hanway. He took the pains to research our benefactor's family tree and visited with his descendants. At his request, the Hanway family agreed to our legally adopting their name, which was confirmed in 1947"

Judge Billings – "Thank you, Mr. Hanway, Mr. Giorgio, you may proceed with your questions."

Bob Giorgio felt like a swimmer drowning in the surf. Mountains of bubbling water laughingly cascaded against his aching body driving him deeper and deeper into the effluvial sand, holding him captive while the aqua world surrounding him suffocated his dwindling efforts at gasping for life-giving air. "He's going to get it in and for all my efforts, I couldn't see it coming. How in hell did I miss that innocent comment?"

The judge's voice was as imperceptible as the muted fart of a shipboard klocsin too many miles away in the fog-shrouded atmosphere hovering crab wise over the countless fathoms above his pounding head.

'I will allow it, gentlemen. You may proceed, Mr. Holleran."

As the attorneys returned to their places the judge intoned. "Objection overruled. Mr. Holleran, you may proceed with the witness."

"Exception."

"Noted, Mr. Sterling."

Now it was Pat's turn. "Could the recorder repeat Mr. Hanway's last response?"

"I was given that name at birth but it was not legally mine until the age of seven."

"Mr. Hanway, I am now showing you a transcript of part of your testimony before the Grand Jury. Please turn to the first page."

"Yes, I have it."

"Could you read the first few paragraphs for us, down to" which was confirmed in 1947.

"Certainly." Joe then read the passage previously referred to before Judge Cumming's bench. As he did so the court filled with an apian buzz of unanswered speculation abruptly ended by the judge's gavel. Pat then countered.

"Thank you, Mr. Hanway. Now, who was Ozuru Timbale?"

"Objection, Your Honor! Objection!"

There was no holding the audience back now. The reporters to a man, erupted from their seats racing for the door and their cellular phones to the outside world. Raul Ramirez jostled his way to the ABC camera crew waiting outside. Judge Cummings didn't bother with the gavel. He rose from his chair and shouted to the courtroom as he rapidly departed to his chambers. "This Court is adjourned until ten Monday morning. Counsels will see me in my chambers at one this afternoon!"

CHAPTER XVII

"THE CRAFTSMAN HAS THE ADVANTAGE OF HIS SKILL"

(Reprise)

All three attorneys sat in the waiting room just outside Judge Cumming's chambers. It was ten after one and each had been in attendance for at least twenty minutes. The prosecutors had passed on lunch in favor of a strategy session in their temporary office at the Federal building. Bob Giorgio had attempted to contact Mike Rawlings for an update on his search at the Library of Congress, but without success. The balance of the lunch hour was spent in a tete-a-tete designed to foresee Pat Holleran's strategy. The assistant prosecutor now knew he was on the right track; that the strategy would be jury nullification on the basis of comparison with an ancient trial involving Joe Hanway's ancestor and the fugitive slave law. Somehow he had to get the details of that trial and forestall the admissibility of that testimony. The first order of business would be to get Cummings to sustain their current objection to the introduction of the name, Ozuru Timbale, whoever he might have been.

In stark contrast, Pat had taken Ted to Marco's to enjoy a light shrimp pasta and complementing glass of Pinot Grigio. Although his curiosity was killing him, Ted managed to remain calm, discussing any number of dissembling but trite bits of conversation. Pat, on the other hand, was relishing not only the moment and the cuisine, but also the camaraderie of his friend as Ted lifted his glass in a playful toast.

"True to my word, no questions. So, here's to Ozuru Timbale, whomsoever he may be or have been."

"Here! Here! To Ozuru Timbale. Seriously, Ted, things have just taken a turn for the worse."

"C'mon, Pat. You've started to cross-examine Joe and already have Sterling and Giorgio in a conniption fit."

"You remember my telling you that your best defense was the hospital's "down" computer but only if the prosecution didn't tumble to the fact that Joe told you who his general surgeon was?"

"Sure! I figure you will get to that later during your summation."

"Ted, that defense is now out the window. This morning, during direct testimony, Sterling got Joe to admit he told you his assigned general surgeon was Dr. Burton."

"So what? Joe didn't know whether or not Dr. Burton was qualified to perform vascular procedures."

"Correct, but once he gave you the name, you did. You knew all about Dr. Burton's privileges. If I had any notion of putting you on the stand I can't now. During their cross-examination you would either have to admit you knew Dr. Burton was qualified to do the surgery or take the fifth amendment to prevent self-incrimination. Nothing good could come from one or the other so that defense is out. As you have alluded to, I have embarked on another avenue and as you well know, I don't want you privy to what goes on until you hear it in the courtroom. Should you wish, I am sure we could still make a deal with the Feds as long as you plead guilty."

"No way, Pat! There will be no plea bargaining. Besides, I'd like to hear whatever tale you're going to spin."

⌒

"The judge will see you now." The secretary smiled and with her right hand indicated the door into the judge's chambers. As the attorneys entered, they were greeted by the grim visage of an uncompromising Judge Cummings. He appeared slightly smaller without his robes, but no less imposing as he controlled the room from behind his desk.

"Be seated. Mr. Giorgio, what is the basis of your objection?"

"The same, Your Honor, inappropriate cross-examination."

"Mr. Holleran, would you please let us in on your secret. Who is Ozuru Timbale?"

"Why, Mr. Hanway's slave ancestor, of course, referred to, but not by name, in Mr. Hanway's Grand Jury testimony."

"Your Honor? The defense is going from evidence given in a most general manner to a specificity not testified to."

"Ozuru Timbale was not generally Mr. Hanway's ancestor. He specifically was Joe's great, great, great, great grandfather who upon gaining his freedom adopted the specific name of his benefactor, Mr. Benjamin Hanway."

"That's enough, both of you. Mr. Sterling, I'm going to overrule the objection. You may continue with your cross-examination, Mr. Holleran, but if your line of questioning strays too far, I won't wait for an objection from the learned prosecutor to strike it from the record. The relevance of whatever testimony is allowed will be appropriately weighed in my charge to the jury. Mr. Holleran has elected not to challenge the testimony brought forth by the prosecution and I will allow him a certain latitude in presenting his defense of Dr. O'Hara. But that latitude is not unlimited. Any questions?"

"Not a question, Your Honor, but perhaps I can make it easier for everyone. If I might indulge your patience for a moment more?" Pat opened his briefcase and drew forth three folders.

"Your Honor, Richard, Bob, each of you now has the written record of case number 15,299, Volume 26, Federal Cases, page 105 – United States vs. Hanway – Circuit Court, Eastern District of Pennsylvania, October term, 1851. Mr. Hanway, a citizen of Lancaster county in the Commonwealth of Pennsylvania had been indicted for high treason against the United States. Interestingly enough, Richard, one of the prosecutors was the Honorable James Cooper, United States Senator from Pennsylvania."

As he accepted his copy, Bob Giorgio revisited the surf and sand as well as the horrible sensation of drowning in their inexorable embrace. Judge Cummings was first to break the silence of the surreal atmosphere attendant upon Pat's revelation. "I will spend an interesting weekend, Mr. Holleran, and look forward to your conduct on Monday."

Upon returning to his temporary office, Giorgio noted that Mike Rawlings had left a message to call. "Hello, Mike, Bob Giorgio here."

"I finally got something for you. The cross reference with Hanway was on treason, not the Fugitive Slave Law; although the indictment was based upon violation of that law."

"I know, Mike, case number 15,299 in Volume 26, Federal cases, page 105".

"Hey, that's right, but if you already knew that, why did you get me all het up?"

"I just learned about it five minutes ago from the defense counsel. He even gave us a copy of the trial which tells me that, other than going through an exercise in futility, no earthly good will befall our team for the trouble of reading it."

CHAPTER XVIII

"WORDS FROM THE WISE MEN'S MOUTH WIN FAVOR."

I ndeed, it had been a most interesting weekend, not only for Judge Cummings but also for the prosecution. For the judge, it was the most stimulating and rewarding academic exercise he had engaged in throughout his entire career on the bench. Unprecedented as it was to be provided this information from the defense attorney it was delightfully challenging to anticipate, or, for that matter, predict which avenues Pat Holleran might explore. Of equal interest was exactly what he, Judge Cummings, would allow him to establish before the jury. Already on the fringes of his mind were the words adequate to guide the jury in his charge to them following the attorneys' closing remarks. What words these might be depended entirely on what the defense planned in the next few days. To a great extent, Pat Holleran had just taken over the trial. In my rulings from moment to moment, I will not permit him to usurp it entirely but I sense he knows that and even welcomes it. He has found his way to argue the law from a different quarter than before and to a great degree I am to be the rearguard protecting his ass from the sniping of the prosecution. Last week may have been boring but the real entertainment starts today.

Richard and Bob had returned to their separate homes outside Washington on Friday evening and each having perused the trial document, had reconvened in their Westbury hotel room on Sunday evening. As he took the file from his briefcase, Richard was first to speak. "That son-of-a-bitch! He's got us between a rock and a hard place. Give me your spin on this?"

"What's my spin? We're spinning in and the plane is about to crash. He's not going to introduce the trial record as evidence. He knows he's on thin ice there. We'll object and in all likelihood Cummings would sustain. So he'll introduce whatever he wants through Hanway. The judge will be so interested – very few of our objections will succeed."

"We could introduce it ourselves. Holleran wouldn't object."

"For what purpose? There's not a scintilla of evidence favorable to our side in that entire document. What are we going to do? Argue for slavery or acquiesce to the charge of treason whenever a white supports freedom for a black. Don't be an idiot! Those arguments were difficult enough between the time the Constitution was ratified and the cataclysm of a Civil War fought primarily because jurisprudence and reason could not reconcile a country half slave and half free. Today, and particularly in this trial, no purpose would be served or advantage gained by removing the scab covering what is at best a festering wound dangerously close to the heart of the body politic. Now we know why he wanted the same jury we did, even more so. The way I see it our only hope is to stick to the facts, quit objecting and trust in "straight arrow, don't screw around in my courtroom," Cummings"

"I disagree. I plan to object as much as possible and hope to restrict what testimony he can get in."

"Why? Every one of those jurors will be on the edge of their seats as Hanway spins his tale. They won't want anyone or anything to interrupt, not a recess, or a lunch break, much less our objections. Every time we stand up they'll look over and you'll read it in their eyes. "Why don't you two shut up and sit down. Stop interrupting. I want to hear every word of this." Don't give them any further reason to hate us.

Cummings won't let Pat go overboard and he'll be quite strict in his charge to the jury. Just stick to the facts we've already established."

"Okay, okay, I get your point but I do intend to call one more witness when Holleran finishes his cross."

"Another witness? Who?"

"Dr. Burton. After Joe's testimony, during direct, I've got to establish that he has privileges in vascular surgery at St. Lucy's."

"Good point. With everything else going on and my days and nights of research, I overlooked that."

"Well, if it's any consolation, I can't see what difference it would have made if you had tumbled onto this ancient trial any sooner."

Monday morning having arrived. Judge Cummings took his seat bringing the court to order with his gavel. "The prosecution's objection at the conclusion of Friday's session is overruled. You may proceed, Mr. Holleran, but as I stated to you in chambers, I will not tolerate your going afield."

"Thank you Your Honor."

"Mr. Hanway, I would remind you that you're still under oath."

Ted heaved a sigh of relief. Whatever path Pat was about to follow had obviously hinged upon the ruling just decreed. He sat forward in his chair; all eyes and ears.

"Mr. Hanway, who was Ozuru Timbale?"

"My ancestor who was befriended by Mr. Hanway many years ago, prior to the Civil War."

"Could you briefly summarize how Mr. Hanway befriended your kinsman?"

"Ozuru was my great, great, great, great grandfather. He was the son of the Chief of the Wasabi tribe in Western Africa when he was captured by slave traders and brought to American in 1845. Upon arrival, he was bought by a Mr. Gorsuch who enslaved him on his plantation in Maryland where he labored for six years all the time chafing at the bonds of his servitude."

"Six years brings us to 1851. What happened then?"

"In the late summer of 1851 Ozuru and another slave escaped and aided by sympathizers in the underground railway began a journey North."

"What happened then?"

"They had reached the town of Christiana in Lancaster County, Pennsylvania where they, along with a small group of other fugitive slaves, were temporarily lodged at a Mr. Parker's house. Mr. Gorsuch had followed and learned of their whereabouts. On the ninth of September, in Philadelphia, he obtained a warrant for their arrest and in the company of a Federal Marshal by the name of Kline, his own son, and several others from his plantation, he proceeded to Christiana. Prior to their arrival at the Parker house a certain Williams, a Negro in Philadelphia who was aware of the warrant, had preceded them and warned the slaves of their danger."

"Go on."

"Kline and the slave owner's party were well aware that Christiana was a hotbed of opposition to the Fugitive Slave Law passed by Congress the year before in 1850. Indeed many political and church groups were militantly anti-slavery. Also within the preceding six months there had been several instances of armed bands kidnapping "free" Blacks to bring them South and sell them into slavery. To say the least Christiana was powder keg with a fuse looking for a light."

"Are you aware of the requirements of the Fugitive Slave Law of 1850 which you have alluded to?"

"Yes, I am."

"Could you briefly explain how they applied to this situation."

"Objection Your Honor."

"Overruled."

"Exception."

"Duly noted, Mr. Sterling. You may continue Mr. Holleran."

"Would you explain, Mr. Hanway?"

"The law provided that a slave owner faced with tracking down a piece of his property not only had the right to pursue the escapee but could seek and obtain a warrant for his arrest from a duly authorized Federal Commissioner, local Sheriff or other official."

"Was there anything else in that law which might be relevant to the scene you have begun to describe?"

"The slave owner, in the process of confiscating his property, could request the aid of any bystander. Upon being shown the warrant, the bystander was required to cooperate and aid the slave owner in his mission no matter what his personal feelings or beliefs."

"Was there a penalty for refusing such help?"

"Refusal could be punished by a fine up to one thousand dollars and imprisonment not to exceed sixty days."

"Would you kindly continue with your narrative?"

"As Mr. Gorsuch's party approached the Parker house, they heard a bugle call. After observing the house for a few moments they saw two Blacks, whom Gorsuch recognized as his runaways, come out into the yard. The slaves saw them and retreated into the house where the Gorsuch party pursued them. Upon entering they noticed the slaves going upstairs where they could hear others loading firearms. Kline read the warrant and then tried to go upstairs assuring those at the top they meant them no physical harm. He was greeted by a sharp object thrust at him whence the entire party retreated to the lawn outside where they could see armed Negroes at the windows. Kline fired his pistol in the air to make it clear they were armed. Again, he called to the fugitives to remain calm, assuring them they had a warrant to arrest two of their number whom Mr. Gorsuch would identify, and that no harm would come to anyone. Someone called down that they wanted fifteen minutes to talk it over among themselves."

"And what happened then?"

"At that moment a stranger arrived on horseback, Benjamin Hanway. Kline approached him asking his identity. He refused his name and his address. Kline explained what was going on and showed Hanway the warrant at which point he requested that he, Mr. Hanway, help his group to arrest the fugitive slaves. Hanway refused stating that he did not approve of the Fugitive Slave Law, and that he believed it to be unconstitutional. He also advised Kline and his group to back away from carrying out the warrant since the slaves were obviously armed."

"Did he leave then?"

"He started to but the Negroes came out and pointed their weapons at the marshal. Kline shouted to Hanway to intercede and prevent them from firing to which Hanway replied they had a right to defend themselves and he would not intercede."

"Was there a firefight?"

"Yes, the Negroes opened fire and attacked the Gorsuch party with clubs. In the melee that followed Mr. Gorsuch was killed, his son seriously wounded, and several others battered and mistreated."

"What happened to Ozuru?"

"In the confusion, he ran off and fortunately contacted representatives of the underground railway who spirited him further North eventually to Canada and freedom."

"What about Mr. Hanway?"

"He was arrested by the Marshal and held over for trial in the Federal Circuit Court."

"What was the charge, failure to obey the Fugitive Slave Law?"

"No, he was accused of high treason."

The spectators reacted noisily as the high-pitched decibels of their questions and comments reverberated from the wood-paneled walls of the courtroom. Some reporters were torn between exiting to rapidly contact their news desks or staying put to learn the rest of this amazing tale.

"Order in the court. Order, or I will clear the room." As sanity slowly returned, the judge turned to Pat. Please continue Mr. Holleran."

"Mr. Hanway, you previously stated that conviction for violation of the Fugitive Slave Law was punishable by a fine as high as one thousand dollars and up to sixty days in jail. Am I correct?"

"Yes, sir."

"But, as we all know, conviction for treason, mandates a death sentence."

"As far as I know, yes."

"Objection."

"On what basis?"

"Hearsay, Mr. Hanway, is not an expert. He is neither a judge, nor is he a member of the legal profession."

"Overruled!"

"Exception."

"Noted. Proceed, Mr. Holleran."

"Did that trial take place?"

"It did, in October of 1851 in the Federal Circuit Court, Eastern District of Pennsylvania."

"Are you aware of the verdict?"

"Mr. Hanway was acquitted."

"No further questions. Your Honor."

Now the reaction was one of a questioning silence, but the intent was loud and clear. "Just a minute, you can't end there. Why bring this testimony forward? What's the connection? Come on, don't leave us hanging."

"Your witness, Mr. Sterling."

"No questions." This time the gavel was useless, the pandemonium generated by dozens of reporters caught in a tangle trying to exit through the double doors at the rear of the courtroom was uncontrollable. Judge Cummings shouted. "This court is recessed until two this afternoon. As the judge exited, Pat noticed an unaccustomed wry smile deforming his lips.

⌐

Once Pat had taken over the trial, lunch breaks had become opportunities to catch one's breath and attempt to decipher the significance of his latest revelation. Today was no different, but infinitely more exciting, as Joe, under Pat's direction, had concluded his tale of slavery and treason. The defense attorney had provided only one answer, namely the acquittal of the original Benjamin Hanway on the charge of treason. As a consequence, the brief moments before noon were abreeze with galeforce questions. Again, Pat had succeeded in getting everyone's exquisite attention, including the national media, who were flooding the airways with reports and analysis even as Pat and Ted entered the grille room at the Country Club.

"Hey doc! You're on every network except the weather channel." Sam, the bartender, using the remote, was proving the same as he spoke. "And Mr. Holleran! Got'em all guessing again, eh? I wouldn't be a bit surprised if you fellas get the highest Nielsen rating this week. Certainly beats the soaps or the business channel. What'll you have?"

"Just a couple of iced teas Sam and menus. Both of us have to get back to the rat race."

"We certainly know who the rats are and you sure got'em racing but where to and why? Come on Mr. Holleran, let me in on the secret? What's coming next?"

"No can do, Sam. Doc's not even in on it, so how can I make an exception for you? Of course I could be bribed but it's too early in the day for Tulamore Dew."

"Not even one little hint?"

"Just stay tuned in, Sam, stay tuned in. What's the soup today?"

"Split pea or clam chowder."

"I'll take the chowder and half a club sandwich. Ted, how about you?"

"Split pea and a burger, medium rare."

"Here comes Betty. I'll relay your order right now."

Five minutes later, halfway through the soup course and just as Bill Harkins closed out the CBS, "*News at Noon*," Ted broke the ice.

"Well, Signor Machiavelli, you've kept everyone in suspense again, only I can't ask you all the questions Mr. Harkins so beautifully summarized just now."

"That's right, Ted. You can't or perhaps I should say I won't answer them if you do."

"Yeah, yeah! I know the drill. I'll get it when the jury gets it and probably with more surprise than they'll show."

"I sure hope so. You've been wanting to hear my golden voice giving a speech since the start of this trial. So don't miss tomorrow's show. It'll be a one-time performance and all the squares will be filled in. You know something? Patience is a virtue. You should display more of it."

"I certainly hope it's worth the price of admission!"

"Court will come to order. Mr. Sterling do you have any further witnesses?"

"Just one, Your Honor. He's not on my original list but I need his testimony to clarify one point. I would like to call Dr. Alfonso Burton to the stand."

"Mr. Holleran, since we lack notification, do you have an objection or do you need time to prepare?"

"No objection, Your Honor.

"You may call your witness, Mr. Sterling."

"Thank you Your Honor. The prosecution calls Dr. Alfonso Burton." A young man in his mid-thirties strode through the gate in the railing separating the working court from the spectator seats and took his place in the witness box. Intelligent eyes surveyed the scene and with the confidence of his youth and education, he seated himself.

"Raise your right hand – ." As the oath was completed Richard approached.

"Dr. Burton, could you briefly state your full name and professional qualifications?"

"Certainly, my name is Alfonso Burton. I'm a surgeon here in Westbury. I received my M.D. from Johns Hopkins in 1994 and took a residency in general surgery at Columbia Presbyterian Hospital in New York City finishing in 2000. I finished a fellowship in peripheral vascular surgery at Yale New Haven Hospital two years later."

"Are you board-certified in any specialty?"

"I became a diplomate of the American Board of Surgery in 2003. After two years of clinical practice and a certain number of major vascular procedures I will become eligible to take an examination for the board in vascular surgery.

"Do you have privileges to do vascular surgery at St. Lucy's Hospital?"

"I do."

"Dr. Burton. Were you on call the evening of the twenty-fifth of August last year?"

"Yes, I was."

Since you cannot be on call for your assigned patients three hundred and sixty five days a year, how does The National Health Administration arrange for coverage?"

"I can only speak for my own specialty. We are sorted into groups of four and cross-cover each other."

"Is Dr. Theodore O'Hara listed in your coverage group?"

"No sir, he is not."

"No further questions."

"Mr. Holleran? Judge Cummings optically nodded in Pat's direction.

"Dr. Burton, how long have you been practicing in Westbury?"

"I came one year ago."

"What type of privileges in vascular surgery did you have when your application for appointment was first approved at St. Lucy's?"

"Class B privileges."

"And what does that mean?"

"It means I had to perform ten vascular operations under the supervision of other surgeons at the hospital with full privileges. When I had done that satisfactorily, I obtained class A privileges."

"During your residency and fellowship training, did you perform any unsupervised vascular operations?"

"No sir."

"How long have you had unsupervised Class A privileges in vascular surgery at St. Lucy's?"

"Six months."

"In that length of time, how many unsupervised operations have you performed for an abdominal aortic aneurysm?"

"Four."

"Thank you. No further questions."

"Redirect, Mr. Sterling?"

"No, Your Honor."

"Do you have any further witnesses to call?"

"The prosecution rests."

CHAPTER XIX

"TIME OUT FOR A BREATHER"

T ony Moreno was comfortably seated in a lounge chair across a low table from two similar, but empty, chairs. In his hand was a notebook, to which he had been referring, but at this moment he was leaning forward, looking full into the camera as his familiar features filled TV screens throughout America. It was 11:45 that night. His program, "Highlights", had just finished a rapid review of the trial happenings in Westbury, as well as a recitation of the known facts in *U.S. vs. Hanway* in 1851. Ted, Pat, Joe and their wives were intent, all eyes drawn to the screen, as Tony continued.

"Ladies and gentlemen, I would now like to introduce you to our guest panelists. First say hello to Mr. Charles Sinclair, currently Attorney General for the State of New Jersey and a former prosecuting attorney. Good evening, Mr. Sinclair. Welcome to "Highlights." As they shook hands Tony indicated the chair for Mr. Sinclair to be seated in. The fiftyish lawyer smiled as he sat to applause, unbuttoning his suit jacket as he did so.

"Next, let's give a warm welcome to Ms. Jennifer Parseghian, a noted defense lawyer from New York City." A younger woman in her early forties entered from backstage fashionably attired in a provocative two-piece suit. Her stride betook confidence and her smile bedazzled. After greeting Tony, she sat down to a higher rating on the applause meter.

Pat interrupted. "I wouldn't relish dueling with her in a courtroom."

"Is that because of what we see or her reputation?" Ted was grinning as he offered the question.

"Both, Ted, both. Let's see if Tony keeps the ball rolling and sparks a good discussion."

"Well Charles and Jenny, both of you heard as much as anyone knows concerning the odd turn of events in U.S. vs. Dr. O'Hara. What do you think, Charles? Where is the defense attorney going here?"

"He's raising a smoke screen, an obvious attempt to gain the sympathy of the jury and turn their attention from the facts of the case established by the prosecution."

"It is true that the defense attorney has not challenged the facts thus far testified to. Jenny; what's your read on this?"

"Well, Tony, it seems quite obvious Mr. Holleran cannot challenge the facts. Prior to the trial he attempted to argue the constitutionality of the law from several standpoints, first amendment rights and restraint of trade, but to no avail. He knew the decision would go against him but he gained a great deal of publicity for his client as witness our discussion tonight. Everything that transpires in that courtroom has a national audience. I have nothing but admiration for his strategy."

"But what about the latest turn of events?"

"I must admit the reference to a trial decided over one hundred and fifty years ago is fascinating, but I haven't quite discerned his reason for bringing it forth. On the surface it would appear he's going for jury nullification, but I sense something deeper. If I were to speculate and somehow hit upon his strategy, I would feel guilty in having let the cat out of the bag."

"Not even some inkling?"

"I have the feeling his arguments will again go to the law but from a different aspect than before. You must remember that a precedent will be set by this jury's verdict. Never forget, in these United States, a panel of twelve citizens – by their decision – can initiate a process which could overturn an existing law. We are about to witness the most significant jury verdict of the new millenium."

"Charles, would you agree the jury has such power?"

"Their duty is to listen to the evidence relative to the case and to weigh its application to the requirements of the law. It's the responsibility of the legislative branch of government to enact or repeal laws, and of the Supreme Court to determine their constitutionality."

"Yes, Charles, I fully agree, but review of a specific law's constitutionality not only may but historically has initiated from a jury verdict."

"Thank you Jenny and Charles. I'm sure we'll have much more to discuss in depth after we see what unfolds in Westbury over the balance of this week. Goodnight everyone."

⌒

"Pat, did Ms. Parseghian stumble on to anything?" Ted posed the question as he used the remote to flick the channel off.

"Not even close, Ted, perhaps a slight hint but the surprises are intact."

"I know my ass is in the grinder, but I must confess I've enjoyed not knowing what's coming next. Every time I think I figured something out, I'm just as surprised as the reporters in the backbenches. However, I did notice one thing this morning. Pat, everything thus far seemed to have hinged on Judge Cummings decision to overrule the prosecution's objection to your introduction of Ozuru Timbale. How did you get him to overrule?"

"Okay Don Quixote, I'll tell you my secret. First, I have to admit I gambled a great deal with your future. Fortunately it paid off. Long ago, I decided your only defense is to negate the law your accused of breaking. As you're aware, I couldn't accomplish this prior to the trial, so the only alternative was to try again once it started. I have to convince twelve men and women the law is unjust to the point that, no matter what the evidence, they will acquit you. Joe's ancestor, Ozuru Timbale, gave me that opportunity, but the problem was how to get the material before the court. That's when I took the gamble."

"No wonder you always win at gin. What do you do? Stack the cards?"

"I wish I could. I didn't cross-examine a single witness until Joe, nor did I make any objection to the testimony Sterling introduced. I wanted the jury to know we had nothing to hide and to have them feel the case for the prosecution to be cut and dried, even boring. I wanted them to look at each other and ask why they were here; to question the punishment being far worse than the crime or for that matter, was there a crime committed? Originally, I had scheduled Joe as our only defense witness so that during direct I could establish the testimony about the trial in 1851, but there were two problems with that. Number one, it made Joe a hostile witness for the prosecution and secondly opened him to a severe cross-examination."

"Aware of the facts involved with his ancestry, prior to Joe's appearance before the Grand Jury, I suggested that when he was sworn in and asked to identify himself he briefly explain where his name, Hanway, came from. Grand Jury testimony is secret and non-admissible in a subsequent criminal trial. However, if during the trial a witness contradicts testimony he gave before the Grand Jury, the judge will admit that testimony when the contradiction is called to his attention. Since the prosecutor is the only legal representative before the Grand Jury, it's almost unknown for a defense attorney to be aware of a contradiction, but he legally has the right to make such a motion. I wanted it to appear that the prosecution was covering up Joe's testimony and I wanted the prosecution's turn at Joe to be restricted to redirect. The rest is history. I canceled Joe as a defense witness which, I might add, confused the opposition no end; and then cross-examined him. When Giorgio objected I was sure that Joe had testified concerning his origin as a Hanway but I wasn't sure Judge Cummings would go along with me. However, he stuck to proper procedural law and allowed it, which gave me at least a limited opportunity to bring forth the facts of that beautiful trial for treason. I even provided the judge and the opposition with the proceedings of the trial from the records of the Federal Circuit Court of Eastern Pennsylvania. Ted, I took a chance with the next five years of your life, but without it you didn't have a prayer of winning."

Ted got up and embraced his friend. "Look, who's talking about tilting at windmills? A Macchiavelli who secretly wants to be Don Quixote. Pat, my friend, I feel honored in your presence."

CHAPTER XX

"More weighty than wisdom or wealth is a little folly."

"The law is clear. A physician cannot provide medical or surgical care to a patient not on his assigned list. The testimony presented to you, ladies and gentlemen of the jury, has demonstrated that, although a computer list of Dr. O'Hara's patients was not available on the evening in question, the patient, Joseph Hanway, knew who his surgeon was and indeed informed Dr. O'Hara of the appropriate name, Dr. Alfonso Burton. In spite of this, he knowingly went ahead with the resection of Mr. Hanway's aneurysm for what may best be described as a semi-emergent indication. The fact that the patient is his good friend or that the operation was quite successful have no bearing before the law. At no point has the defense challenged these facts. Indeed, Mr. Holleran has neither objected nor cross-examined any of the prosecution's witnesses except for Mr. Hanway and Dr. Burton. And what did his cross-examination of Mr. Hanway demonstrate? A tale which was entertaining to be sure, and what a cast of characters! A runaway slave and his owner, the underground railway, a Federal Marshall and a citizen of Christiana Pennsylvania who befriended the slave and for his trouble earned an indictment for treason which ended in his acquittal. I cannot predict what use the attorney for the defense will make of such testimony but it is my duty to remind you that it is colorful history and that is all. It has absolutely no bearing on the indictment in this trial. It is your sworn duty to analyze the testimony in evidence before you and apply it to the content of the law in question. If you find the defendant has transgressed the letter of the law beyond a reasonable doubt, you must return a verdict of guilty. In this decision, you must not consider the sentence or degree of punishment. This is a matter for your further deliberation should you find Dr. O'Hara guilty. The law is straightforward, the evidence clear and uncontested. I trust in the justice of your decision. Your Honor, the State rests."

The courtroom was standing-room only. The contestants were in their accustomed places after a late start as Richard Sterling slowly returned to the prosecution's table. The clock indicated 11 A.M. and all eyes turned to Pat, as he rose to address the bench. "Your Honor, I would respectfully request a recess for lunch. My closing remarks should take about an hour. Should you agree, I would prefer not to have them interrupted."

"Court is adjourned until 1 P.M."

"All rise!"

CHAPTER XXI

"I HAVE SEEN UNDER THE SUN ANOTHER EVIL,
LIKE A MISTAKE THAT PROCEEDS FROM
THE RULER; A FOOL PUT IN LOFTY POSITION."

"Ladies and gentlemen of the jury, seventy years ago, several years before Dr. O'Hara and Joe Hanway were born, the Social Security Act was passed in Congress and signed into law by President Franklin Roosevelt. Section 208, paragraph 8 stated as follows: "Whoever discloses, uses, or compels the disclosure of the Social Security number of a person in violation of the laws of the United States, shall be guilty of a felony and upon conviction thereof shall be fined under title 18, U.S. Code, or imprisoned for not more than five years, or both."

"Change a few titles, and it sounds familiar, doesn't it? Ask yourselves right now, this moment, how many times in the past month have you personally had to reveal your Social Security number? Did you do so when you applied for a job or when you filed a tax form? How about that time last week when you checked by phone on the balance in your banking account? Or perhaps when you applied to renew your driver's license? We disclose it, and are compelled to disclose it, literally on a daily basis. And, what of the government sworn to uphold the laws of the land? Allow me to share a secret with you. In all of those seventy years the government has never once prosecuted an individual soul for revealing that hallowed number nor a single institution for compelling anyone to trade those sacrosanct digits to obtain a service or seal some sort of transaction. And why is this? Why has the federal government never in a single instance prosecuted such a felonious crime?"

"They never intended to. Paragraph eight was attached to the bill to ease its passage and answer the objections of those legislators who feared the possibility of everyone having a national identity number. The government knew full well that with the passage of time paragraph eight would soon be forgotten. It was never their intent to enforce this section of the law. Then why now? Why this rush to prosecution under Section X Paragraph 3 of the law creating the National Health Administration? Why dispense kangaroo justice to the very first villain who dared to operate on an unlisted patient when infractions of the Social Security Act occur millions of times each day and have done so increasingly for seventy years. Ladies and gentlemen, isn't it obvious? The Government is scared to death! The fabric of their law is in danger of being pricked by a tiny thorn. Should you acquit Dr. O'Hara, that prick could become a larger tear leading to the unraveling of the entire law. How would that sway the balance if, at some future date, they were to decide to restrict your choice of clergyman or God forbid, your lawyer."

"To be absolutely clear, let me quote the pertinent section of the National Health Security Act:" Any physician providing medical or surgical care to a patient not assigned to him by the National Health Administration shall be guilty of a felony and upon conviction thereof shall be subject to a fine not to exceed $100,000 or imprisonment from three to five years or both."

"The prosecution has told you that in your deliberations you must not consider the sentence which would attend upon a guilty verdict. It would be a subject for your further consideration. I beg to differ. The defense maintains that punishment for violation of the law under question is the most essential consideration which you, the jury, must weigh in determining Dr. O'Hara's guilt or innocence; more than the evidence presented by the prosecution, more than circumstances, more than motive, and why do I say this?"

"You should be fully aware these penalties are not automatic or cast in cement. Indeed, should you recommend clemency, Judge Cummings has it within his authority to lower or eliminate the fine as well as to suspend or modify the jail sentence: A guilty verdict under such flexible circumstances would seem to confirm the facts in this case but would it serve the cause of justice?"

"Please recall what I quoted just a moment ago: "Any physician providing medical or surgical care to a patient not assigned to him by the National Health Administration shall be guilty of a felony-". The operative word is felony. The crime is not a misdemeanor and it warrants a penalty far greater than the slap on the wrist inherent in a fine or a few years in jail. Under the laws of the State of Connecticut, a physician who is convicted of a felony shall have his license to practice medicine revoked. There is no appeal. His profession would be lost to him forever. Imagine! No debate, no extenuating circumstances, no recommendation for leniency, just a simple mathematical equation: $A+B=C$. Any physician convicted of a felony forfeits his license to practice his profession; Dr. O'Hara has been convicted of a felony; therefore Dr. O'Hara forfeits his license to practice his profession."

"Another consequence the prosecution has failed to mention is loss of citizenship until such time his debt to society has been paid. He could not vote, hold office, bear arms or serve his country in time of need. Indeed, he could not serve on such a panel as you do now. You would do well to remember these facts. Conviction would deprive Dr. O'Hara of all these things, his ability to practice his beloved surgery, his professional stature, indeed his very livelihood! All in this courtroom have heard the sworn testimony of many of the prosecutions witnesses alluding to the honor and respect in which Dr. O'Hara is held. So let us explore his life further. Exactly who is Dr. Theodore O'Hara?"

"I see him as a very proud man but not in the sense of being egotistical. On the contrary, he is quite humble but proud in his confidence to dispense his art to a needful patient, a confidence born of years of training and further decades of experience giving freely of himself to his hospital and to his community. He has served as chief of the section of General Surgery, chairman of the Department of Surgery, Director of the residency program in General Surgery at St. Lucy's Hospital, and president of its medical staff. For many years he has had an academic appointment on the clinical staff at Yale Medical School and has been an active member in various medical and surgical societies, local, state, and national. Throughout his career, with all the constraints and obligations just mentioned, he has maintained an active clinical practice. Indeed, I would be remiss if I did not mention to you he has performed over four hundred unsupervised resections of aortic aneurysms."

"The essence of his life is responsibility, to his patients, to the ethics of his profession, and to his community. He doesn't seek accolades or rewards but rather quiet satisfaction in the knowledge that he applied his skills to obtain the best outcome possible for all his patients. He would deem it a singular honor that his best friend, when faced with a serious malady, would have no one else perform surgery on him. Truthfully, he is today's embodiment of the same traits which motivated two men sharing the name of Benjamin Hanway over one hundred and fifty years ago."

"The first Benjamin Hanway, the son of a Presbyterian minister, a citizen of Christiana, Pennsylvania, believed in the evil of slavery and the injustice of a law forcing anyone to abet the return of a fugitive slave to his master. In 1851 he befriended just such a slave and by his refusal to obey the dictates of the Fugitive Slave Law, he gave Ozuru Timbale his freedom and indirectly his own name. Ozuru knew the evils of slavery first-hand and longed for the freedom which Mr. Hanway risked his own life to give him. These also were proud men. They did not seek vainglory, but were resolute in the courage of their convictions and determined not to forsake them in time of crisis. And how do I know this? Allow me to digress and briefly relate the destinies of the Misters Hanway following their fateful meeting in 1851."

"After his acquittal for treason, Mr. Hanway continued to aid runaway slaves through his participation in the underground railway. His trail was difficult to pursue until the Civil War when, soon after hostilities began, he volunteered and became an officer in the ranks of the Army of the Potomac. By 1862, he was commissioned a colonel in command of a regiment of Pennsylvania volunteers. On the 17th of September that same year, the Union forces under General George McClellan found themselves facing the Confederate Army, under General Robert E. Lee, across Antientain Creek on the outskirts of Sharpsburg, West Virginia. The rebel forces were attempting to flank the Army of the Potomac and invade the North through the hilly terrain of Southern Pennsylvania. The strength of Lee's position was a sunken road, which offered his soldiers the protection of a natural trench. Colonel Hanway's regiment was given the unenviable task of assaulting this hornet's nest. Forever after in written chronicles, this bit of country dirt and gravel has been known as "the bloody lane."

"The lead companies of the Pennsylvania regiment suffered near annihilation from the massed Confederate musketry and artillery. It was only the final rush of the last remaining battalion led personally by Col. Hanway that gained the road itself where hand-to-hand combat lasted for what seemed an eternity. Hardly a survivor did not recall seeing Col. Hanway, sword in hand, urging and leading them to engage the soldiers in gray. Though grievously wounded in his left shoulder, he organized evacuation of injured comrades, even at the height of the bloody struggle. As the last of the rebels scampered from the sunken road, Col. Hanway grasped the regimental flag and, leaping upon the parapet at the far side, led his men in cheering their victory when a mini-ball passed through his neck. He was dead before his body crumpled upon the bloody gravel mounded with blue and gray corpses."

"A grateful nation honored him with the Congressional Medal of Honor and buried him with full military honors in Arlington Cemetery. The man once accused of treason at last found peace having sacrificed his own flesh for a cause he had pursued his entire adult life. Two years later, in 1864, the Supreme Court found the Fugitive Slave Law unconstitutional. The prime precedent cited by the Chief Justice in presenting the unanimous opinion was the United States vs. Hanway, October 1851. Rest in peace, old soldier!"

"But what of Ozuru Timbale? As I mentioned, in Canada, he adopted the name of his benefactor, married and sired two sons. He learned to read English and kept abreast with the news from the former colonies he had escaped from. Thus, he became aware of President Lincoln's

Emancipation Proclamation which, through issued in 1862, did not take effect until January of 1863. Armed with this knowledge, his moral certitude of the evil of slavery, and his acknowledgement of the debt of honor to his namesake in Pennsylvania, he and his family emigrated to Massachusetts where he volunteered for service in the 54th Mass. Infantry regiment – an all black unit under the command of white officers. Up to that time, former slaves and free blacks had been utilized by the Union for menial tasks in support of combat troops. Many officers, all the way to the high command, had reservations as to their possession of the courage and discipline necessary to deport themselves as an effective fighting force. The 54th represented a huge experiment, if not a gamble, to debunk this demeaning theory.

"The first test came on the 18th of July, 1863. The 54th had been given the task of subduing Fort Wagner near the entrance to Charleston harbor as part of a plan to capture that important Southern port. Ozuru, I should say Benjamin Hanway, had been promoted to Sgt. Major in the 2nd battalion which had been selected for the assault upon the fortified towers to either side of the main gate."

"History has recorded the bravery displayed to a man by this famous regiment on that day. The task of seizing a position fortified with a moat, backed by an earthen rampart and reinforced with a wooden stockade was nearly impossible. Strategically placed towers along the walls provided mutually supporting fields of fires. The 1st and 3rd battalions in disciplined ranks crossed the seaward side of the moat and climbed the earthen works only to be slaughtered before they could reach the fortification."

"Meanwhile the 2nd battalion's assault on the main gate to the inland side had been timed to coincide with the climax of the seaward battle. The same carnage was inflicted upon the Union soldiers as they tried to close with the defenders massed in their towers and behind the walls. As luck would have it, some of the Confederates had been shifted within the fort, to aid in repelling the 1st and 3rd battalions. His officers had all been killed or wounded and Benjamin took command of the survivors. Sensing a lessening of the fire opposing them, he rallied those still able to function and personally led a final charge, which for a brief instant breached the Confederate line gaining access within the fort."

"The 54th failed to capture Fort Wagner that day but had gained the respect of the soldiers in gray and the admiration of the Union when accounts of the bitter struggle were reported in the Northern press. Ozuru failed to survive. At the breach in the ramparts his lifeless body, pierced with multiple bayonet wounds, was found surrounded by eight corpses clad in gray, all of them dispatched by means of crushing blows to the skull. The only weapon in Ozuru's hand was an intricately carved Wasabi war club. The warrior son of his chieftain-father had sculpted it from teak wood while working as a carpenter in Canada."

"For his courage, the Black Benjamin Hanway was awarded the Silver Star and given a hero's burial in Arlington Cemetery. He had paid his debt to another Hanway whose physical remains had been interred a year earlier in this same hallowed ground. May both Benjamin Hanways rest in peace, side-by-side, comrades in arms."

"So, ladies and gentlemen, what are we to make of this? One hundred fifty four years ago, a slave was befriended by a man of principle, a proud man who felt obligated to live according to his beliefs for which he was accused of treason. The slave gained his freedom but felt a debt of honor to his benefactor, a debt which he paid for with his life. And who was the villain of the piece? Was it Mr. Gorsuch, the slave owner? We may not admire nor agree with him, but he believed in the institution of slavery and the United States Government, in 1850, affirmed his right to do so. I should say reaffirmed, since this odious institution had legally existed in this country since the ratification of our Constitution. Why not Marshall Kline? No villain there. He was a public servant authorized to enforce an existing law."

"No, the villain was the government. Expediency to save the Union swayed the Congress to pass a law upholding the right of an individual to own another and, as a corollary, had the right to reclaim his property should such an indentured one escape from his custody. Certainly, this compromise totally neglected a discussion relative to the morality of slavery. But the Government could not leave well enough alone. As a part of that law they required any citizen, no matter what his conviction or belief, to provide assistance in capturing a fugitive slave when asked to do so by a slave owner or authorized agent with an appropriate warrant. The law gave absolutely no shrift to the moral ethos of a citizen placed in such a situation. The penalty for refusing was a fine of one thousand dollars, a substantial sum at the time, and incarceration for a maximum of sixty days."

"When Benjamin Hanway refused to help Mr. Gorsuch reclaim his property and warned him of the consequences of his persistence in doing so, he was not accused under the Fugitive Slave Act. The government again made an autocratic stretch and indicted him for treason. Conviction would have forfeited his life."

"None of us are accustomed to attribute despotic motives to those who enact or enforce our laws, but our history is replete with more than a few examples of the same. I would argue that the *United States vs. Hanway* has the dubious distinction of representing the most inglorious effort of such governmental persecution from the time of our revolution. The United States is and indeed has been "The last great hope of mankind." But perfection in this world remains impossible and citizens must remain eternally vigilant to keep its democratic institutions intact. The jury deliberating in the Federal District Court of Eastern Pennsylvania needed but a brief moment to return a verdict for acquittal and found their decision more than justified when it was cited as a precedent thirteen years later, in 1864, when the Supreme Court unanimously determined that the fugitive Slave Act was unconstitutional."

"What comparison can we make in the case before us, the *United States vs. O'Hara*? Who are the characters and what do they represent? I would put to you that Dr. O'Hara is the slave? If we accept the definition of slavery as a lack of freedom we may also agree that there can be all degrees of that loss. A black man in the South prior to the Civil War was in total slavery having lost all of his freedoms save his ability to think privately. Dr. O'Hara is a slave to the extent that he has lost the freedom to choose his patients, a fact under the present law which also applies to Joseph Hanway who has lost the freedom to choose his doctor. Indeed all of us – myself, Attorney Sterling, Judge Cummings, each and every one of you sitting on this jury – have lost the same choice and therefore to that extent are also slaves. Dr. O'Hara became a fugitive when he apparently chose to ignore what makes him a slave and operated on his friend, Joseph Hanway."

"And who is the modern-day villain? Is it the prosecution? I think not. They are performing their duty under the existing statute just as Mr. Kline did over one hundred fifty four years ago. No, I would suggest to you that the villain of the piece is again the federal government. They served a warrant intending not only to restore Dr. O'Hara to his former status, but also to force him into abject slavery. The Pharisees in Washington have made violation of section X, paragraph 3, of the National Health Security Act a felony, and if convicted, Dr. O'Hara will lose the freedom to practice his profession as well as the freedom to exercise his rights as a citizen. Never mind a fine and time in prison. They are nothing in comparison."

My friends, that same government could have made this infraction a misdemeanor punishable by a reasonable fine and even a short prison sentence but again they have chosen to by tyrannical and outsize the punishment to the offense. They want to deprive Dr. O'Hara of his life, not his physical life as with Benjamin Hanway, but his entire professional and political life. Surely, he will continue to breathe the same air as we, appreciate his senses, think and converse, but is there truly any difference between such an existence and that which Ozuru Timbale endured under Mr. Gorsuch?"

"One character in this macabre scene remains to be identified. Who is the citizen, the innocent bystander, asked by the government to assist in serving the warrant to return Dr. O'Hara to his slave status? Ladies and gentlemen of the jury, it is you. You have come upon and become an integral part of the drama. In truth you are only one citizen because you must speak with unanimity either for conviction or acquittal. A majority opinion will not suffice. You have the singular choice to deprive Dr. O'Hara of his life or to find him innocent. That momentous decision should be based not only on the evidence you have heard but also upon your intelligence, your conscience, your faith in this country, your ties to those who have gone before you and made their marks to assure that these United States, in spite of their many faults, remain a bastion of freedom in a world increasingly dedicated to destroying itself. You may choose to identify yourselves with the panderers and the toadies, the sycophants, the Uncle Toms and the oreos, or you can align yourselves with those heroes who have made this country great; with

Benjamin Hanway, with Ozuru Timbale, with all those who have followed their conscience and succeeded in overturning a hateful law; who gave their lives in service to a cause they cherished. You can forever join with those who have been witness to the reality of "Duty, honor and country." God help this country when it no longer produces such titans among its citizens, for, when that day comes, The United States will cease to exist."

"I implore you to consider the enormity of your decision and place proportionate weight to your conscience and God-given insight. It's true that there are only two ways to nullify an existing law. The Supreme Court can find it to be unconstitutional or Congress can vote to repeal or change it."

"However, my appeal to you would not be complete without suggesting that, just as judgment for acquittal in the case of the *United States vs. Hanway* led to the demise of the Fugitive Slave Act, your decision could open the door for the ultimate judicial review of Section X, paragraph 3; of the National Health Security Act."

"As for me, I have faith in this country, hope in the freedom for which it stands, and both faith and hope in the charity of your decision. Thank you."

"Your Honor, the defense rests."

An unnatural stillness pervaded the small courtroom on the second floor as the participants and spectators slowly returned after a half hour's recess. Brief attempts at conversation were rare and disjointed as everyone shared in the adrenaline deprivation attendant upon the cessation of Pat's emotion-draining speech. There would be time for the mind to analyze and evaluate the arguments he set forth, but for now one felt it in the gut, that dull sub-diaphragmatic awareness that something of great significance had just occurred; that you were present and witnessed it; but for the moment neither could nor needed to appreciate that significance. Just to return and be seated in the same arena was enough and, although you were cognizant that everyone there shared in the same mystery, you wanted to be alone to deal with that intestinal void by yourself.

Lawyer and client had reclaimed their seats at the defense table. "Pat, we've known each other since kindergarten and shared good times too numerous to mention, even survived the bad ones too, but today you've given me something far beyond friendship, far beyond a lawyer's duty to his client. I have a feeling you and the original Mr. Hanway would have gotten along very well. You both specialize in saving foolish idealists."

"You don't have to be an idealist to want to be free."

"All rise. The second district court is now in session, Judge Harold Cummings presiding."

Everyone's attention centered on Judge Cummings. "Mr. Brown, would you bring the jury in."

The bailiff opened the door to the jury room allowing each one to silently file in, identical masks of emotional exhaustion on their faces. Once all were seated, the Judge leaned forward, hands folded on the desk in front of him. He commanded their immediate attention with the mere probity of his demeanor, the fixation of his dilated pupils, and the tone of a voice resonating in a friendly yet authoritative manner.

"I would like to thank you for your patience and attention throughout this trial. When you were first impaneled, several weeks ago, I instructed you in the duties of a juror; how you were to listen to the evidence and form an opinion as to the defendants guilt or innocence. In a very few moments, you will retire to the jury room to decide Dr. O'Hara's fate. Now it is my duty, not to influence your decision in any way, but to inform you concerning the rules of this court in arriving at your verdict. The law requires that your deliberations remain totally secret until your verdict has been announced in open court. You may take as much time as you wish to thoroughly discuss the evidence, which will be available to you in written form at all times. You are not to discuss the case with anyone outside of the jury room and that includes the bailiff, Mr. Brown, and myself. If you have a question that deals with the interpretation or significance of anything relative to Section X, Paragraph III, of the National Health Security Act, you may transmit that question through Mr. Brown for my consideration. I will get back to you with a written answer as soon as possible. To facilitate these housekeeping matters, your first order of business will be to elect a spokesperson. He or she will be your contact with the bailiff and myself, and will be the person to announce your verdict publicly in this courtroom. You are to be completely at ease and must feel at liberty to bring up anything in your discussions. At various times during your debate formal votes may be called for by your spokesperson. Majority votes may rule how your deliberations may be conducted but when it comes to your verdict the vote must be unanimous, either for acquittal or conviction. There will be no middle ground. Should you arrive, after prolonged debate, at a standoff, I will have no alternative other than to declare a mistrial, and at a future date in a different jurisdiction, it will be done all over again. The three alternate jurors will be confined with you, but cannot voice an opinion or vote, unless, due to extenuating circumstances, one or more of you must step down. That decision is reserved solely to my judgment. Now then, have I explained the format to your satisfaction? Do any of you have any questions regarding what I've said thus far? Yes, Mrs. Rodrigues?"

"Your Honor, will we be able to pose questions to the prosecutor or defense attorney to clear up any of the testimony?"

"No, Mrs. Rodrigues. I will be the one to answer any such question. Mr. Sterling and Mr. Holleran have both rested their cases. Anything else? "

"Fine. Now allow me to explain to you how the law applies to the case before us. In a number of ways, you have been witness to a very unique and unusual trial. To begin with, as the prosecution presented its case, through the testimony of a number of witnesses, the defense attorney chose not to cross-examine any of them until the final two, namely Mr. Hanway and Dr. Burton. Indeed, in the case of Mr. Hanway, the defense made no effort to dispute his remarks; nor did they argue against Dr. Burton's statements; but rather chose only to develop them in further detail. In addition, Mr. Holleran brought forth no witnesses of his own."

"Legally, what does this mean? Quite simply, you must accept the sworn testimony of the prosecution's witnesses as truly representing the facts of this case. In your deliberations, you cannot challenge the validity of these facts for whatever reason. That was the duty of the defense which, for reasons of their own, they chose not to do."

"Secondly, in his cross-examination of Mr. Hanway, Mr. Holleran seized upon a proper legal precedent to introduce testimony concerning an ancient trial for treason which involved transgression of The Fugitive Slave Act of 1850. Having established the details of this antique indictment and the verdict rendered in the Federal Circuit Court of Eastern Pennsylvania, he went further in his closing remarks to draw a comparison between that trial and the one we are considering today. To be sure, all of us, myself included, listened to these arguments with rapt attention. However, no matter how much you or I identify with Mr. Holleran's symphony; agree or disagree with his arguments; you cannot consider them in making your decision for guilt or innocence. The defense has legitimately introduced this evidence to argue against the constitutionality of Section X, Paragraph III of the National Health Security Act. They have done so as a basis for appellate review of that section of the law should you arrive at a verdict against the defendant. Since it is not your duty or privilege, but rather that of the Supreme Court, to decide the constitutionality of a law, you cannot and must not consider such evidence in deciding the fate of Dr. O'Hara."

"So, where does that leave us?" You have two weeks of the prosecution's testimony to sift through and analyze. You must then put yourself in Dr. O'Hara's place. What was his intention when he operated on his friend, Mr. Hanway? Was he fully aware that it was illegal for him to do so? Did the fact that the hospital computer was down provide enough confusion in deciding who should perform the surgery? Did Mr. Hanway's revelation of Dr. Burton's name as his assigned surgeon provide sufficient information to Dr. O'Hara for him to back down from being the responsible surgeon? To find Dr. O'Hara guilty you must do so "beyond a reasonable doubt." The evidence that the prosecution has presented, and that evidence alone, must establish that Dr. O'Hara acted with full knowledge that he was transgressing the law, and that he did so willingly. If there is a question in your mind that the prosecution has established these facts, you must find Dr. O'Hara innocent. In addition, that doubt must be a reasonable one. What do I mean by that? Simply put, any adult with intact mental faculties acting without preconceived prejudices and without outside influence should be expected to arrive at the same conclusion. That may seem wishful thinking and quite impractical to you, but that is the law. I would ask you to think long and hard about the concept of reasonable doubt. In the final analysis, it is the cornerstone of justice in this democracy. You are twelve individuals who must speak with one voice. No one else in the universe will be privy to the conversations and debates you will engender in that room. I implore you to thoroughly discuss the evidence, listen to the arguments put forth by your fellow jurors, enter into the discussion, but in the end vote your conscience. Bailiff! The jury will now retire."

"All stand. This court is now in recess until further notice."

CHAPTER XXII

"PERSPECTIVE"

"Good evening ladies and gentlemen, welcome to "Highlights." You're all familiar with my guests. On my right is Charles Sinclair, Attorney General for the State of New Jersey, and on my left Ms. Jennifer Parseghian, a prominent defense attorney from New York City."

It was eleven thirty in the evening and the earlier newscasts had been rife with reports from the courtroom in Westbury. They had detailed the closing arguments from the adversarial attorneys as well as Judge Cummings instructions to the jury, which was scheduled to begin deliberation the following day. Having their appetite suitable whetted by factual citations, a substantial portion of the national viewing audience was tuned in to appreciate an analysis of the day's events and to understand what different interpretations might be offered by Tony Moreno's guests.

"Today, Dr. O'Hara's fate has been placed in the hands of the jury. The State has summarized the evidence against the good doctor and Attorney Holleran has rebutted by arguing against the law itself, and what an elegant discourse it was. Jenny, let's start with you. What do you think of today's phenomena?"

"I witnessed one of the most amazing closings in the annals of courtroom drama. Mr. Holleran paid no heed to the facts established by the prosecution and by so doing let the jury know that in no way would their verdict be based upon them. His good fortune in gaining admissibility of the details pertinent to that ancient trial for treason hamstrung the prosecution. Essentially, their choice was to remain boring, emphasizing facts only, or begin a crusade in favor of slavery and governmental abuse. Mr. Sterling's closing remarks reflected the dullness of his choice. Consider how Mr. Holleran, having dismissed the facts, immediately brought the prosecution up short on the one bit of advice they had offered the jury, namely; "Do not consider the punishment in your deliberations." In an instant, the defense portrayed the prosecution as holding back, not telling the complete truth. The punishment would not be just a fine and imprisonment, but loss of citizenship and the license to practice surgery. At that point the jury and we, the public, got answers to the questions left in the air when the defense finished their cross-examination of Joe Hanway. And what answers! Two Civil War heroes both named Benjamin Hanway and both interred in Arlington. And the final question? Why bring all this up? The answer, an analogy between Benjamin Hanway's trial for treason and Dr. O'Hara's inquisition. By the final paragraph, I could see the flags waving and John Philip Sousa marching his band through the courtroom."

"I agree the oratory was masterful and exciting but, in the end, isn't the defense going for jury nullification? Attorney Holleran wants the jury to ignore the facts and render a verdict on the basis of sympathy. Judge Cummings, in his charge to the jury emphasized three items: First, they have to analyze the evidence relative to the existing law; Second, that guilt has to be judged beyond a reasonable doubt; and third, it is not their right or privilege to repeal that law. He did acknowledge that their verdict, pro or con, could precipitate a proper review of the law by those constitutionally responsible for doing so, namely the Congress or the Supreme Court. Indeed, he emphasized that in this trial the burden of proof rests upon the prosecution. The jury cannot annul the testimony as presented by the prosecution and then decide on acquittal because they don't like or agree with the law. I agree with the judge and, in my opinion, Attorney Sterling has demonstrated guilt beyond a reasonable doubt." Charles Sinclair seemed content and self-satisfied as he relaxed following his rebuttal to Jenny's remarks.

"But Charles, can't you see what the defense has accomplished? As things now stand, it doesn't matter what the jury decides. All along, Pat Holleran has wanted to argue the law. He did so before the trial when he knew he couldn't win. He did so again during his summation thanks to the admission of testimony relative to Joe Hanway's ancestor. All the while he has had the riveted attention of the entire country. Can you honestly find anyone who doesn't have an opinion about Dr. O'Hara's situation? He already has what he wanted. If the jury returns a guilty verdict he will appeal and, the mood of the country being what it is, that appeal will end up in the Supreme Court. At that point, consider the ammunition he has: first amendment rights, restraint of trade, and the precedence of a pre-Civil War trial which accomplished the identical purpose he has in mind, namely, repeal of an onerous statute. And the appellate arguments won't be disputed behind closed doors in a legal tete-a-tete. No, they have already been hashed over every day for four months in homes, offices, restaurants, bars, gyms, you name it." And what if the verdict is acquittal? I would think public opinion will force the Congress to at least review one aspect of the National Health Security Act. Pat Holleran has known all along he could not argue the facts before the existing law. He had to void the law in order to exonerate his client and thus far he's performed beautifully in accomplishing that task. I have nothing but admiration for his skill, My hat is off to him."

It was Tony's turn. "Thank you Jenny, Charles, again you've given us a great deal to think about. Jenny, I would agree that Attorney Holleran's summation wasn't strictly that, but truly an oration which found its audience prepared to accept the marching orders which it laid down. I can't wait to hear tomorrow's polls. In any event Charles, if Jenny is correct, we won't have closure for many months or even years to come. So long as the topic is relevant we expect and welcome your frequent return to share you insight in these matters. My thanks to both of you again. We'll be back tomorrow night with a surprise guest."

CHAPTER XXIII

"I HAVE SEEN SLAVES ON HORSEBACK WHILE PRINCES WALKED ON THE GROUND LIKE SLAVES."

It was three in the afternoon the following day and the jury had been isolated since 9 A.M. The morning had been devoted to electing a foreperson and a review of the prosecution's testimony. A Mrs. Angela Pulanski had been elected forewoman, a retiree, seventy-four years of age who had lost her husband to a stroke two years previously. Prior to her marriage many years ago, she had started a banking career as a teller. When her youngest child was ten, she returned to the Westbury bank and at the time of her retirement had attained the position of Assistant Director of the commercial loan department in the main office opposite the Elton Hotel on the green. A small pension, and whatever social security added to it, kept her comfortable without frills. Her quiet life was made all the more enjoyable by frequent visits to her eight grandchildren, all of whom lived within a thirty-mile radius of Westbury. As their chosen leader, she was doing a credible job in leading the discussion concerning the cut-and-dried facts of the case. Indeed, there was very little to discuss. By lunchtime everyone unanimously agreed that Dr. O'Hara in truth had operated on Joe Hanway with the full knowledge he was not the assigned surgeon under the rules of the National Health Security Act. But the afternoon had proved to be quite a different matter. Mrs. Pulanski had called for a vote based upon the evidence reviewed that morning but several members of the panel immediately objected. Ruby McQueen, who, it was rapidly becoming clear, was the spokesperson for the five black members, took the floor.

"Hold on a minute! We haven't touched upon the defense testimony at all. It just wouldn't be fair to take a vote now before we've heard everything Mr. Holleran had to say. I want to hear what you all think about that old trial before the Civil War. And how about the punishment in this case? Seems rather too much to me. Mr. Holleran thinks it is and he certainly thinks the law is wrong."

Diego Montero joined in. "Yeah, I want to talk about those things and what about discrimination here? Most of the people in my neighborhood like to keep their heritage intact and their language alive. They don't understand why they have to go to a doctor who doesn't speak Spanish. I want to go to a doctor I pick out not one selected by some candy-ass in Washington."

"That's right. If I feel more comfortable with a black doctor, I should be able to choose him on my own." This time it was Joe Morgan, a black juror, voicing his objection." That Mr. Holleran is one smart cookie. His story of Mr. Hanway and Ozuru Timbale was right on. As Diego just said, these candy-asses in Washington could learn a lot from it. My vote will be "Innocent."

"Now, now! Everybody will get their turn and there's no need for swearing or crude language. Mr. Zino? You raised your hand?"

A spare, gray haired seventy-year-old stood to address his fellow panelists. "It seems to me everyone has agreed that Dr. O'Hara knowingly disobeyed the Social Medicine law but whether we find him guilty or not will really depend on everything Mr. Holleran brought up. As for myself, I am living on my Social Security pension and, frankly, I don't want to rock the boat. I've got a bad heart and high blood pressure and don't want to jeopardize my medical care in any way, shape or form. A hero I'm not. It doesn't take a long memory to recall what managed care and the HMO's did to us only two years ago. What do you say, Mrs. Pulanski?"

She was taken by surprise. Her mind had been wandering as she thought of an appointment with her own physician, Dr. Buonocore, at 5 P.M. that afternoon. She had seen him three weeks previously and had the return appointment to hear the results of some tests he ordered. When she had been called for jury duty his office had been quite cooperative in shifting her time to five o'clock. As the argument became more heated, she began to consider if she would be on time. "Yes Mr. Zino. What did you ask?"

"You know. Do we go by the evidence or do we heed Mr. Holleran?"

"Well, I can't contradict the prosecution. Dr. O'Hara did operate wrongfully but to me the punishment is excessive. I realize later on we can recommend leniency but there's no getting around his loss of citizenship and medical license. Because of his age, I suppose the license part isn't as bad as Mr. Holleran made it out to be. As to whether we should take it upon ourselves to change this part of the law. I would have to agree with Judge Cummings who charged us not to do so."

Thus the comments went back and forth for the balance of the afternoon. It soon became obvious that the Blacks and Latinos had been won over by the defense attorney's argument from the past. It was equally apparent that the four retirees, though in a quandary relative to the sentence to be imposed, were not swayed by the same defense strategy dating back to 1851. They were not willing to throw down the gauntlet to the government. By four o'clock Mrs. Pulanski was becoming concerned about making her appointment with Dr. Buonocore. During an unaccustomed lull, she recommended the first vote to be taken.

Fifteen minutes later, the sense of the group was confirmed when the tally was eight to four for acquittal. The ballots for conviction came from the three retirees and Mrs. Pulanski. A request to adjourn met with the judge's approval and Angela breathed a sigh of relief as she hurriedly donned her coat, rapidly exiting to the parking lot. Dr. Buonocore expected his patients to be on time.

"Mrs. Pulanski, the doctor will see you now."

Angela had arrived with five minutes to spare. Three weeks before, she had come complaining of an episode of pain in her right upper abdomen radiating to the scapular area on the right side of her back. The pain had lasted for thirty-six hours but had subsided by the time of her visit. It had been the third such attack over the past year, each of them associated with nausea. During the most recent attack, she had also vomited several times.

After a physical exam, Dr. Buonocore ordered some blood tests and an ultrasound of the abdomen which she had managed to fit in piecemeal at infrequent breaks during the trial. Three days after the ultrasound had been done, upon returning home in the evening, there was a message on her answering machine from Doctor Buonocore's secretary stating the time and date for one further test, a CT of the abdomen and pelvis. She had barely managed to fit this in her busy schedule and, at this moment, was quite curious as to the results.

"Mrs. Pulanski, it's good to see you. How have you been since I saw you last? Any further episodes of pain and nausea?" The doctor was dressed in a white lab coat and, in spite of the lateness of the hour at the end of a busy afternoon, his appearance was impeccable.

"No doctor. I've been fine. But I am anxious to hear the results of all those tests, particularly the extra one you ordered, the CT. I don't have cancer, do I?"

"No, no. You don't have cancer. Do you remember our discussing the possibility of your symptoms being caused by stones in your gallbladder?"

"Yes I do. Do the tests show that?"

"The blood tests were all normal but the ultrasound did highlight stones in your gallbladder."

"What does that mean? Do I need to have the stones removed or my gallbladder taken out?"

"All things being equal, I would recommend removal of the gallbladder. However, the ultrasound showed something else, which was the reason I ordered the CT scan."

"Something else! What? You just told me I don't have cancer."

"It picked up an aneurysm of the abdominal aorta. That's a condition where the aorta loses its elasticity, thins out, and expands like a balloon."

"I know what it is doctor. Aren't they apt to rupture and bleed? How large is it?"

"The scan indicates it's limited to the aorta below the takeoff of the arteries to the kidneys. It measures nine centimeters at its greatest diameter, that's bout four inches, and yes – the danger of not fixing it is rupture and bleeding. With one this size, the risk of hemorrhage is fifteen to twenty percent per year. Surgery performed when it's actively bleeding has a much higher mortality rate than when correction is done electively."

"So, if I don't have anything done, I'm truly gambling with my life."

"That's one way to put it. Ordinarily, such a decision would be based upon a comparison of the risks of surgery versus the risk of hemorrhage. In your case, the government has made the decision more urgent."

"What do you mean? Can't I think this over a bit?"

"Well, Mrs. Pulanski, you're seventy-four years old and, according to my chart your seventy-fifth birthday is only two months away. Under the National Health Security Act, no one seventy five years or older may be operated on for an aneurysm on an elective or emergent basis."

"What about my gallbladder?"

"If it were only your gallbladder, it could be removed laparoscopically. You've probably heard of this band-aid type surgery with three or four tiny incisions and the surgeon operates by looking at a video camera. The aneurysm will require the abdomen to be opened, but the gallbladder can be removed at the same sitting, two for one so to speak."

"Whose list am I assigned to for this kind of surgery? You're telling me it has to be done within the next two months?"

"That's right Angela, within two months." He rang for his secretary on the intercom."

Yes, Dr. Buonocore. May I help you?"

"Ruth, would you kindly check on the computer whose list Mrs. Pulanski is on for peripheral vascular surgery?"

"Certainly, doctor."

"We'll have your answer in a few moments. I should mention that there is a method of handling these aneurysms without an open procedure. It's all done from within the artery by means of an expandable graft over a balloon. From what I hear it's rather tricky. But I hesitate to go into any further detail since the National Health Agency has to approve it on a case by case analysis of anesthetic risk. Since you're basically in good health, you wouldn't qualify.

"Doctor?" It was Ruth on the intercom. Dr. Alfonso Burton is Mrs. Pulanski's surgeon."

"Thank you Ruth."

"Not at all, doctor."

"Well, there you have it, Angela. Shall I set up an appointment with Dr. Burton. He's new in town but a fine surgeon. He trained in the best places."

"I know I have only two months but let me think this over for a few weeks. As soon as I make a decision I'll call. Is that all right, doctor?"

"Certainly, Angela. You let me know. In the meantime, about that gallbladder. Stay away from fried fatty foods or anything too spicy. Okay?"

"I'll let you know as soon as I know, doctor."

Angela had slept only fitfully that night, her mind befogged in that eerie stratum between consciousness and the distant realm of Morpheus. Sanguine images of the surgery she so desperately needed alternated with depictions of Dr. O'Hara being variously tortured by small, red devils sporting forked tails. Oddly these imps rhythmically chanted the numbers four and four hundred, over and over again, as they painfully pricked the doctor's flesh with small hot pokers. Dr. O'Hara's parched lips mimicked the same dirge, four and four hundred, but no sound came forth to mix with the Stygian chorus. Despairing of solving the riddle, she shifted the scene to an operating suite where she was the patient asleep on the table. The drapes covering her were emblazoned with the repetitive numbers four and four hundred. The same ritualistic chant, coming from the throats of the operating team, suffused the entire room. Confusion and obfuscation spun her exhausted mind from one scene to the other. Somehow, she sensed that a part of her already knew the answer but that it would remain a mystery until, when fully awake, an appropriate suggestion could provide germination to the seed already implanted. With a serene aura of redemption, she finally succeeded in voiding the images and fell into a brief but regenerative sleep.

The alarm awakened her at seven. As the morning ritual of bathroom ablutions was completed, she donned her robe and descended to the kitchen to recharge the coffee maker, allotting the correct ratio of water to grounds in the filter. Orange juice in hand, she opened the front door to retrieve the morning edition of the *Gazette*. There on the front page was a photo of Dr. O'Hara next to a byline entitled; "First day of jury deliberation fails to bring a verdict." Her recognition of the familiar headline coincided with the last swallow of the sweet nectar in her glass. Returning to the kitchen, she placed the empty glass in the dishwasher and obtained a coffee mug from the cupboard. Still looking at the newspaper she reached for the silex pot. There was something oddly disturbing about Dr. O'Hara's photo. He was too composed, too comfortable and the edge of her awareness was prodded by a different scene, something not so orchestrated or peaceful. Her brow furrowed perceptively as she slipped the pot from beneath the filter and the steamy essence of the wakeful brew escaped into the room. What magic the aroma of freshly brewed coffee could weave. The beatific Mesmer, from the night just ended, had chosen his trigger perfectly. With the visual of Dr. O'Hara imprinted on her retina and the comfort of morning coffee in her nostrils, Angela's mind revved into high gear. The serum of the subconscious injected into the conscious during her disturbed sleep, along with these sensory perceptions, suffused her anterior cerebra with the logic behind the decision now all too obvious to her.

First and foremost the two problems before her, namely the verdict and the surgery, were inexorably bound. Accomplishing one required an affirmation to the other. Four and four hundred? Dr. Burton may be well trained but he is not experienced as yet. Dr. O'Hara has both training and experience. Dr. Burton has done only four unsupervised resections of an aortic aneurysm; Dr. O'Hara has done over four hundred. With only a few months remaining to do the operation, I want Dr. O'Hara as my surgeon. There is only one way. Acquit Dr. O'Hara and nullify patient lists.

Attorney Holleran was totally justified in submitting testimony relating to Mr. Hanway's lineage. Although it doesn't bear directly on the indictment, it has energized the vast majority of American citizens and inspired them to analyze the law and its propriety, not only pertaining to Dr. O'Hara but also to themselves. These same citizens are fortunate in that they can make their own decision, pro or con; after all they're not on the jury. We have to decide based upon the law, hateful though it may be. But there is something else, something within us, something that has nothing to do with Benjamin Hanway, Ozuru Timbale, or a trial for treason. That wonderful story prepared us to search more deeply into our very souls to provide true justice for Dr. O'Hara.

To be sure more than a few world-changing decisions have been made by heroes for the most selfless of considerations, but far more have been decided quietly for comfortable and practical reasons. The celestial hypnotist had done his job. Everything made sense. Once Joe Hanway had told Dr. O'Hara his listed surgeon was Dr. Burton, Dr. O'Hara knew of his training in vascular surgery but he also knew of the cockeyed experience ratio of four to four hundred. Without further thought, he unilaterally decided to proceed with the operation. Attorney Holleran recognized Dr. O'Hara's logic in making that momentous decision. His intent to prep the jury for doing the same, with the tour-de-force of an indictment for treason and the Wagnerian feats of the two Benjamin Hanways, got our juices flowing and now witness what's in the process of happening."

"Yesterday, the blacks and latinos on the jury were obviously sympathetic to the defense strategy but what did their spokespeople give voice to? A treatise about slavery or governmental despotism? No, Ms. McQueen spoke only to the convenience and desirability of a black citizen having the choice of a black physician. And what of Mr. Montero? Did he wax fervently on the issue of slavery and its victims? No indeed. He merely petitioned for members of his community to seek care from doctors who shared their ethnic background and spoke Spanish.

"And what of me? Yesterday, I, with the other retirees, shared an overwhelming fear that if we were instrumental in changing the National Health Security Act we could somehow be in danger of losing accessibility to the medical profession altogether. I know that's why I voted for conviction and I know damned well that's why the others did too. The four of us had also been well attuned to the martial music created by the defense but old habits and older fears had prevailed. This morning I can see beyond that. There are probably a thousand different reasons for choosing a doctor; race, ethnicity, language, charisma. You name it, it's there. Today, I want to choose a surgeon based solely upon his experience and I want the man over whom I have the power to save or destroy.

"Angela, forget a second cup of coffee! Get dressed and get yourself to that courtroom. You've got to convince Mr. Zeno and two other white-hairs that you're right."

⤿

"Ted, this is Pat. You're a hard man to track down this morning."

"I had a pancreatic resection starting at eight. Didn't finish until a few minutes ago. What time is it?"

"Twelve noon."

"Sally beeped me about an hour ago but I couldn't check on the message until I finished. What's up?"

"Well hang on to your hat. I hope you can delay office hours this afternoon. I got a call from the courthouse a little over an hour ago. Judge Cummings wants everyone there at one. The jury's arrived at a verdict."

"Consider office hours canceled as of now. Now that doomsday has arrived, I'm numb; don't know what to say. What's your guess?"

"No guessing, Ted. We'll know one way or another in a little over an hour. Meet me at my office at a quarter of one and we'll walk over together. You might want to alert Laura. I'll arrange to save her a seat."

"Sure thing, Pat. What about Joe? Will he be there?"

"I've already talked to him, Ted."

CHAPTER XXIV

"FOR MILDNESS ABATES GREAT OFFENSES.
"MORE WEIGHTY THAN WISDOM OR WEALTH
IS A LITTLE FOLLY."

At 1 P.M. it was standing room only in the Federal Courtroom. Laura was seated in the front row, behind the railing backing up the defense table where Pat and Ted had taken their seats. Next to Laura, Joe Hanway anxiously kept his thoughts to himself. Ted had turned his head, nodding to his friend as his eyes sought the assurance afforded by his mysteriously calm mate. For their part, Richard Sterling and Bob Giorgio fought their anxiety as they nervously conversed at the prosecution's table.

"All rise!"

There was a shuffling of feet and an occasional cough as the audience responded to the bailiff's request. The judge rapidly gained his chair behind the bench and seated himself.

"This court is now in session. Ladies and gentlemen of the jury, have you arrived at your verdict?"

The bailiff indicated to Mrs. Pulanski that she should rise. As she did so, she replied. "We have, your honor."

"The bailiff will bring the verdict to me."

Anticipating the request, the bailiff had already crossed to where Mrs. Pulanski stood and took the folded piece of paper she offered him. He then strode to the bench where he passed it to Judge Cummings. He in turn, unfolded the document; read it; and returned it to the bailiff who returned it to Mrs. Pulanski.

"Will the defendant please rise."

"How does the jury find Dr. Theodore O'Hara?"

"Your honor, in the matter of the United States vs. Dr. Theodore O'Hara charged with violation of Section X, Paragraph 3 of the National Health Security Act, we the jury finds the defendant not guilty."

Absolute pandemonium broke out as a great cheer erupted from the gallery, spreading rapidly to the larger group outside in the hallway and beyond to the crowd awaiting news on the street adjacent to the Federal Building.

Ted and Pat were on their feet and a grateful client embraced his friend and savior. Laura and Joe hugged each other, faces aglow, jumping up and down in sheer relief when Ted turned to lift Laura over the railing. Prior to their extended embrace, a brief touching of their souls, occasioned by the meeting of their eyes, short-circuited further use of sight and hearing. Thus isolated amidst the bedlam surrounding them, the sense of touch communicated all that was necessary to share this exquisite moment of triumph and vindication.

The prosecutors were aghast staring at each other in disbelief. However, a more discerning observation of Bob Giorgio's demeanor betrayed a glimmer of resignation, even relief.

Judge Cummings remained inscrutable without emotional response whatsoever. After an eternity of only several minutes, he rose and furiously rapped the gavel. "Order in the court! Order in the court! There will be order in this courtroom!" His voice had risen to a decibel far in excess of any he had used before during the trial. Gradually, the onlookers began to respond, some taking their seats.

"Order in the court! Bailiff, you will please remove anyone who does not take their seat and remain silent." This last threat gained a grudging response and the room soon became quiet. All eyes transfixed the Judge expecting him to thank the jury for their time and effort.

"Madame Forewoman, ladies and gentlemen of the jury, I am dismissing you and setting your verdict aside. You have obviously not heeded my instructions and acceded to making judgment, not on the law, but upon you own sentiments. You do not have the thanks of this court. I hereby declare a mistrial and will schedule a new one when it can be arranged in another jurisdiction."

There was absolute silence. Everyone, participants and spectators alike, sat immobilized, stunned by the words penetrating their consciousness. The prosecutors were the first to react. They again turned to each other in disbelief but this time with mutual grins displaying relief at having been delivered from a level of hell far beyond Dante's imagination. Next to stir were Laura, Ted, and Joe; who, having recovered from mutely staring at Judge Cummings, simultaneously turned their ashen faces to Pat Holleran. Their unspoken questions permeated the dank atmosphere now palpable throughout the room. "What's happening? We don't understand. Wasn't Ted just acquitted? How can the judge do this?"

Pat was the single individual in the courtroom who was not surprised. As he faced his friends, he appeared totally relaxed, a man completely in command of the shipwreck surrounding him. Raising his hand in a reassuring gesture to Ted, he turned to confront the bench.

"The defense will appeal, your honor. The proper documents will be forwarded to the circuit Court by tomorrow afternoon."

"So noted. This Court now stands adjourned."

As Judge Cummings dismounted to the level of the courtroom floor, his eyes sought those of the defense attorney. As they made contact, they each nodded to the other with a slight smile whimsically curling the corners of their lips for the briefest instant.

At that moment, when thoughts throughout the courtroom were in complete disarray, Pat's were perfectly logical and clear. Judge Cummings had just acknowledged their passage to the Supreme Court. If the jury's verdict had stood, Ted, of course, would be free and a precedent against the National Health Security Act would have been established. Any further recrimination would await the indictment of another doctor charged with the same offense. All of the enthusiasm for change engendered by the publicity of this trial would have been for naught. Pat's assessment of Judge Cummings had proven to be correct. He was eminently fair (after all he had acquiesced to the defense's strategic testimony.) But he was also a stickler for the rules of jurisprudence (jury nullification would not be permitted in his courtroom.) Now, Sousa's marching band would go all the way to the Supreme Court where the issue would be decided once and for all and all the cards would now be on Ted's side. Poor, Ted! Right now the guy is really on the ropes, from supreme elation to total despair in an instant. I'll get Laura, Ted, and Joe over to my office as soon as I can to fill them in on what a great victory we actually did just win.

～

"Ted, if you didn't believe everything I said in my office today, perhaps you'll feel better after you listen to a second opinion. You doctors know all about second opinions, don't you?"

"Pat, it's all gradually sinking in. Just be patient with me. You're right. I'm very familiar with second opinions but I must confess, not from the standpoint of the one seeking it. Where am I going to hear this opinion?"

They had all gathered late that evening, after picking at a nourishing but forgettable dinner. The stalwart six, the O'Hara's, Hanways, and Hollerans, had been listening to the TV newscasts in a vain attempt to decipher them and, despite Pat's cheerful attitude, the majority emotions remained shock and worry.

"Just flip the remote to channel eight. It's time for '*Highlights*' I'll eat my hat if we don't get a humdinger of a second opinion from Jenny Parseghian."

The program was already in progress and Tony Moreno was concluding his opening remarks.

"So, in an unending series of surprises we have been treated to more fireworks from Westbury. The jury came in with a verdict for acquittal only to have it thrown out by Judge Cummings who declared a mistrial on the basis of jury nullification. Then the defense registered an appeal. I don't know about you two but I feel like I'm on a roller-coaster. What's coming next?" The other two were, of course, Charles Sinclair and Jennifer Parseghian. "How about it, Charles, Where is this all going to end?"

"Well, Tony, Judge Cummings made the right decision. The verdict was based upon jury nullification and should have been thrown out. There is no place in our legal system for this abomination to survive."

"Fighting words, Jenny?"

"You're right Tony. I still hear Sousa's marching band in the background. Although I did not foresee a mistrial and, as you know, I had predicted the defense's appeal of a guilty verdict! But this is even better. It's almost as if the judge and defense lawyer planned the whole thing. Twelve tried and true behind closed doors unanimously acclaimed the good doctor to be innocent. Then the judge called it all nullification. Remember, no one came to him complaining about the conduct of one or more jurors. The deliberations were entirely secret until now. The judge threw it out on his own recognizance. It will be interesting to interview the jurors and find out why they voted as they did. They're no longer under oath to keep anything secret. But beyond that the judge has given the accused a free ticket all the way to the Supreme Court, not following a guilty verdict, when only the law would be on trial, but now the law and the judge will be on the docket. Full steam ahead! The question is not only the constitutionality of the law but was Judge Cummings within his rights and duty to declare nullification? I recently took my hat off to Mr. Holleran. Now I bow to him."

"Ted, I rest my case. Can you get a better second opinion than that?"

CHAPTER XXV

"THE WISE MAN'S UNDERSTANDING TURNS HIM TO HIS RIGHT."

I t began very slowly, just a few instances within the first week, hundreds of times daily within a fortnight and a full scale revolution by the end of the month. Annie may not have been first but she was one of a very few when she referred Mrs. Clark to a gynecologist, Dr. Stanley. Her patient needed a hysterectomy and, based solely on reputation, wanted Dr. Stanley to do it. Annie agreed with her and, in spite of the fact Dr. Stanley was not on Mrs. Clark's list, she made the referral.

The spontaneity of this Hippocratic rebellion spread from the East to West coast almost within hours, certainly within days, and rapidly enlisted the cooperation of hospitals without which it would have died a natural death. It not only involved the surgical specialties but the gamut of medical specialties as well. The National Health Administration, recognizing their only hope to stem the tide was to threaten the administrative cohorts of medical institutions, put the pressure on. They soon realized they were talking to the enemy. These same professionals had suffered enormous financial losses when they had been usurped by the Federal behemoth; their salaries had been universally cut; and the burden of red tape had proven to be almost unbearable. They welcomed the doctor-patient revolution.

Like a large, brown bear stirring ever so slowly after a winter's hibernation, the medical profession finally realized the power it had always possessed to rule its own destiny. But pay attention to how this came about. The nature of the beast has always been individuality. Have you ever seen a herd of bears, much less such large groups with a single purpose in mind? Everyday a physician makes any number of decisions, critical or inconsequential, for which he accepts total responsibility. Medicine by committee is anathema to him. Yes, he has his local, state, and national organizations who, for the most part function as lobbyists posturing for positions, decided upon by a minority of their members. The fact is, because of their individuality, doctors have never unified and promulgated a given stance to the government or the populace. It is simply against their nature to do so. Then what was different now? One of theirs had run the gauntlet and survived. No matter all this nonsense about jury nullification, their Dr. O'Hara had been found innocent. Each and every one of them could identify with that stellar beacon, that green light which they lost no time in emulating, one by one. Within a month, the collective effect of their treasonous activity was infinitely greater than any similar effort arrived at after debate and referendum. But most of all, it was something that each of them could do. It was in their nature to do so. The effect in Washington resembled the carnage of a dozen runaway Amtrak locomotives bursting the bonds of Union Station and laying waste to the Senate and House Chambers in the Capitol Building across the street.

CHAPTER XXVI

"THE FOOL'S UNDERSTANDING TURNS HIM TO HIS LEFT."

Richard Sterling and the Attorney General, John Bruckner, had been ushered into the Oval Office where they awaited the appearance of the President of the United States. When John had alerted him to this meeting, Richard immediately consulted Bob Giorgio relative to their strategy in pursuance of Dr. O'Hara's appeal. A five-page summary resided in the brief case at his feet. Indeed, the Attorney General was as familiar with the document as he. Both came to their feet as the President entered from the door leading from his private quarters. He was accompanied by his Chief of Staff. Harold Churchill, a constant companion when politics were on the table. The President seated himself behind his ornate desk as Mr. Churchill spoke.

"John, Richard, please sit. Thank you for coming so promptly. The President has asked for a few moments of your precious time to discuss this matter of Dr. O'Hara and the National Health Security Act."

"Yes, Mr. President, we can provide you with a brief, up-to-date strategy the Justice Department will be pursuing in this case." The

Attorney General was about to receive the aforementioned document from Richard Sterling, when he was interrupted by the President.

"Never mind that now, John. This thing has gotten out of hand. We've got to cut our losses and plan a strategy for the upcoming national elections. God knows the economy, with its recent recovery, will not be an issue, and foreign policy is foreign policy. The world outside the United States has suddenly become less important last week. The only inferno I'm aware of is right here. Did you see the polls today? Seventy percent of the population is in favor of complete repeal of the National Health Security Act. Harold, break the news to them."

"John, we're not going to pursue the appeal. Attorney Holleran has managed to make fools of us all and it's difficult to predict what new trick he has up his sleeve, so we're going to take away his forum. The jury verdict has also awakened the sleeping giant of the medical profession who is best dealt with politically, not in the courtroom. Another danger is going before a Supreme Court, five of whose members remain Republican appointees. There will be no further legal pursuit of Dr. O'Hara or any other physician. Next week, on the floor of the House, Representative Atkins of Connecticut will introduce a bill to repeal section X, paragraph 3 of the National Health Security Act. Richard, the President wants you to arrange one further session in the Second District Court. Let me know when the arrangements have been made and I'll give you further instructions."

The Attorney General broke in. "Mr. President, are you quite sure? Don't you want to at least peruse Mr. Sterling's document? I can leave it with you now?"

"For Christ's sake, John! I don't give a damn what strategy you've got. It can't be any better than the one you used in the trial. We're Simon Legree and Beelzebub wrapped up in one. The legal battle is over. The political battle has just begun. The best way to rid ourselves of Dr. O'Hara and especially Attorney Holleran is to drop the charges; cut them off at the pass. Eighty percent of the upcoming election is going to center on medical issues and I need ideas. If you have any good ones let me know: Otherwise your end of it is over. Any further questions?

"None, Mr. President."

CHAPTER XXVII

"FOR MILDNESS ABATES GREAT OFFENSES"

(Reprise)

"**P**at, what are we doing back here? I thought Judge Cummings threw the verdict out and you appealed his decision. Isn't the appeal coming up in the Circuit Court, in about a month?"

Pat had informed Ted the afternoon before to meet him in Judge Cummings courtroom at ten this morning. He had received a summons for both of them to be there but no explanation had been given. That being so, Pat had to assume that the judge was also in the dark.

"I don't have an answer for you. I could guess, but then in another fifteen minutes we'll know for sure. So why should we play games? Besides, this should be duck soup for you. You've gotten quite used to surprises."

"Okay, okay, Macchiavelli. I'm sure it won't be the last. I guess one more won't hurt too much."

As Ted was speaking, Bob Giorgio had entered the chamber and taken his accustomed seat at the prosecutor's table. Richard Sterling's absence spoke volumes to Pat and the expression on his face changed to a broad smile as the Judge entered a courtroom deserted save for the bailiff and those already accounted for.

"All rise. The Second District Court is now in session, Judge Harold Cummings presiding."

"Well, Mr. Giorgio, I hope the Justice Department has an adequate reason to interrupt my court, however briefly. Is Mr. Sterling to be expected?"

"No, your honor. Mr. Sterling will not be in attendance. I will be acting for the United States."

"Mr. Holleran, do you have any questions or comments before Mr. Giorgio informs us why we are here."

"No, your honor, none."

"Well, Mr. Giorgio, you have our undivided attention."

"If it pleases the court, I am here to deliver an affidavit signed by the Attorney General of the United States dropping all charges, criminal or otherwise against Dr. Theodore O'Hara, a resident of Lakeview, Connecticut."

Ted was stunned. Pat only broadened his grin as he embraced his good friend, a gesture not only of camaraderie, but practical as well as it aborted Ted's collapse into the chair behind him.

"Is there any further business before this court? Mr. Giorgio? Mr. Holleran?"

"None, your honor."

"None, your honor."

Harold Cummings, now with a grin to rival Pat's, stood as he rapped the gavel. Case dismissed." Without further, comment he exited to his chambers.

"Hey! What just happened here? What's going on? Did I just hear what I thought I heard? After all this time and effort? Just like that?"

With the last question, Ted had snapped his fingers which seemed to have awakened him from his dream-state and he too began to smile. Even Bob Giorgio was smiling as he came over, offering his right hand to them.

Pat interrupted. "Yes, Ted, you heard it right. It's over except for one thing, buddy. I hope you saved these golf winnings because my bill is going to be on your desk tomorrow morning."

"Please, don't take more than half my retirement, Shylock."

First Pat and then Ted shook Bob Giorgio's hand. The peace treaty had been signed and there was time for pleasantries before each side began to analyze the motives behind the signatures. Bob was first to speak.

"Pat. May I call you that, Mr. Holleran?"

"Sure. Why not Bob. I'm sure you know Dr. O'Hara, er, I mean, Ted."

"Yes, and please! I'm not going to say no hard feelings or anything else that inane. I did my job to the best of my ability. Pat, you forced me to think about the consequences of this law as much as anyone else throughout the country. I'm not going to reveal what conclusion I've arrived at, because, that's my business. But I can honestly say, in retrospect, it did not interfere with my prosecution of Dr. O'Hara, excuse me, Ted. I honor my profession enough to realize that's a plus. I can also recognize when a fellow attorney turns in an historic performance. Pat, my congratulations. It was even difficult for me not to march to the music of your final oration. Just as a teaching experience, if for nothing else, I'd like to sit down with you sometime in the near future and have a post-mortem. By the way, you beat me by only ten minutes to Benjamin Hanway's trial in 1851. What bothers me still, to this day, is that it wouldn't have made any difference if I had."

"Thanks, Bob. That's high praise comingas it does right after your team lost. I'm sure we can arrange some time soon to rehash it, but for now, would you settle for a drink? Come on Ted, I'm sure Sam might have some Tulamore Dew up at the grille room. But first I've got to call the *Gazette* and give them an exclusive."

As Pat reached for his cell phone, Ted sought his own and dialed Keane Manufacturing Company.

"Good morning, Keane Manufacturing Company. Irene speaking."

"Irene, is the most ravishing, supremely intelligent, and sexiest CEO in the entire universe there? The world's luckiest surgeon wishes to speak to her."

"God, I wish my man talked to me like that. Hold on. I'll get wonder woman."

"Thanks, Irene. It's a very special occasion."

After thirty seconds of silence Laura's familiar lilt filled his ecstatic brain.

"Well, hunk, it better be a very special reason to interrupt me at the busiest part of the day. What did Cummings want? To say he was sorry?"

"Sweetheart, you should be far more respectful of Harold and his office. No, he didn't say he was sorry, but Bob Giorgio did better than that. He announced Uncle Sam is dropping all the charges against me. I'm free as a bird."

"Oh Rhett honey! Are you sure? They're just walking away from it after all the fireworks? It's almost as if General Sherman arrived in Atlanta without matches."

"There you go again. Which side of the Civil War were you on anyway, Scarlett? Yes, by God, it's true but we may have to mortgage Tara if we hope to pay Macchiavelli's bill."

"To hell with Tara; to hell with Pat's bill! You get home early. Do you hear? We're going to celebrate tonight. Any smoke seen rising from the O'Hara residence tonight will not have come from the striking of a match."

"I assume you mean the kind with combustible sulfur on the end of a wooden stick."

"You assume whatever you wish. See you later, Rhett."

CHAPTER XXIII

"A Promise Kept."

The ides of March had arrived and it was five minutes of nine in the morning. The first tee at Mattatuck National Golf Club was just beginning to show brave new tufts of green intermittently scattered on the bleak, wintry tundra beneath their feet. It was a chilly but sunny morning with a quickening breeze out of the Northwest. The layered look was definitely in fashion as Frank, Harry, and Mike were stretching and taking their practice swings. Frank was anxiously peering beyond the pro-shop to the club storage area where he spotted an electric cart being driven by George, the starter, with Ted O'Hara in the passenger seat.

"All bets are on, boys. Our medical hero has arrived. Remember, he's my partner. Ted, great to see you. I understand it was a tough winter."

"I've had better. Frank, Harry, Mike, how are all of you? Ready for another season?"

"Sure thing, Ted. I'll wager the best of it was that headline last week. So the bastards gave up after all."

"As I recall, I agreed that if my residence was not Danbury Federal Prison I'd make this a foursome today. Correct?"

"Congratulations, Ted. It's not easy talking to a hero and whether you acknowledge that sobriquet or not, you are." When the handshaking and backslapping were over, Frank brought them back to reality.

"No arguments, Ted. I won the toss before you arrived and you're stuck with me. We're partners. Three dollar Nassau, five ways, automatic pushes, and a dollar apiece for all the funnies, chippies and sandies included. What's your handicap, Ted?"

"It's still fifteen, I couldn't have a better partner. Who's low man? I could use a few shots."

Mike spoke up. "I'm a twelve so you'll get three shots but nothing extra for your trials and tribulations. No pun intended."

Harry and Mike were the first to tee off on the straightaway par five. Both drives avoided the fairway traps, right and left, settling two hundred twenty yards down the middle of the mounded greenery. Frank and Ted managed to duplicate the feat and clambered aboard their cart. Frank immediately made his pitch.

"Ted, how old are you?"

"I'll be sixty-six in October. Why do you ask?"

"After the trial and everything haven't you just about had enough? Ready to pack it in?"

"You hit the nail right on the head as far as the National Health Administration is concerned. My problem is, I'm like an old fire horse. I still love to do surgery and listen to patients with their problems. Unless I find an adequate substitute for that in retirement, I'll go bonkers!"

"Perhaps I've got a solution. I've known you for years and am well aware of your status in the profession. Lord knows how many times we've talked about the problems of financing medicine. I' think I've helped shape your thinking just about as much as you have mine. I value your medical opinions beyond any other."

"I appreciate that Frank, coming from you, but remember I'm married to another tycoon and, although on a different scale she faces the same problems as you. If occasionally I come up with a contrary opinion, it probably comes from Laura. We're a good team, you know."

"No argument there. Laura's changed my opinions more than once. Between you and me, it's hard not to. What I have in mind is to do the same on a more formal basis."

"What do you mean?"

By now they had all struck their second shots. At their ages, no one had the distance to reach the green in two but each of them was within, at most, an eight-iron from a three-tiered green, tucked into a small hillock left of the fairway and surrounded by three inviting traps.

Ted called out. "Am I right? No shots on this hole?"

"On the nose, Ted. It's the seventh handicap hole and Harry gets the most, six. Who's away?"

Again Ted spoke up. "I think I am. According to what's left of my eyesight that pin appears to be in the back. You read it the same?"

"Sure do, partner. I'd say it's about one hundred fifteen yards. An eight iron? That's what I'd use."

"Already have it in my hand, Frank. Keep an eye on this. Would you? I'm going directly into the sun."

"Gotcha!"

Considering it was the first day of the season, Ted applied a remarkably smooth swing to the ball which arched high into the invigorating ocean air to land softly fifteen feet to the right of the flag.

"Great shot, Ted. Who's next? I'd say it's you, Mike."

Amazingly everyone had gained the putting surface in regulation three. Frank and Ted were in the cart again.

"What I mean is I want you to meet with a group of my business associates in Boston. With all the hullabaloo your friend Pat Holleran has stirred up throughout the country, we think there's a chance the entire Health Care Administration will implode. Just yesterday, a Representative from your State introduced an amendment to repeal the section of the law you broached. There's not much else going on in the world or with the economy so guess what's going to be on the front burner throughout the upcoming campaign for the national election in the fall?"

"What do you have in mind?"

"Just as I alluded to, a formal airing of various notions and opinions what to offer the public as a private alternative to the socialized flop in Washington. More than that I want to offer you a position on an ad-hoc committee to iron out a strategy to counter the President's during the campaign. So far he's taken Mr. Holleran's platform away by withdrawing your indictment and yesterday offered the public a bone in the House of Representatives.

"Sounds interesting. May I come without committing myself? I know Laura would be more than curious."

"Of course! I've already sent an invitation to your friend, Pat Holleran. That man is amazing. What he's accomplished, not only for you but for all of us, demanded an intelligence and charisma very few are capable of. I won't compare him to Abraham Lincoln but the names do easily roll off the tongue together. Some of my friends are business leaders in Connecticut and they have a unique plan to restore Mr. Holleran's national platform so rudely taken from him last week. I'd appreciate it if you were to lend your support in getting him to come, without commitment, of course,"

"Sure, Frank. When does this conspiracy take place?"

"Ha! Always one with the appropriate word. How about a week from next Tuesday? It'll last three days and I already have rooms booked at the Ritz for you, Laura, and the Hollerans. Now, let's see if we can get one-up on the first hole."

"No problem, Frank. Putting is the best part of my game."

CHAPTER XXIX

"COME TO THE PUB AND TALK A LITTLE TREASON."

It was late on Saturday night the day after Ted played that fateful round of golf as Frank's partner which as one might have guessed, they won handily. The triumphant six, the O'Haras, Hollerans, and Hanways had all gathered in Chatham for a celebratory weekend and were relaxing after a memorable dinner at the Quitnessett Bars Inn. They had retired to the upstairs piano bar at Captain Ahab's for coffee, dessert and the anticipation of an after-dinner libation. Ray Koontz, the locally popular pianist, had just completed a half hour of memorable show tunes and got up to take a short intermission. Having espied Ted and Laura at the table adjacent to the grand piano, he came over to greet his old friends.

"Doc and Laura, good to see you. I know you've been busy and haven't had the time to stop by but let me add my congratulations. Everyone here was rooting for you and when we heard the good news last week, the boss even broke down, led the cheers, and bought a round on the house."

Ted rose to shake Ray's hand. "Thanks, Ray. I think you know everyone here. The Hollerans, Pat and Mary, and the Hanways, Joe and Vicky."

"Sure. Say, Mr. Holleran, A special thanks to you. What a great job you did in bailing out my friend here, old public enemy number one. Jeez, what's this country coming to when people like doc here find themselves on the wrong side of the law? Anyway, thanks for a great job. I'm sure you saw yesterday's headline. By an overwhelming majority Congress repealed patient-doctor lists."

"I appreciate that, Ray, but don't be too impressed by the majority vote. The Republicans were eager to repeal it but the Democrats were under orders from the White House. They want to mend fences and cut their losses. From here on to the election in November, you're going to see one helluva donnybrook about that entire law."

Okay, Mr. Holleran, I'll pay attention. Doc, when I return from my break, why don't we get together for a few songs? Just let me know what you want to sing."

"I'd like that, Ray. Haven't had a chance for a long time."

"You're on. By the way, when you finish your coffee, cordials are on me. Congratulations, Doc."

"Thanks, Ray. See you back here in ten minutes."

"That was nice of him. I always did like Ray, and what a master of the keyboard!" Joe had finished a sip of coffee and was about to devour another forkful of key lime pie. "By the way Ted, I meant to ask you earlier. How is Mrs. Pulanski doing? You doctors are all alike; never miss a chance to drum up business, even at your own trial."

"Hey! God bless Mrs. Pulanski. Without her, I wouldn't be sitting here. She's doing just fine. I discharged her from the hospital two days ago and she's coming along even better than you did Joe. But then she's a lot tougher and has a better disposition. I never did thank you Pat, for contrasting the number of aortic resections Al Burton and I had done. Al is a fine surgeon but still a little green behind the ears, just as I was at his age."

Pat nodded acceptance of Ted's gratitude. "You know it never ceases to amaze me how some unpredictable circumstance can determine the outcome of any given trial. I had done my damnedest to convince that jury the law was abominable. I used all my guns, the Social Security Act, Benjamin Hanway, Ozuru Timbale, a trial for treason, the American Flag, and Mom's apple pie. That bit about Dr. Burton's inexperience contrasted to Ted's was just a nail in the shoe of the horse the king rode into battle. But when the jury took their first vote, they were deadlocked, eight for acquittal four against. Then along came fate. Mrs. Pulanski had been elected the foreperson and she, with the other retirees, were the four against. She had an appointment at five that afternoon with Dr. Buonocore, Joe's physician. She got the bad news she had a giant aneurysm and most amazing of all, her surgeon was Dr. Burton. It was early the next morning that the four and four hundred hit her squarely between the eyes and it didn't take long to convince her fellow senior citizens to give her Ted as her surgeon. So, Ted you got to steal two cases from Dr. Burton, – cases which would have almost doubled his experience with aneurysms. He must be a bit pissed off at you."

"You got it all wrong, pal. Al and I get along just fine. We just had lunch together the other day and he was quite happy with the way things worked out since he hates socialized medicine as much as I do. However, he did say something about taking away my masculinity, if I ever steal another patient from him."

"An Ivy League surgeon insinuating castration. I don't believe it. Okay to talk about it, but, if he ever acts on it, he'll have me to deal with." Laura's rebuttal elicited guffaws around the table.

Ray had returned to the piano and signaled for Ted to join him. "I haven't had a chance to do this since last summer. Honey, I've got a couple of songs meant just for you. Unfortunately, the rest of you guys will have to listen too."

"Always the ham. Go on, get up there. I hope our conversation doesn't disturb your warbling." Joe playfully pushed Ted on his way as Vicky came to his defense.

"Joe, you mind your manners. I love to hear Ted sing. Sure wish my man had a talent like that."

"To each his own, baby. I haven't heard too many complaints."

"We'll just see about that later."

"You ask how much I need you? Must I explain."

Ted's baritone blended with the chords the piano wafted throughout

228 | WILLIAM F. QUIGLEY, M.D.

the room. Background conversations quieted as everyone attuned their ears to listen.

"I need you oh my darling like roses need rain."

"At last, everything's back to normal. Ted's singing and we're all having a grand time. I don't know about the rest of you but I'm stuffed. That swordfish was fantastic." Mary rolled her eyes in mock satisfaction.

"You ask how long I'll love you? I'll tell you true."

"My rack of lamb was also out of this world. Mary, remind me to bring you to the Quitnessett Bars more often."

"How about every Saturday night Romeo; and then sing to me afterwards."

"Until the twelfth of never, I'll still be loving you."

"Just like that, Pat."

"Then I'd better hire a tenor. There are some things I can't do."

"Not many, darling, just a few."

"Hold me close. Never let me go. Hold me close. Melt my heart like April snow."

"Laura, when Ted gets back to the table, remind me to apologize for keeping him in the dark throughout the trial. I could have let him in on a lot more than I did, but his natural surprise at appropriate times definitely made its impression on the jury."

"I'll love you till the bluebells forget to bloom. I'll love you till the clover has lost its perfume."

"No need, Pat. Ted understands perfectly."

"I'll love you till poets run out of rhyme. Until the twelfth of never and that's a long, long time."

Laura was slipping into a trance, totally focused on the lyrics, but was prodded awake by the continuing repartee.

"Until the twelfth of never and that's a long, long time."

The applause was appreciative as Ted finished, nodding to Laura who was now beaming. "Ray, how about something from, "Camelot", *"If ever I would leave you."*

"Sure, Ted."

Laura momentarily closed her eyes reminiscing on another occasion when Ted sang the same melody to her.

"If ever I would leave you. It wouldn't be in Summer."
This time Pat's voice brought her back.

"Joe, there's something that's been bugging me ever since Ted called me to his office in September. I can't put my finger on it, but perhaps you can help me out."

"Seeing you in summer I never would go."

"It's been a constant itch in the back of my brain where I couldn't scratch it and it's been driving me crazy. Everything you and Ted told me made sense, but then it didn't make sense. And that was true all along the way. All the parts that made sense fell neatly into place as I planned Ted's defense, but that aggravating bugaboo danced like a firefly in the dusk, always there, but never there; always a question, but never an answer. Joe, I have a feeling you can help me out on this one."

"Your hair streaked with sunlight. Your lips red as flame."

"Counselor, what could you possibly mean?"

"Don't give me that crap, Joe, I've got you back in the witness box and you're under oath."

"If ever I could leave you, it wouldn't be in autumn."

"Right from the start something didn't add up. Things were too cut and dried. You had an aneurysm, Ted was available. You didn't tell the hospital who your surgeon was, but you did tell Ted. Without a flicker he operated. Friendship is one thing, but five years in jail is another, not to mention the rest of the punishment I brought up at trial. I have to ask why, Joe? I haven't been able to decipher it."

"Knowing you in autumn I never could go."

"You say I'm under oath, Pat?"

"That's it, unless you want to perjure yourself."

"In that case, you've got me. Your instincts haven't failed you. I guess that's why Ted wanted you as his lawyer from the start."

"I've seen how you sparkle when fall nips the air. I'd know you in autumn, and I must be there."

"Out with it Joe. Scratch that itch for me."

"From the start, counselor? Yeah, from the start! Ted and I had played golf the day before he operated on me and when we finished, I told him about an uneasy feeling I had been experiencing in my upper abdomen, and how at night in bed, when I was completely relaxed, I was aware of a prominent pulsation in the same location. He had me lie down on the bench in front of our lockers and felt my abdomen. Right then and there he diagnosed the aneurysm."

"And could I leave you running merrily through the snow."

"So what? So he made the diagnosis a day earlier. Brace yourself Mary. Armageddon is on the way."

"It's not that bad, Pat. We were both fed up with socialized medicine; me with paying through the nose for it; and Ted with slaving under its restrictions. So we cooked up the scheme – the details of which you are totally familiar. Ted knew my family history which, when coupled with your hobby, the Civil War, earned you the honor of being his defense lawyer. In his own mind, he felt that you could take this information and be creative in organizing a defense for what seemed a hopeless situation. At first I was against it since Ted was taking all the risks, you know, the fine and the possibility of jail time. Anyway he remained willing so finally I gave in."

"Or on a wintry evening when you catch the fire's glow."

"Well, I'll be damned. It was all a conspiracy. Come to think of it: I should have been alerted when I told Ted I had to interview you to confirm the facts of what had happened in the hospital. He countered that you had not returned to work as yet and I should arrange to see you at home. What should have rung a bell was that you played eighteen holes of golf with us several days before, and, of course, it was in your den that I first met Ozuru Timbale."

"You don't know the half of it. It took Vicky and I a week and a half of searching through the garage and attic to find that ancient photograph and my grandmother's family treatise. Needless to say, from now on they will always occupy a place of honor in the Hanway household."

"If ever I should leave you. It couldn't be in spring time."

"You mean to tell me Ted risked his entire life on this scheme and trusted me to get him out of it?"

"Briefly, yes."

"Sorry, smart ass, but my lawyer's brain is running overtime. That bugaboo keeps coming back and itching. Scratch it again for me. All of us know that computer systems have periodic downtimes on an unpredictable basis. I'm not quite sure I'm ready for this answer, but explain it if you will. Why did it just happen the hospital computers were down that particular night, after the backup system at the National Health Administration was unavailable after five in the afternoon?"

"Seeing how in spring time, I'm bewitched by you so."

"Can't fool you, can I, Pat? You're right again. It was no accident but rather a stroke of genius on Ted's part. He could tell you better but it went something like this. Several months before the charade began, Ted was having some difficulty accessing his assigned patients on the office computer. In the hospital, after rounds one day, he posed the problem to Eric Grunwald, the administrator's dot.com whiz responsible for the hospital's entire computer system. I don't know if you have ever met Eric, but let's just say he's the typical nerdy type one might expect in this position. As Eric entered the physician's referral database to research the problem, Ted happened to note what password he used. You'll have a good chuckle when I tell you what it was. I suspect Eric sees some perverse humor in it also. The word was 'Dumb Dork.'"

"Oh no, not in spring time."

"Ha! Ha! Get to the point."

"During office hours, the afternoon before my operation, Ted entered the entire physician referral database with Eric's password. With his own password, he could have only accessed the patients assigned to him. My record would not have been available. Anyway, he rapidly scanned to the 'physical' end of the file beyond the 'readable' end where he recognized an 'end of file' marker. This was an unprintable character of two overlapping triangles. He then 'copied' this marker into the 'clipboard' computer file and backed up the database to my file. He tabbed down to a box where he could enter text and typed in some innocuous medical gerbilese. More significantly, he 'pasted' the 'end of file' unprintable marker into the same box and logged out after 'saving' the results."

"So what? Get to it, Joe."

"When Dr. Curtin logged onto my file that evening in the emergency room, the computer attempted to read back the unrecognized 'end of file marker' and froze. It saw the file as corrupt, in a sense it had a nervous breakdown and printed out gibberish."

"summer, winter, or fall."

"Well, I'll be damned!"

"Enough of Sherlock Holmes, chauvinism, and male bonding!" Vicky's words riveted everyone's attention. "Sure you guys gambled and laid all the bets on Pat who, you knew, given a few suggestions here and there, would come through for you. But you're forgetting the real hero of the piece, or should I say heroine. Please! Let me introduce Mrs. Laura O'Hara. Yes she runs a business and chafes as much as Joe under government control of medical costs but Ted asked her to acquiesce to a cockamamie scheme which could take him away from her for five years. Can anyone tell me how much she loves him to agree to that?"

Before anyone could answer, Laura was on her feet rushing to join Ted beside the piano.

"No never could I leave you at all."

As his voice trailed off and the piano chords subsided, the entire room burst into applause. Ted and Laura embraced, sharing a prolonged kiss.

As their lips parted, Laura, *sotte voce,* inquired. "Ted, how's your adrenaline level?"

"Sweetheart, ever since the charges were dismissed, it's bottomed out at a level lower than whale dung, and that's at the bottom of Nantucket Sound."

"In that case, why don't you make our excuses while I go powder my nose? Let's go home and burn Atlanta again."

"Frankly, my dear, that's what I wanted to hear."